Praise for
## *The Quality of Silence*

"An eerie eco-tale of disasters both real and man-made on the frozen tundra of Alaska may make you rethink the popular perception of snow as innocuous white fluffy stuff. The isolated woman on her own and in danger is standard thriller fare, but here it is given new life. . . . The alternating voices of mother and daughter are so compelling, it's hard not to want to go along for the ride. . . . The book skates smoothly over issues of environmentalism, tribal rights, and the relationship of the deaf and hearing worlds. . . . The temperature drops, the action heats up, and the suspense builds with the storm."
—*The New York Times Book Review*

"Much like *The Revenant* and *The Hateful Eight,* Rosamund Lupton's suspense novel *The Quality of Silence* pits its characters against a heartlessly cruel Mother Nature. . . . About half of this teeth-chattering novel is narrated by the indomitable Ruby, who is profoundly deaf—and a model of girl power. . . . In this tale, the deadly cold and treacherous road are no match for the fiery heat of enduring love."
—Carol Memmott, *Washington Post*

"A compelling and beautifully written journey into the darkest of hearts."
—*Seattle Times*

"An elegantly visual novel . . . The level of detail throughout the story breathes life onto each page. . . . A heartwarming and thought-provoking story."
—*Free Lance-Star*

"A tight, claustrophobic thriller that will enclose readers in a world of cold from which there's no escape . . . The author evokes a sense of absolute isolation that hovers at the edge of every scene. . . . Lupton uses powerful, evocative language to craft a literary novel that sets a knife-edge of danger on every page, as readers follow mother and daughter through the forbidding landscape t̶

"Lupton delivers in spades. . . . T

strongly in the emotional conflict between family members both present and absent. . . . *The Quality of Silence* comes absolutely recommended, offering thrills and family drama in equal measure along with some important real-world issues and emotion strong enough to take your breath away."

—Addley Fannin, *Fairbanks Daily News-Miner*

"A heart-stopping page-turner from bestseller Lupton . . . Lupton limns a starkly beautiful story at once as expansive as the aurora borealis and as intimate as a mother and daughter finally learning to truly hear each other."

—*Publishers Weekly* (starred review)

"Nail-bitingly suspenseful and chilling . . . Lupton demonstrates her mastery of the suspense genre in this dazzling tale of human resilience."

—*Library Journal* (starred review)

"The strongly visual story hits the ground running. . . . This journey is paced like a bullet. . . . Lupton is at her best when describing the dark, wintry wilderness and pitting her two female protagonists against all comers. . . . Delivers an engrossing wallop of readable escapism."

—*Kirkus Reviews*

"A rip-roaring read full of both beautiful descriptions of the tundra and harrowing passages on the dangers of subzero temperatures."

—*Booklist*

"I loved *The Quality of Silence*. It was scary, suspenseful, and so exquisitely, evocatively written I often found myself shivering as if I were there in Alaska with Ruby and her mother. It was everything you want in a wonderful novel."

—Liane Moriarty, bestselling author of *The Husband's Secret* and *Big Little Lies*

"Like a breath of icy air, this relentlessly tense thriller is also a child's-eye family drama like none other. Not since *Smilla's Sense of Snow* have I shivered like this."

—Emma Donaghue, *New York Times* bestselling author of *Room*

ALSO BY ROSAMUND LUPTON

*AFTERWARDS*

*SISTER*

ROSAMUND LUPTON

# The
# Quality of Silence

A NOVEL

B\D\W\Y
BROADWAY BOOKS
NEW YORK

Copyright © 2015 by Rosamund Lupton
Reader's Guide copyright © 2016 by Penguin Random House LLC.

All rights reserved.
Published in the United States by Broadway Books, an imprint of the Crown Publishing Group, a division of Penguin Random House LLC, New York.
crownpublishing.com

Broadway Books and its logo, B \ D \ W \ Y, are trademarks of
Penguin Random House LLC.

EXTRA LIBRIS and colophon are trademarks of Penguin Random House LLC.

Originally published in hardcover in the United States by Crown,
an imprint of the Crown Publishing Group,
a division of Penguin Random House LLC, New York, in 2015.

Grateful acknowledgment is made to Penguin Random House LLC for permission to reprint "No Possum, No Sop, No Taters" from *The Collected Poems of Wallace Stevens* by Wallace Stevens, copyright © 1954 by Wallace Stevens and copyright renewed 1982 by Holly Stevens. Used by permission of Alfred A. Knopf, an imprint of the Knopf Doubleday Publishing Group, a division of Penguin Random House LLC.
All rights reserved.

Library of Congress Cataloging-in-Publication Data
Lupton, Rosamund.
    The quality of silence : a novel / Rosamund Lupton.—First American edition.
        pages ; cm
    1. Widows—Fiction.    2. Deaf children—Fiction.    3. Mothers and daughters—
Fiction.    4. Wilderness survival—Alaska—Fiction.    I. Title.
    PR6112.U77Q35  2015
    823'.92—dc23        2014048641

ISBN 978-1-101-90369-8
eBook ISBN 978-1-101-90368-1

Printed in the United States of America

*Book design by Lauren Dong*
*Cover design by Ervin Serrano*
*Cover photographs: (frost) Bajrich/Shutterstock; (people) Arcangel: Lee Avison/Arcangel Images, Inc.*

10  9  8  7  6  5  4  3  2  1

First Paperback Edition

For Tora Orde-Powlett

It is deep January. The sky is hard.
The stalks are firmly rooted in ice.

It is in this solitude, a syllable,
Out of these gawky flitterings,

Intones its single emptiness,
The savagest hollow of winter-sound.

WALLACE STEVENS

My name is a shape, not a sound. I am a thumb and fingers, not a tongue and lips. I am 10 fingers raised old—I am a girl made of letters

R - u - b - y

And this is my voice.

**Words Without Sounds** @Words_No_Sounds – 1h
*650 followers*
EXCITEMENT: Tastes like popping space dust; feels
like the thud-bump as a plane lands; looks like the
big furry hood of Dad's Inupiaq parka.

It's FREEZING cold; like the air is made of broken glass. Our English cold is all roly-poly snowmen and "woo-hoo! it's a snow day!"—a hey-there friendly kind of cold. But this cold is mean. Dad said there were two main things about Alaska:

For one, it's really really cold, and

For two, it's super-quiet because there's thousands of miles of snow and hardly any people. He must mean the north of Alaska, not here by Fairbanks Airport, with cars' tires vibrating on the road and people with suitcase wheels juddering along the pavement and a plane scissoring the sky. Dad is a big fan of quiet. He says it's not that I'm deaf but that I hear quietness.

Mum is keeping close to me, like she can wrap me up in another warm layer of her, and I lean right back into her. She thinks that Dad's snowmobile broke down so he missed his taxi plane. She says his sat phone must have run out of charge, otherwise he'd have definitely phoned us.

Dad was meant to meet us at the airport. Instead there was this policewoman who "Can't Tell You Anything Yet, I'm Sorry." Now she's striding off ahead of us like we're on a school trip and the museum's about to close with the girl gang calling after her, "Five minutes in the gift shop, miss!" but when a woman walks like that you know she's not going to slow down.

I'm wearing goggles and a face mask. Dad was super-bossy about what we had to bring with us—*proper Arctic gear, Puggle*—and now with the broken-glass air I'm glad. I never cry, least not when people can see me, because if you start down that slippery slope you could end up wearing a pink tutu. But crying in goggles doesn't count as public, because I don't think anyone can see. Dad says that up in the north of Alaska your tears can freeze.

Holding her daughter's hand, Yasmin stopped walking towards the airport's police building, causing the young police officer to frown, but for a short while she could pause what was happening. All around them snow had fallen, snow on snow, covering what had once been there in its monotone color and texture; a scene made of plaster of Paris. By her feet she saw the delicate markings of a bird's footprints in the snow and realized she was staring downward. She forced herself to look up, for Ruby's sake, and was startled by the clarity around her. The snow had stopped falling and the air was dazzling, bright and crystalline, the lucidity astonishing; one more turn of the dial to more clarity still and you'd see each atom of air defined around you. It was as if the scene hovered, too in focus to be real.

The policewoman just took a newspaper off the table, like I'm a little child who's not allowed to read newspapers, so I hold up all my fingers to show her I am ten but she doesn't understand.

"A senior police officer will shortly fill you in," she says to Mum.

"She thinks I'm a coloring book," Mum signs to me. People often miss Mum being funny, as if people who look like movie stars can't tell jokes too, which is really unfair. She hardly ever signs to me, she always wants me to read her lips, so I smile too, but our smiles are just carrier bags; inside we're not feeling smiley.

Mum says she'll be back soon and to come and get her if I need anything. I sign "OK," which is raising my thumbs. It's a sign hearing people use too, which is probably why Mum doesn't tell me to "USE YOUR WORDS, RUBY."

When I say "I said" I mean I signed, which is hand-talking, or I typed, which is another kind of hand-talking. Sometimes I use an American sign, which is like people using an American word when they speak with their mouth.

There's 3G in here but I've checked and I haven't got an email from Dad. It was stupid to even *hope* there would be as:

For one, his laptop broke two weeks ago, and

For two, even if he's borrowed a friend's there's no mobile signal or Wi-Fi in the north, which is where he must be because his snow-mobile broke down, so he'll have to use his satellite terminal to send me an email and that's super-hard to do when it's freezing cold.

"Puggle" is the name for a baby platypus. Dad films wildlife pro-grams and he loves platypuses. But a platypus, especially a baby one, wouldn't survive two minutes in Alaska. You need to have special fur that keeps you warm like an Arctic fox and feet that stop you sinking in snow like a snowshoe hare or be like a musk ox with big hooves that can break ice so you can get to food and water. And if you're a person, then you need goggles and Arctic mittens and special clothes and a polar sleeping bag, and Dad has all of those, so even if he has broken down in the north where your tears freeze he'll be all right, just like the Arctic fox and the musk ox and the snowshoe hare.

I completely believe that.

And he'll come and find us. I know he will.

On the plane from England, which took HOURS and HOURS,

I kept imagining what Dad was doing. I was thinking, *Dad will be leaving the village now; Dad will be on his snowmobile now; Dad will be getting to the landing strip.*

*"In the middle of nowhere, Puggle, and the thing about the middle of nowhere is that it is very beautiful and empty because only very few people find it."*

*Dad will be waiting for the taxi plane now.*

*"Like a letter for the postman, you need to be there on time or you're not collected."*

I fell asleep for ages and when I woke up I thought, *Daddy will be at Fairbanks Airport now, waiting for us!* And I wrote that tweet about Excitement being Dad's furry Inupiaq parka hood and the thud of the plane landing, although we hadn't actually landed yet but I thought that would be the most super-coolio feeling ever: bumping down and Dad being so close.

Then the flight attendant came busybodying towards me and I knew he was coming to tell me to switch off my laptop, which would've made Mum happy, because she hates thatbloodylaptop. I asked Mum to tell him that I'd put my laptop on flight-safe mode. I wasn't sure Mum would, because she'd have been super-happy if I'd had to turn it off; but the flight attendant saw me signing to Mum and realized I was deaf and did that thing people do, which is to go all mushy. Dad thinks it's the combo of beautiful Mum and little deaf girl (me!) that makes them like that—like we're in a movie on a Sunday afternoon. The mushy flight attendant didn't even bother to check I was on flight-safe mode after that, just got me a free Twix. I hope there aren't any terrorists who are ten-year-old deaf girls or they'll just be giving them free sweets.

I'm nothing like the little girls in those films, and Mum isn't like a movie star either, she's too funny and clever, but Dad is quite like Harrison Ford. You know, the kind of person who can disarm a terrorist if he has to but still reads the bedtime story? He finds that really funny when I tell him. And even though he's never actually had to disarm a terrorist—well, duh—he always reads me a story when he's home, even now I'm ten and a half, and I love falling asleep with his fingers still making words in front of my eyelids.

Then we landed—thud-bump of the wheels and me super-coolio excited—and I linked up to the free Wi-Fi and posted my tweet and we got our luggage off that roundabout for cases, our legs a little funny after being on a plane for so long, and we hurried to Arrivals. But instead of Dad waiting for us there was a policewoman, who "Can't Tell You Anything Yet, I'm Sorry," and she brought us here.


The senior police officer had been delayed, so Yasmin went to check on Ruby. She and Ruby were coming out to spend Christmas with Matt in just four weeks' time, but after her phone call with him eight days ago she'd needed to see him face to face immediately—as immediately as is possible when you have a child at school and a dog and cat who need looking after and Arctic clothes to buy. She'd been worried about taking Ruby out of school, but since Matt's father had died there was no one who Ruby would stay with happily.

She looked at Ruby through the glass in the door, watching her shiny, erratically cut hair falling forward over her face as she bent over her laptop. Ruby had trimmed it herself last Wednesday evening in a Maggie Tulliver moment of hair-cutting independence. At home, Yasmin would ask her to turn off the laptop *and enter the real world,* but for now she'd let her be.

Sometimes when Yasmin looked at her daughter time seemed to hit an obstacle and stop, while everyone else's time moved on without her. She'd missed entire conversations before. It was as if the contractions, begun in labor as pain, continued afterwards as something else, equally strong, and she wondered if this labor had an end to it. Would she still feel this when Ruby was twenty? Middle-aged? Would her mother feel this for her now? She wondered how long you could go on missing being loved by your mother.

The young policewoman strode up to her—the woman never went anywhere slowly—and told her Lieutenant Reeve was waiting for her and that her suitcases were safely stored in an office, as if the logistics of luggage had equal weight with what Lieutenant Reeve would say to her.

She went with her to Lieutenant Reeve's office.

He stood up to greet her, holding out his hand.

"What's happened to Matt? Where is he?"

She sounded angry, as if she was blaming Matt for failing to turn up. She'd been so deeply angry with him that her voice had not yet attuned to this new situation, whatever this situation was.

"There are a few things I'd like to confirm with you," Lieutenant Reeve said. "We have records for foreign nationals working in Alaska."

Since Ruby had been diagnosed as totally deaf (very rare, they said, as if her baby's deafness was a type of orchid), Yasmin had seen sound as waves. As a physicist, she should have done that before, but it took Ruby to comprehend the truth that sound was physical. Sometimes, when she didn't want to hear what a person was saying—audiovestibular specialists, thoughtless friends—she imagined surfing over the top of their words, or diving through them, rather than letting the waves hit her eardrums and turn into decipherable words. But she had to listen. She knew that. Had to.

"According to these records," Lieutenant Reeve continued, "your husband has been staying at Anaktue. Although originally we had him staying at Kanati?"

"Yes, he was there for eight weeks in the summer, at an Arctic research station, making a wildlife film. He met two Anaktue villagers and they invited him to stay in their village. He returned to Alaska in October to stay with them."

An unnecessarily detailed, procrastinating answer, but Lieutenant Reeve didn't hurry with his response either, as if he too didn't want this conversation to go any further.

"I'm afraid that there has been a catastrophic fire at Anaktue," he said.

*Catastrophic.* A word for immense devastation, for volcanoes and earthquakes and meteorites striking the Earth, not for the tiny village of Anaktue, more of a hamlet even than a village. The stupid thing was that she'd been coming out here to row with him, to issue ultimatums that she'd intended to carry through. She'd traveled halfway round the globe to tell him that he had to come home, right now, that she didn't believe him that nothing more would happen with the Inupiaq woman and she wasn't going to stand by on the other side of the world as this woman destroyed their family. But that had made Matt seem so lily-livered weak, this other woman and herself determining his loyalties and future, that she had become angrier still so that not a single item in hers and Ruby's cases was folded but hurled and crammed inside, ready to burst out when they were unzipped in Alaska in a fury of down feathers and Gore-Tex.

"We think gas canisters for a heater or cooker exploded in one of the houses," Lieutenant Reeve said. "And the fire spread to a stockpile of snowmobile fuel and generator diesel, which caused another much larger explosion and a devastatingly intense fire. No one at Anaktue survived. I'm sorry."

She felt knifed by love, winded by the sharpness of it. The sensation was oddly familiar, a harsher version of the pain she'd felt in their early days, long before marriage and a child, before there was any tangible security that he'd still be with her tomorrow. And time was no longer stretched out and linear but bent back on itself and broken into fragments so that the young man she'd loved so passionately was as vividly recalled and equally present as the husband she'd argued with eight days ago.

She remembered the low winter sun slanting through the windows, the slow quiet voice of the philosophy professor, the thick walls of the lecture hall cushioning them from the cawing of birds outside. Later, he would tell her they were starlings and dunnocks. He was sitting a few empty places away from her. She'd seen him twice before and had liked his angularity; his way of walking quickly and preoccupied, as if his mind was dictating his pace; the sharp planes of his face. When she clicked her knitting needles he'd glanced towards her, and their eyes had a jolt of irrational recognition. Then he'd looked away as if looking any longer would be a reproof for the clicking. When the lecture finished he came over to her as she put her knitting away, baffled.

"Is it a snood for a snake?"

"A railing."

Later he said he thought she was barmy but wanted to give her the chance of a defense.

"You're a fruitcake, right?"

*That was your idea of giving me a defense?*

"An astrophysicist," she'd said.

He'd thought she was joking, then he'd seen her face.

"A knitting astrophysicist in a philosophy lecture?"

"I'm learning about the metaphysics part of physics. In Oxford you can do a joint degree. And you?"

"Zoology."

"So what are you doing at a philosophy lecture? Apart from questioning my knitting?"

"Philosophy's important."

"To animals?"

"To how we think about animals. Ourselves. Our environment and our place in it." He caught himself and looked abashed. "Not normally so heavy. Not so quickly."

"I've come a long way to do heavy quickly."

Her school had been brutally underachieving. She'd survived it by becoming hidden and anonymous; fortunately, her high-cheekboned, small-breasted looks had no currency with teenage boys. She'd hugged the secret of being clever close to herself, deliberately underperforming in exams until A-levels, when she'd spectacularly pulled a glittering four As out of a bag everyone presumed contained a collection of unshiny Cs and Ds. She'd had to hide her nerdiness for years; now she was celebrating it.

She put away her long thin piece of knitting.

"Eight o'clock. Outside the UL. I'll show you."

Lieutenant Reeve leaned towards her and she realized that they were both sitting at a table, opposite each other; she hadn't remembered sitting down. He was handing her something.

"A state trooper from Prudhoe found it at the scene. He brought it to us to show you. From the initials inside we think it may be Matthew's?"

She stroked the touch-warmed solid metal of his wedding ring. Inside were hers and Matt's initials; half of the first line of a vow. She felt the second half of the vow under her wedding ring imprinted on the soft underside of her finger.

"Yes, it's his," she said.

She took off her wedding ring and replaced it with Matt's, which was much too big for her finger. She put hers on again, hers now keeping Matt's safe, because maybe one day he might want to wear it again. It was impossible for him to be dead, not with that knife inside her; not with Ruby sitting next door. She could not—would not—believe it.

She noticed Lieutenant Reeve watching her hands.

"He takes off his wedding ring when he's working. Puts it some-where safe."

The explanation Matt had given to her, weeks ago, when she'd spotted his bare ring finger in a photo he'd emailed to Ruby. Thank-fully Ruby hadn't noticed.

She didn't tell Lieutenant Reeve that she hadn't believed Matt's excuse.

A few hours after the philosophy lecture, already dark, they'd walked away from the historic part of town, inhabited by students and tourists, to a retail park on the edge of a housing estate, the tarmac and concrete impersonal, the shadows forbidding. He saw that there were knitted tubes around signs and railings and a bike rack. He hadn't been beguiled solely by luminous eyes, long limbs, and generous smile, but by soft wool around hard metal, yarn coloring aluminium and steel in stripes and patterns.

She told him that she was part of a group of guerrilla gardeners, stealthily changing concrete roundabouts into small flower meadows in the middle of the night, but she hadn't done that for a little while.

"Only so many roundabouts?" he'd asked.

"The wrong time of year to plant," she'd replied. "And you can't garden in lectures."

"So is this your secret passion?" he asked.

"Knitting snoods for railings? Fortunately not."

"So?"

But she didn't trust him enough yet to show him.


Lieutenant Reeve was unsure whether to put a comforting hand on hers but felt awkward as he started the gesture. She was being so dignified, none of the fuss he was expecting. Unfair, fuss; he meant emotion he wouldn't know how to deal with—grief.

"A plane saw the blaze yesterday afternoon," he told her, thinking that she'd want details. He would in her place.

"The pilot flew over Anaktue just before a storm hit. The North Slope Borough state troopers and public safety officers mounted a search-and-rescue mission, despite the storm and terrible flying conditions. And they kept searching until the early hours of this morning, but tragically there weren't any survivors."

"Yesterday afternoon?" she said.

"Yes, I don't have any more details, I'm afraid. It was the state troopers and PSOs in the north who were on the scene."

"He phoned me yesterday. Matt phoned me. At five p.m. Alaskan time."

She'd known it all along, but now she had the proof. As the policeman made a phone call she remembered fragments of their conversation as they'd walked back towards their colleges together and how all the time another conversation was going on, in the way he leaned in closer to her, the way she subconsciously matched her pace to his; she noticed the faded checked collar of his shirt against his neck, with the protruding Adam's apple, as if he was still in the process of being formed, this man-boy.

He saw the harsh streetlights land on her brow and cheeks and mouth, and saw the woman she would be in ten years and it was just like that, he told her later. *Bam! A magic trick. A miracle. The woman I want to be with.*

She'd had less confidence in his imagined future. But as she walked with him she felt the solitariness of her old life, the one in which she was the oddity, the only person in her family and school and estate to go to university, recede a little behind her.

## 2

In the remote northern community of Prudhoe Bay, Captain
David Grayling was alone in his office, bone-heavy tired. The
electric lights were glaring down and he longed for the gentleness of
daylight. Two more months till there'd be a morning here. It eroded
a man's soul. He was thinking about Timothy. Was it because of
Timothy that he'd become paternal towards the young officers in his
charge, as he knew everyone thought? He'd always seen himself more
as the musher of a team of enthusiastic young huskies, holding the
lead lines to guide them in the right direction, a canvas dog bag on his
sled in case any were injured and needed carrying to safety.

But at Anaktue, he had been neither father figure nor musher. The
men had seen him vomit, over and over, each corpse appalling him
anew. The storm had raged over the blackened village, their chopper
only just able to land, the wind chill biting at their faces like a half-
starved animal. *Blow winds and crack your cheeks.* They'd set up their
blindingly bright arc lights, glaring into the wrecked houses, illuminating the barely recognizable remains of men, women, and children.
To Captain Grayling, the darkness surrounding their lights had seemed
infinite.

They'd worked in silence, a whole team of men, most of them still
boys to Grayling, not talking or joking; no banter to shield them as
they bagged and photographed and documented. *"You sulphurous and
thought-executing fires."* Lear's words creeping into his mind, but a

blasted heath was a soft option compared with Anaktue, and thought-executing fire was only true for those who died; those who had to sift through the carnage would think far too much.

Years ago, a working lifetime, Grayling had wanted to go to university and study literature. But his father had wanted him *to do something*, not "namby about with poetry." It was a criticism that had hit home. He'd thought if he was going *to do something*, then it would be something that would benefit his beloved Alaska. For a little while, he'd hoped to do medicine but couldn't master the necessary chemistry, so he chose to be a state trooper. He was the only one on the training course for whom it was a second choice. He discovered three weeks in that he had the wrong kind of brain to be a state trooper, filled as it was with all sorts of irrelevant information and ideas. So he cleaned it out, ridding it of what he no longer needed (a moot point as to whether he'd ever needed it). So he hadn't thought of the blasted heath for years. But Anaktue was different. Anaktue delved into some deep part of him that couldn't be cleaned out.

When they'd seen the scale of the disaster, and when the storm had eased enough, more state troopers and PSOs had joined his team. Grayling himself had led the search party for survivors. Using a search beam on the chopper, they'd done a radius around the village, moving farther and farther out, but found no one. Grayling had been informed that there were twenty-three people in the village. He only stopped searching when the troopers at the village had counted the remains of twenty-four bodies. Grayling would have to find out the identity of the twenty-fourth victim.

Finally, the sickening business of it all was done. He was the last one out, taking the lights with him in the chopper. Behind him, Anaktue turned invisible in the blackness.

Later today he had to give more press interviews to journalists, in their heated, well-lit TV and radio studios, who would sleep without nightmares.

His phone rang and he was put through to Lieutenant Reeve from Fairbanks. It was about Matthew Alfredson, their twenty-fourth victim, whom they'd identified from computerized visa records: the wildlife filmmaker whose wedding ring Grayling had found glinting in the wreckage. Everything else had been destroyed, metal twisted into ugly shapes, but this one ring remained a perfect eternal circle. Grayling knew from his brief foray into chemistry that platinum could withstand intense heat, but this undamaged ring still seemed little short of miraculous. It hadn't been found near any of the bodies, so although the metal was an unbroken circle, Grayling surmised that the marriage itself was less enduring and he'd hoped he was right, because it might lessen the tally of grief.

But at five o'clock yesterday, while they were searching through the charred remains of Anaktue, this man had phoned his wife. How could this be possible? My God, was this man still out there somewhere, alive? He needed to talk to the wife.

To Yasmin, Captain Grayling sounded like an archetype of a state trooper, his voice self-assured and deep. She imagined him broad-shouldered and rugged-faced to match his voice.

"Did your husband tell you where he was?" Captain Grayling asked.

"No. But I think he was at the airstrip, waiting for a taxi plane. Lieutenant Reeve said there was a storm yesterday afternoon and terrible flying conditions, so the taxi plane wouldn't have come. He might still be there."

"We searched a wide area that included the airstrip."

"It was dark, though, surely, and stormy; you could have missed him?"

He heard the hope in her voice, this grasping at a different outcome, and felt sharp compassion for her.

"The airstrip is flat and pretty easily visible," he said. "We had powerful lights and we went over it thoroughly."

He didn't tell her that he'd flown over it himself, half a dozen times, checking and rechecking.

"Does he use a snowmobile?" he asked.

Anaktue was miles from anywhere, across virtually impassable terrain, so it was surely the only option, but he needed to be sure.

"Yes."

He had asked his team to piece together the heat-softened fragments of snowmobiles. Those fragments would now be frozen solid.


Yasmin remembered Matt telling her and Ruby that he'd bought a snowmobile from a villager who'd wanted to upgrade. She'd thought it strange that Inupiat men hunted caribou using snowmobiles, but Matt hadn't found it odd.

"Do you know how many snowmobiles were at the village?" Captain Grayling asked.

"Three," she replied. There was Matt's, the new upgraded one, and one that belonged to a villager working at the wells at Prudhoe Bay. She and Matt had spoken about it: a safely neutral subject in front of Ruby.

She waited for Captain Grayling to say something and in the silence knew that they'd found three—the remains of three—at the village. So he wasn't on his snowmobile, alive and well and at this very moment almost at Fairbanks, about to burst in, with hugs for Ruby and she could tell him she loved him. But it had been absurd to think he could get all the way to Fairbanks by snowmobile. She was just so impatient now to see him.

"He could have been traveling by dog sled," she said.

A few weeks ago, he'd emailed Ruby about going out with an Inupiaq man on a sled pulled by huskies. She'd doubted his enthusiasm, not understanding why anyone would want to travel by sled in Arctic temperatures, but maybe his enthusiastic tone had been genuine.

"The kennels were also destroyed in the fire," Captain Grayling said.

"He could have been away on a filming trip when there was the fire and taken the dogs with him."

"Filming trips in midwinter?" Captain Grayling asked. "In the dark?"

"He's making a film about the wildlife in Alaska during winter. He was really just using Anaktue as a base."

She didn't say how skeptical she'd been about Matt's reason for staying at Anaktue, nor that she hadn't confronted him. But he could have been telling her the truth.

"Even if he was on a filming trip," Captain Grayling said, "surely he'd have come back to Anaktue, or the airstrip, in time to get to Fairbanks to meet you?"

"Something must have gone wrong with the sled or a dog," she said.

"You said your husband didn't tell you where he was when he called?"

"No."

"Any clues at all as to where he was?"

"No."

"Can I ask what he did say to you?"

"We didn't speak."

"I'm sorry?"

"We lost the connection before he could say anything."

"He didn't say anything at all?"

"No. As I said—"

"So how do you know it was him?"

"It was two in the morning in England and he's the only person who calls me at that time. We often lose the connection. He has a satellite phone and needs a clear line of sight to the sky. Or maybe his phone just ran out of charge. As he hasn't called again, I think that's the most likely."

"Could it have been someone else calling you? Maybe a wrong number?"

"No. It was him."

She didn't tell Captain Grayling how surprised she'd been that Matt had called her. Apart from that terrible call eight days ago, he'd virtually stopped phoning her, though he steadfastly emailed Ruby. During a rare phone call between them a month ago, she'd accused him of not bothering anymore and he'd told her that he couldn't phone her from Anaktue, he had to trek for two miles and climb an icy ridge to get a satellite link. Oh, and it was also winter so pitch-black when he made the trip, and at that moment he was speaking to her in minus eighteen Fahrenheit. She hadn't pointed out that he did that trip every time he sent an email to Ruby, which was frequently; just glad that he did. There'd been a storm yesterday. It would have been an even harsher journey.

She wished she could believe in some rewind in their relationship, unknown about by her, that meant he'd walked for two miles in the Arctic cold and dark to speak to her, but knew that wasn't true. She didn't know why he had called her, especially when she'd been getting on a plane with Ruby in just a few hours' time and he'd see her face-to-face.

"Which satellite phone company does your husband use?" Captain Grayling asked.

So he intended to check out what she'd told him with Matt's phone company. She gave him the name of the company and hoped it wouldn't delay their search.

She waited to feel some kind of relief, but none came. Perhaps, after all that anxiety, she needed to actually touch him to feel relief.

She hadn't yet asked either Lieutenant Reeve or Captain Grayling if Corazon was a victim of the fire. She hadn't wanted to say her name.

**Words Without Sounds** @Words_No_Sounds – 12m
*650 followers*
ANXIETY: Looks like a chessboard with the squares
quickly moving about; feels sweaty and shivery;
tastes like prickly ice cream.

I usually don't do very well with speech therapists but there was one man, he was really young, I think he was still learning to be a doctor, and he asked me if I saw words, as clearly I couldn't hear them. Mum doesn't like me saying, "No shit, Sherlock," but Dad finds it funny. And the young sort-of-doctor did too. I hadn't told anyone this before him, but I do see words and touch them and taste them too. I know that's weird but this young sort-of-doctor didn't think so. He thought I should tweet about it and I said, "Great plan, Batman!" (as I knew he liked book characters brought into our chats). He was my first follower and now I've got hundreds, which is weird (WEIRD—Looks psychedelic; tastes dip-dab-sherbet-fizzy).

That tweet I did about "Excitement," the one when I thought Dad was waiting for us at Arrivals? It's funny because I said the word "Excitement" looked like the furry hood of his Inupiaq parka, but in October when he went out to Alaska I tweeted "Sadness," and Sadness looked like his furry parka hood too. So I think how you see a word, just like what it means in a sentence, is all about context and timing. At school I wouldn't use a word like "context" because people think me being in the "Gifted and Talented" program is as weird as being "Special Needs"; being both is super-weird and not in a dip-dab-sherbet-fizzy way.

Usually it helps to tweet a feelings word.

But it didn't help.

———

The policewoman was checking Yasmin's contact details when Lieutenant Reeve came in. He told her that Captain Grayling was waiting to speak to her on the phone in his office. She went with him and picked up the phone.

"I'm sorry," Captain Grayling said. "We've made a terrible mistake."

He sounded gentle. She made his face softer, his physique less bulky.

"A satellite phone was recovered near one of the burned-out houses by a junior member of the search team. He called the last number. He was hoping it would locate someone who might still be alive, a possible casualty."

"I don't understand."

"It was a public safety officer who made the call to you, not your husband. He managed to get a second or two's connection. I'm sorry. It was a confusing scene and he's young and inexperienced. He should have reported this to me straight away. He's being disciplined, of course; he should never have done it."

"Matt's alive," she said to Captain Grayling. "Whether he made the call to me or not."

"Mrs. Alfredson—"

"He must have dropped the phone when he got out of the fire."

"But he wasn't there when we searched."

"He must have gone to call for help. It's what Matt would do. He'd have tried himself and, if he couldn't, he'd go and get help. And he dropped his phone but didn't realize. He has to trek for miles to get a proper signal and—"

"I'm sorry, Mrs. Alfredson, but—"

"Or he was away on a filming trip," she said, "like I told you, and dropped the phone before he left and—"

Captain Grayling interrupted. God, how he hated doing this. "Twenty-four bodies were recovered from the scene. The village had twenty-three residents at the time of the fire. I was given this information yesterday and have checked it again today."

"You can't be totally certain about the number of people there," she said, and heard the fast desperation in her voice, the measured certainty in his.

"There were plans to install new generators at Anaktue, so a detailed survey was done on every household. There was also a survey carried out for a possible new Inupiaq school. It was very specific on the numbers of villagers living there and at what times of the year."

Captain Grayling sounded so reasonable and kind. She saw Lieutenant Reeve watching her; he must have spoken to Captain Grayling first. He had a glass of water ready for her. Captain Grayling was continuing, the sound waves relentlessly hitting her eardrums and turning into words.

"Of the twenty-seven villagers, four of the young Inupiat men are away working at the wells in Prudhoe Bay as they do every winter, which means there were twenty-three villagers remaining. And as I said, we recovered twenty-four bodies."

"You haven't identified Matt, though, have you?" she said.

"You told Lieutenant Reeve the wedding ring was his."

"But he wasn't wearing it, was he? And you haven't done proper forensic tests, you can't have done. You would have told me."

Grayling felt compassion for this woman coursing through him, threatening to dislodge the dead weight of grief always present inside him, so precariously balanced. He wished there were a way of telling her that wasn't brutal.

"The fire was very intense," he said. It had left some bodies barely identifiable as human, let alone as a person with a name and family. It was unlikely they'd even be able to get dental ID for some of them.

"I wish I hadn't been the person who had to tell you, but your husband is dead. I'm so sorry. I know that Lieutenant Reeve will look after you."

He hung up the phone.

———

The phone call from Matt had simply been tangible evidence of what Yasmin had already known, carried on the tip of a knife and now in the core of her: that he was alive.

In truth, she hadn't been surprised to learn the phone call wasn't from him; the surprise had been when she thought he'd called her. She wished he had, not because it would be a sign of reawakened love for her, but because then the police would have to believe her and she wouldn't be in an Alaskan police building next to an airport with no clue, really, as to what she should do.


Mum's just come in. She's crouching down, so her face is close to me and I can read her lips easily. She tells me that Dad is fine. There's been a mistake, but she will sort it all out. She looks too tight, like when you miss hitting a Swingball and the cord wraps itself round and round the post. I pretend not to notice and smile at her.

She tells me that Dad dropped his phone, which is why he hasn't been able to call or text us. An older policeman comes in and asks Mum to go with him. She says she'll be back soon. As they leave, the older policeman puts his arm out towards her, then drops it again without touching her. Lots of people don't know how to behave towards Mum—her looking so lovely puts them off—but it's completely clear she needs an arm around her.


In his office, Lieutenant Reeve tried to usher Yasmin Alfredson to a chair, but she wouldn't sit down.

"Matt's not dead," she said. "The state trooper in the north, Captain Grayling, has to search for him."

Lieutenant Reeve had read somewhere that there were four stages of grief, denial being the first.

"I'm sorry, he doesn't think there's any point."

"So he just gives up? How hard can it be to go and look for someone?"

He was afraid that her voice would break into a scream or a sob and kept his own voice calmly firm.

"If Captain Grayling thought there was the remotest chance, then he'd go. He flew a helicopter himself to Anaktue, despite the storm. Wasn't even on duty but came in anyway. And he was the last person to leave; spent nearly twelve hours in minus thirty, searching."

The man was a maverick in Fairbanks terms, running the show up in the north as if he owned the place, often with scant regard for rules. But he would always go the extra mile, never abandoning a search-and-rescue mission while there was any hope left. People said it was ever since his son had died in Iraq.

Yasmin had fallen silent. Still not saying anything, she got up and left the room.


My bracelet vibrates, which means there's a loud noise. It's like a James Bond gadget for deaf people so I know if someone's shooting at me (the man in the special shop said that and I thought it was pretty funny). It's meant to let you know if a car's coming, in case you forget to look both ways.

Mum comes in with our suitcases; it must have been the door banging shut behind her that made my bracelet vibrate. She doesn't smile at me. She always smiles at me when she sees me, even if I've only seen her five minutes before; like every time she sees me she smiles because she's super-pleased to see me again. Some people think she's aloof. I've lip-read them saying that. The mean words are easier to lip-read than the soft warm ones. I think if she didn't look so beautiful they'd see her better.

She tells me that Dad is OK but there's been a terrible fire at Anaktue. She says the police are being idiots and slowcoaches so we're going to have to go and *find him ourselves*.

They left the police station, dragging their suitcases across the compacted snow. The cold felt sharper now. She and Ruby were wearing liners inside their Arctic mittens, their face masks pulled up.

Where was he?

She had to think it through, calmly, rationally, as the scientist she'd once trained to be.

Captain Grayling had searched the airstrip thoroughly and it would presumably be a flat open area, so relatively easy to spot someone. Captain Grayling was probably right and Matt wasn't there.

So where was he? Think. Logically. Forget the cold and Ruby's face looking at her. Focus.

If Matt was at Anaktue when the fire started, what would he do? He'd try to help and, when he couldn't, he'd go to call for help. In his haste she imagined his phone dropping from his pocket and falling silently onto the snow. So, not noticing, he trekked on through the storm for two miles, then climbed the icy ridge to get a satellite connection. And then what happened? He felt in his pocket for his sat phone and it wasn't there. Maybe he started retracing his steps, looking for it, not knowing he'd dropped it right back at the village. How long did he search for it? Perhaps he then tried to walk to get help. He'd have been desperate. There were children in the village. Corazon. If he walked too fast he'd sweat and his sweat would freeze against his skin and he'd get hypothermia. But he understood the danger of hypothermia. It wouldn't help him for her to worry. Focus. But she saw his eyes as he realized that there was no town or village or house to go to, no help for a hundred miles, but he kept walking anyway as if he could make it different, before finally knowing it was futile. She wanted to put the warm palm of her hand against his face.

Focus. And all the time the police were searching Anaktue and the airstrip and it was dark, stormy, and their lights never spotted him because he wasn't there. How long till he returned to Anaktue, to find it deserted and the police gone?

Ruby was patting her arm; her suitcase had got caught in frozen slush at the edge of the pavement. Yasmin helped her to right it.

There was a better explanation. He'd gone on a filming trip, just like she'd told Captain Grayling. There were in fact all sorts of animals to film, the Alaskan winter wilderness teeming with them. She'd been wrong not to believe him. And then something had delayed him: a dog getting injured, or the sled breaking. It didn't matter. The point was he was nowhere near Anaktue when it was on fire. And, just as importantly, *he'd have his emergency kit with him*. And the phone? As he'd set off with the huskies he'd dropped it and didn't notice; silencing snow again, lost objects dropping into it and making no protest. If he was in a sled it must be difficult, leads to the dogs tangling maybe, lots to think about and distract you from a dropped phone. And then? He got back to the village after the fire, after the police had searched, last night perhaps, this morning even, to find it burned to the ground and deserted.

She had studied physics and astrophysics, not medicine, so she didn't know how long he could survive.

She wasn't going to allow Captain Grayling's body-count evidence; it was unproved, not verified. It was incorrect. It *must be* incorrect. And here was the base of illogic on which she built the rest of her cogent hypotheses—that he had to be alive because she loved him: an emotional truth so keenly felt and absolute that it couldn't be dented by rational argument.

Helping Ruby with her suitcase, they headed towards the airport building. She would get on a plane with Ruby to the north of Alaska and they would find him.

As they reached the terminal she saw that the light had dimmed dramatically since they'd first arrived, that spell of dazzling daylight over. She knew that there were carefully calibrated words for dusk and nightfall here. She and Matt had spoken about it on the phone when he first came to Alaska—a good call, one of very few good calls. This light was called "nautical twilight," with the sun between six and twelve degrees below the horizon. Soon the sun would dip to twelve to eighteen degrees below the horizon, and it would be "astronomical twilight." And then it would be simply black.

## 3

**Words Without Sounds** @Words_No_Sounds  – 1h
*650 followers*
NOISE: Looks like flashing signs, neon-bright;
feels like rubble falling; tastes like other people's
breathed-out air.

It's horrible here. There's loads and loads of people with suitcases and trolleys. I'm writing Mum's mobile and email address on little cards and keep getting jogged. On the back of the card there's a taxi company, but Mum says they're only open in the summer. She says we'll give our cards to anyone who might be able to help.

I was a bit worried about the police being slowcoaches, but now I think it's really good because it means Mum is going to get Dad, and so he'll see how much she loves him. He might not know that because she's hidden it under lots of crossness.

Yasmin asked the five people queuing at the North Airlines counter if she could queue-jump, and they must have seen her desperation because they kindly stood aside. She faced the scowling woman at the counter.

"Do you know how I get to Anaktue?"

"There's a line, ma'am."

"But—"

"You have to wait your turn, lady."

Yasmin stepped away. The hostility of the woman would clearly only be appeased by queuing. She signed to Ruby, asking how she was getting on with the cards, and Ruby signed that she'd finished, a silent conversation that crossed the noisy hall. She'd given Ruby the task to make her feel useful, but also in the long-shot chance that someone would take a card who knew something about Matt and Anaktue.

She noticed a sign up for tour parties to the Arctic Circle to see the aurora borealis. For a few seconds she was interested before remembering that Anaktue was hundreds of miles further north and, in any case, the tour didn't operate during the midwinter months.

```
To: Matthew.Alfredson@mac.com
Subject: We're coming!!
From: Ruby.Alfredson@hotmail.co.uk


Hi Dad, Mum is coming to find you and I'm coming too.
We're at the airport and Mum's going to get us plane
tickets. Mum really really wants to see you. I can't
wait to see you too.


Love you megatonnes
Puggle
```

I know Dad's laptop is broken but his satellite terminal works so he'll just need to borrow someone else's laptop. If Dad's OK, then some of his friends in the village must be too and they'll have taken a laptop. Inupiat people aren't stuck in the past like some people think.

They hunt caribou and make aputiat, but they have snowmobiles and laptops too; it's not an either/or thing. And someone's bound to have taken their laptop when they got out of the fire. I would. After Bosley, who's our dog, and Tripod our cat, my laptop would be the next thing I'd take. So Dad'll be able to check his emails.

Dad and I think that when I go to secondary school I'll be too grown-up to be called Puggle, as it's a baby name. But he agrees that I can't become a grown-up Puggle and be called Platypus, so we're still working out what he'll call me.

When I emailed Dad I saw I'd got emails from people at school, but when I'm actually at school most of them don't talk to me. It's not coolio AT ALL to talk to "the-deaf-girl," which they say like it's one word, like that's my name.

Tanya, head of the girl gang, is the most nasty—"Oh look, here comes the-deaf-girl wanting a goss"—I can read her lips really clearly and she's started wearing pinky lip balm and that's what I look at while the girl gang laugh. And then I say, "Why would I want to goss with you? You have the personality of a toaster! And anyway gossiping is horrible."

They go on laughing because they don't understand sign and think it's funny I'm doing-weird-things-with-her-hands. But Jimmy understands signs and he laughed because "personality of a toaster" was funny.

(NASTY: Feels like barbed wire; looks like a rabbit with its leg in a trap; tastes like whispering glittery lip balm.)

When I email or Facebook, people who can't sign understand me straight away and get my jokes. Also they tell me jokes and I get them straight away too, which is important for a joke. (Not people like Tanya, but people who email or Facebook me.) And people tell me private things too. Max, who's been in my class since Reception, is upset we've only got two and a half terms left in Wycliff Primary. He's really worried about secondary school, like me. But at school we don't ever talk to each other. It's like there's two worlds, the typed one (like emails and Facebook and Twitter and blogging) and then the "real" one. So there are two me's. And I'd like the real world to be the typed one because that's where I can properly be me.

Dad got me my laptop. Mum hates it and right away called it that-bloodylaptop. She always glares at it, like the laptop could glare back at her and she could win the glaring competition.

Mum thinks if I could mouth-talk, everything will be better. She tells me that almost every time we walk home from school. Instead of arguing, I hold her hand. But sometimes I do argue with my voice—my hand-voice so I can't hold her hand anymore—and I say, "No it won't," or "You don't understand!" Because

for one, I'll never sound like they do, and

for two, that'll be the other thing about me; I'll be the-deaf-girl-with-the-stupid-voice, and it's bad enough being the-deaf-girl without being the-anything-else-girl too.

I'd rather be the-showy-off-brat-girl, the-nerdy-know-it-all-girl, any of those sorts of things, because those sorts of things you can try to change, if you want to. Or not. Up to you.

Being deaf isn't something I can change. Mum doesn't understand this but I don't know if I even want to. It's my Ruby-world, a quiet world that I look at and touch and sometimes taste but don't hear. Dad says quietness is beautiful. So maybe my world is lovelier than other people's. And maybe making sounds I can't hear in my quiet world would spoil everything.

Max is really worried about changing schools, has an upset tummy about it and everything. I'm worried too, but my tummy's been OK.


Yasmin reached the front of the queue and the hostile woman.

"I need to get to Anaktue."

"I don't know where that is, ma'am."

"About five hundred miles north of here."

"We don't cover it."

"The nearest town then? Deadhorse, I think?"

She'd remembered it was the place Matt flew to when he came to Anaktue, that he'd get a taxi plane from there.

"I told you, lady, we don't cover that region."

"Can you tell me how to get there? Please?"

"I do North Airlines check-in; I'm not a travel agent."

A man came up to Yasmin. About forty, he was dressed in overalls, a peak cap with "Am-Fuels" on it, a 9/11 pin.

"You'll need Arctic Airways," he said. "But their last flight for the day left ten minutes ago."

She felt rising panic, and he must have noticed because he looked at her with kindness.

"I might be able to get you on a flight to Deadhorse," he said. "From Deadhorse, you can get a taxi plane to most places in the north." He paused a moment. "Aint Anaktue the place that's been on the news?"

"I imagine so."

She didn't volunteer anything more, and he didn't press her.

"Can you wait a little bit while I see my daughter onto her flight?" he said.

Behind him was a young woman, eighteen or nineteen, looking excited, eyes darting around, a smile reappearing every few moments, a rucksack on her back.


Mum's handing out the little cards I've written, asking people if they know anything about Anaktue, and she gets really funny looks. Some rude people just put theirs in the bin right in front of us. I'm writing some more now, on the back of a different taxi place. I'm a bit worried that people will phone or email Mum thinking she's the taxi.

I'm still thinking a bit about the nasty girl gang at school and gossiping.

Dad told me about this film where a preacher tells people why gossiping is so terrible. He says that when you say a bit of gossip, you're emptying a feather pillow out of a high window into the wind, and if you want to take the gossip back you'd have to find every single feather and you could never ever do that. But it would be good if that was true of Mum's cards and they go all over the place, and someone will know something that will help us find Dad really soon.

Fifteen minutes later, Yasmin saw the man in the peak cap threading his way through shoals of people towards them. She thought he looked anxious.

"Jack Williams," he said, holding out his hand. "Sorry to take a while but I wanted to see my daughter through the departure gate. She hasn't been away from home before. Not for more than a week anyway."

Yasmin liked him for being anxious.

"Freedman Barton Fuels are flyin' a load of us worker bees to the wells south of Prudhoe, via Deadhorse," Jack continued. "It's a charter. I know the pilot and gave him a call. If you want to hitch a ride it's fine with him. 'Course it probably ain't legal, but he's not goin' to tell anyone. There's a couple of spare seats."

"Thank you," Yasmin said.

He smiled at Ruby. "I wish all daughters could stay put at your age. Not get all grown-up and want to go off travelin'."

Yasmin wasn't sure how much of that Ruby had understood, but Jack spoke clearly and didn't put his hand to his mouth, so she'd have got most of it.

"Come on, I'll show you the way. Those your cases?"

———

I don't like this man. Don't trust him for a second. He's all smiley-smarmy. He's got our cases and his sleeve has wrinkled up and you can see an Omega watch. Dad has one like it, quite like it, that Grandpa left him. He says it's much too precious to wear every day, so why's this man wearing it on just any old day? Now he's seen me staring.

Yasmin had seen Ruby looking at the watch, more like glowering at it. No wonder Jack noticed.

"I used to buy presents for my wife," he said. "When you work at the wells, it's ugly and dirty and you want somethin' nice at the end of it. I'd get her pretty things. Right before our twentieth anniversary, she took a heap of her jewelry back to the store. Swapped it with this. Gave it to me."

And his wife died, Yasmin thought, so he always wore her watch. She felt compassion for him in a way that before today she couldn't have imagined.

They followed Jack as he led them along a corridor and into a small departure lounge. There were fifteen to twenty men, most wearing F.B.F. caps and overalls, a few with Am-Fuels caps. Yasmin took hold of Ruby's hand. She feared the day men like these would no longer see Ruby as a child. To her relief, the men didn't notice their arrival; they were focused instead on a slight man wearing a suit, his back towards them, his blond hair shining in the artificial lights. Yasmin could sense their hostility towards the suited blond man, almost feel its abrasiveness against her skin.

"Fuckin' tree-hugger," one of them said to him.

"Ain't no trees up in North Alaska, no one told you that?" said another.

The blond man met their aggression with superiority. "Aren't you concerned, or at least interested in what you're working with? Carcinogens that cause cancers, radioactive chemicals—"

A man with a tattooed face interrupted, towering over the blond man. "Do we look sick?" He turned to the other workers. "Comes here and does his song and dance routine every fuckin' week."

Yasmin could see the blond man's face now and was surprised that he was in his fifties, his eyebrows gray, his skin pallid.

The man with tattoos continued, "Heard it all before, fella. Know what F.B.F. stands for? 'Frack Baby Frack.' Sarah Palin. The lady had vision."

The blond suited man's tone was still superior. "You've been taken over by American Fuels, so you can't make that joke anymore."

Yasmin saw that Ruby, lip-reading, was intimidated by these men and their language.

"He said 'frack baby frack,'" she told Ruby, finger-spelling "frack." She asked her not to lip-read anymore; she'd tell her if there was anything important.

The men were now staring at her. Jack came closer.

"This lady and her daughter are gettin' a ride with us to Dead-horse," he said.

One of the men laughed. "Got a mall now, has it?"

"We want to get to Anaktue," Yasmin said. "We're getting a taxi plane from Deadhorse."

"Ain't you seen the news?" a muscular man said to her. "It's burned to fuckin' toast, everyone and everythin'." He looked around at the others. "Said on the news, stupid fuckers stored fuel right by their houses."

"Hydraulic fracturing may have caused the fire," the blond man said, his pallid face animated as if this stimulated him. "Anaktue is only forty or so miles north of Am-Fuels' wells at Tukapak."

"Wouldn't know 'bout that," the muscular man said. "But I'd be guessin' it's forty or so miles of fuckin' *snow*."

"People have set fire to the water coming out of their faucets," the blond man said.

"Yeah right," the muscular man said. "It ain't fuel explodin' like the news said, it's water burned everythin' down."

"The fumes could well have ignited," the blond man said. "That's always a risk."

"Oh, for cryin' out loud," Jack said, and Yasmin was sure he was moderating his language because of her and Ruby. "You're tellin' us fumes from a frackin' well went *forty miles* across northern Alaska, in minus thirty, in high winds without breakin' up, then got to Anaktue and exploded? *Spontaneously?*"

"It's possible," the blond man said.

"That's bullshit and you know it," Jack said. He stared at the blond man's face, as if reading him a line at a time. "Jesus. You'd *like* it to be a frackin' accident. You want somethin' like this to happen."

"OK, you're right," the blond man said. "Hydraulic fracturing is an accident waiting to happen; a disaster waiting to happen. Better a small village in Alaska has everyone die than a highly populated area. So yes, if wiping out a village is what it takes to permanently stop hydraulic fracturing, then yes."

Yasmin was repulsed, but she had to talk to him because he knew where Anaktue was—*"only forty or so miles north of Am-Fuels' wells at Tukapak."* Anaktue was a tiny place, so how did he know?

She went over to him, holding Ruby's hand. She found his unflinching eye contact with her invasive.

"Silesian Stennet," he said to her, holding out his right hand, plump and freckled with age spots. She didn't take it.

"I was finance director of a hydraulic fracturing company," Silesian continued, not breaking eye contact. "But I couldn't in all conscience continue, not with the knowledge I had of the risks. But some people just don't want to be warned."

"How do you know where Anaktue is?" Yasmin asked. "Do you know people there? Have you heard from someone?"

"Like I said, I worked for a hydraulic fracturing company. Anaktue is sitting on hundreds of thousands of barrels of shale oil. It's only thirty-five miles from the Trans-Alaska Pipeline, so the infrastructure is almost in place to ship out the crude. All the hydraulic fracturing companies know where Anaktue is. They'll have source rock samples, 3D seismic data, and drilling data for Anaktue."

Jack watched Yasmin with Silesian Stennet and wondered if he should warn her about the son of a bitch; tell her that he'd been convicted of sabotage at a fracking site; that he was just lucky no one got hurt. Several inches taller than Silesian, Jack could see that his blond part had gray streaks running in a line on either side. He wanted to be a young man with a cause, but he was a middle-aged zealot embracing obsessions.

No one's mouth is open, no one is speaking, and Mum has gone like the Swingball again. She's forgotten she'd tell me if someone said something important or interesting.

The man with the blond hair says in sign, "Do you want me to tell you what's happening?"

It's super-coolio when someone knows sign language and they're not deaf. Like when President Obama signed "Thank you" straight back to someone who'd signed to him, like it wasn't a big thing. Mum hasn't even noticed because she's listening to whatever it is.

The blond man finger-spells "Announcement" and now he's signing something about a dead horse. He means the place; the place where we're going to so we can find Dad.

In American Sign Language the sign for a horse is putting your hand to your head and wiggling your pretend ear, like the puppet horse in War Horse. In British Sign Language you pretend you're holding the reins while you gallop, which is more fun to do. I think about the story of the sign, not what it means, because I'm worried it means something bad.

The blond man is holding out his phone. He's typed something for me to read. I go closer to him, which isn't very far, so Mum won't mind. I read what he's typed:

> "There's been a crash at Deadhorse airport. A cargo plane has spilled its load. No flights landing till it's cleared up. Might be tomorrow or the day after."

I feel sick. Like in the plane when I walked down the aisle and thought that underneath the floor was miles of sky.

The blond man says, "Why are you going to Anaktue?" and he finger-spells "Anaktue."

"To find Dad," I tell him.

"At Anaktue?" he says, and his face is kind of smiling, like he thinks it's funny.

"Yes."

I don't like being close to him. When he put his phone near my face to read, his hands smelled like old fish.

You know how I said that Jack guy is creepy? Well, he isn't, not really. I was just annoyed with him for being with us, when it should be *Dad* with us. Was even annoyed with him helping us, which is stupid, because we need his help to get to Dad. So even though I find this blond man creepy, I'm not going to trust my creepy-monitor.

I go closer to Mum. A man's talking to her, but she's still forgotten she'd let me know anything important, so I'll lip-read him. I can't make out every word but quite a lot.

He says small taxi planes will still fly from Deadhorse because they don't need the main runway. We can still get to Dad!

There's another man, the one with lots of tattoos, saying something about getting to Deadhorse from here, but I can't read his lips very well because he mumbles. And now another one is smiling like it's really funny.

"And how's she supposed to do that?" he says, and then he sees me and stops for a moment. "Get the effing bus?"

And now he's looking at Mum and he's saying something I can't lip-read, then he says, "You can't drive there. It's five hundred miles on an ice road."

I tug at Mum, making her look at me. "What will we do?" I say. "How will we get to Daddy?"

She tells me to wait a moment. The blond man comes closer to me again and shows me his phone:

"Why does your mother wear two wedding rings?"

I look at Mum's hand. She always has her wedding ring on and sometimes her engagement ring or the ring Dad gave her when I was born, which is made of a stone called peridot, which is green and means joy, and Mum says is the same color as my eyes so she can look at her ring when I'm not there and imagine my face really clearly, but Dad says it also means he was on a bit of a tight budget.

She doesn't wear Dad's wedding ring too because *he* wears his ring. I don't understand. It's like the floor of that plane is just soggy paper and I'm falling through it.

Mum is grabbing the man's phone and snapping it shut and shoving it back at him. She bends down so that her face is close to mine. "Daddy takes off his ring when he's working," she says. "Which is why a policeman found it. And now I'm keeping it safe for him." She's mouth-speaking and signing at the same time. "Daddy is OK."

The blond man is watching her sign and it's like he's stealing something from me.

———

Wheeling her suitcase with one hand and holding Ruby's hand with the other, Yasmin walked away from the departure lounge along a long corridor towards the exit. Ruby was struggling to keep up, her suitcase tipping over on its wheels.

She must think of a plan. There had to be a plan. Had to be. If she couldn't think of a plan, would that be the moment someone would tell her to face facts? And who would that someone be? A policeman? Someone from England? As long as she was on her way to find him, Matt was alive. And it wasn't some reactionary grief, fueled by a need in her, but because if she stopped believing he was alive, if she let people and their facts crowd around her, he'd be left alone in the northern Arctic wilderness and wouldn't survive.

Mum says that we need a team talk. Dad used to do our team talks till he came here, then Mum took over. At home, Mum says she and Bosley are "Team Ruby" and it's a let-it-all-out time, because it's not good to keep things bottled up and I should have a good old cry if I want to (rather than risk crying in public, which she thinks is embarrassing too). And, when I do, Bosley wags his tail, bumping it against me, and it's like he gives me some of his tail-wagging happiness. Sometimes Tripod is there instead of Bosley and he purrs with trembly happiness on my lap and that's really nice too, but usually it's Bosley.

Mum says we're going to go to a hotel, but I thought we were going to find Dad. She says that a good hotel is bound to have a sitter service. For a little bit I don't know what she's talking about. And then I do and I say, "No!" She's never left me with a sitter before. I don't want to be left with a sitter. She says it won't be for very long. And she'll make sure that the sitter is nice.

The blond man is right behind us and he's been watching us sign. It's like he's been stealing again but I didn't even know. He must have run some of the way, because his face is all shiny and his blond hair has got dark sweaty streaks in it.

He comes in front of us so we can't walk down the corridor anymore. He's staring at Mum, not saying anything, just doing that "OMG! She's so GORGEOUS! I'm going to turn myself into a total dork by just staring at her" thing. But they always look more dorkish by not saying anything for ages and ages. Mum never notices. *"Mum's romantic roadkill,"* Dad calls it. *"She's a hit-and-run driver."*

*"No, she's not, because she doesn't even know she's hit them,"* I say, defending Mum, which makes Dad laugh.

That sounds like they tease each other all the time, but they hardly ever do.

The blond man is speaking now, and I can see his lips.

"I can help you find a good hotel here," he says.

"We're fine, thank you," Mum says. But she doesn't mean the "thank you."

She takes my hand and we walk along the corridor away from him.

But he's coming too. He reaches out to touch her, like she knows him already, like she's his wife or girlfriend, but she doesn't let him because she doesn't even like him.

"You've never been here before," he says, "so you don't know what places rip you off."

Yasmin tried to get Ruby away from Silesian Stennet, but he was blocking their path.

"You need a sitter, right? I'll look after the girl. Keep her safe for you."

"I said we're fine."

"It's no trouble. I live here in Fairbanks. Just a block away. Professional sitter service would be expensive. I'd be happy to do it for free."

As she looked at his face she remembered that this small town had a high rate of violence against women. He took hold of her arm. "You wouldn't be beholden."

Jack had hurried up to them, and Silesian let go of her arm.

"Are you all right?" Jack asked her, and she nodded. Jack turned to Silesian. "Leave this lady and her daughter alone, you got that?"

"Thank you," Yasmin said to Jack. She turned to Ruby. "OK?" Ruby nodded and they carried on, pulling their cases towards the exit of the airport.

Jack was physically barring Silesian from following them, and Yasmin was grateful to him.

She wished that she had left Ruby at home in England, but since Matt's parents had died she hadn't trusted anyone to look after her, and Ruby was fearful of being away from home. Few people could talk to Ruby or understand her and there could be unintentional cruelties, like turning out her nightlight so Ruby wouldn't know if they said something to her as they left her room, those final good-nights that she needed. So how could she possibly leave her here, in this violent town on the other side of the world from home, with strangers, and that disturbing man nearby?

We're next to the big doors of the airport. Each time a person comes in, the doors slide open and cold dashes inside too and it makes my face hurt. I'm worried the blond man will come after us. Mum must know because she says, "He's just a slimeball and we don't need to worry about slimeballs."

I showed her the sign for "slimeball" ages ago. I made it up and it's a bit gross: you put your finger in your nose. It's the first time Mum's done it. I know she wants to make me smile, so I do.

"I really don't want to stay in a hotel with a sitter," I say. Mum nods, like she understands. I think she's a little bit worried about the slimeball man too. Like he might come and find me. She doesn't say anything for quite a long time. Four lots of people with trolleys of cases come through the doors, and each time a jet of cold air blasts in with them.

Mum says that she's come up with two scenarios, and she finger-spells "scenarios." I can tell we're a proper team now. Our scenarios are:

One, Dad got out of the village and went to get help, but he wasn't able to find any and when he got back all the policemen had gone home again.

Two, he was away filming and took longer than he meant, and when he got back to Anaktue it was terrible because it had burned down and all the police had left.

In both scenario one and scenario two, he's at Anaktue waiting for us and now we just have to get to him.

I'm super-happy about the "we" because I know for definite now that she's not going to leave me behind.

Mum says if it's scenario two, Dad might have been using huskies and a sled and I hope that he was, because he'll have huskies to stop him being lonely. He's told me all about them. One of them is called Pamiuqilavuq, which means "Wags-his-tail," and I think he must be a lot like Bosley; I hope Dad has Wags-his-tail with him.

We're at the place where you get a taxi now. I thought we were going to get a taxi all the way to Dad, but Mum said we can't do that because cars can't drive across Alaska in winter. Mum's on her phone, so there must be 3G here, and I think she's sorting out our plan.

In northern Alaska, Captain Grayling hung up the office telephone, ending his conversation with Yasmin Alfredson. The poor woman had phoned them on her cell phone, near Fairbanks Airport from the sounds of it. She'd come up with scenarios, creating stories for herself in which her husband was alive. Then she'd demanded they search again. He'd recognized what she was doing because he'd done the same when they'd told him about Timothy—refused to accept it because acceptance was impossible to bear. Denial was a melting ice floe but you clung to it anyway. He'd needed to spell it out to her, force her into the drowning ocean; there were twenty-four bodies and twenty-three villagers, her husband's phone and wedding ring had been found at the scene of the fire, the long and thorough search had found no survivors—because there were no survivors. She had become silent on the phone and then hung up. He hoped that she could get a flight home quickly and that her relatives and friends in England would look after her.

It was up to her to find Matt, she knew that now. Just her.

A long-repressed memory surfacing with the smell of whiskey and unwashed clothes; the shadowed damp grass of the cemetery cold through the thin soles of her shoes. She was twelve, visiting Mum's grave. Wanting to press a switch and make it light outside. Her father taking a bottle out of his coat pocket and drinking it, right there, right by her headstone. They were shutting up the cemetery car park by the time she got him to the car.

She got into the driver's seat. Dad too drunk to even notice.

The Elephant and Castle roundabout, three lanes of traffic, too much of it, too fast, too noisy; beaten-up cars like theirs, vying for space and not letting her turn, shouting their horns at her. She'd watched Dad drive all those trips to and from the hospital, watching how he drove so she wouldn't think about what was happening to Mum. Along the Old Kent Road, high-rise council flats crowding around her, graffiti, half standing to reach the pedals. Stalling. Cars honking at her. A man peeing on the pavement. Traffic lights turning red. Crying with fear, shaking with it, but getting them home.

She'd tried to forget and had been too ashamed to tell anyone, even Matt. But it had been up to her and she had got him home.

Years later she'd got a summer job at a cousin's stables where rich kids kept their ponies and horses. She'd been asked to drive a horsebox as a one-off "emergency" that continued for the rest of the summer. She didn't have a license, but nobody checked. Her cousin called her mental. Her mother would have called her brave.

She put her arm around Ruby against the vulturine cold. By Fairbanks Airport, sharply bright lights lined the pavements and roads; softer lights from buildings shone out. Tomorrow there would be a morning with daylight. In the remains of Anaktue there would be no lights at all, and that far north there would be no morning but a polar night for another two months. Matt would be in darkness until they reached him.

## 4

Mum said we'll get a lift in a lorry to Dad and now we're in this place with DREADNAUTUS MEGATRON trucks. I bet in the night they all transform into huge thinking robots. There are tankers, which are as long as *our whole road* in London. Jimmy would think this place is *AWESOME SAUCE!* (My friend. Used-to-be friend. We had our favorite words for things.)

Mum says that nearly all the trucks are going to the oil wells at Prudhoe Bay, and Deadhorse is just before it, so they'll go there on the way.

The first two places we went, Mum asked the receptionist if one of their drivers could take us with them to Deadhorse. NO! Taking passengers is AGAINST THE RULES! You have to imagine that bit underlined in red to match the expressions on their faces. Like they were also saying, "You are so DIM to be even asking this question." Then she talked to a few drivers, and they said the same thing, but instead of the underlining-in-red expression, they smiled at her and took ages to say it. She's been offering the money Grandpa left Dad and her, but it doesn't do any good. I think she should tell the drivers how good she is at physics. She doesn't tell people usually, but if they knew that about her they'd see that she would be useful if their truck broke down. But she just gives them one of my cards. We've hardly got any left.

We're off to the repair shop now. She says a driver with a truck needing repairs will need our money more and take us with him, even if it is breaking the rules.

Inside the repair shop was the smell of diesel, flashes of sparking welding tools, grime and oil ingrained in the ridged concrete floor. Pop music was playing. Like the company calendar on the reception desks, the music made the place feel like it could be anywhere at all. Only the seeping cold reminded you it was Alaska.

As she dragged their cases across the ridged concrete with every man in the place staring at her, Yasmin remembered that people had once found her daringly independent; they'd admired her for being so self-sufficient and so strongly her own person. But since Year Four of primary school there hadn't been a choice.

Lots of kids didn't have a father at home, but it was only Yasmin who didn't have a mother; a centrifugal absence, flinging her to the edge where she was different and apart. She'd watch, giddy with longing, as other people's mothers waited at the school gates, their snacks and hugs ready, while she walked home to a silent, empty flat, or music blaring out as if she belonged to a family of teenagers. That was glossing it kindly. Russell in prison by nineteen, Davey permanently excluded, Dad's brain mashed by booze and grief. Every morning she came downstairs to the smell of last night's food not yet in the bin, the remains hardened onto the plates. She'd wash up, then make herself breakfast. She'd longed to find a breakfast table already laid because that would mean homework checked and clothes that were clean and a story before bed. The girls who wanted a glass slipper and a prince's kiss to wake them up clearly had school shoes that fitted and a mother kissing them good night and didn't have a clue.

Until Matt, for all those years, she had felt weightless with loneliness.

Two drivers at the repair shop had now turned her down; their vehicles belonged to the haulage company and they didn't have to pay for repairs. They were like the other beer-gut-thrusting, combat-wages-earning drivers, keen to say no but keener still to first have a female audience for their machismo as if they were rocketing off for intergalactic warfare rather than driving a road. Now a third driver was turning her down. As she listened, knowing it was pointless, but unable to abort the effort until it was confirmed, a young man slid out from under a lorry on a kind of low go-kart.

"You're the second person bin askin' for a lift."

With Deadhorse Airport out of action, she supposed that other people would be resorting to hitching lifts too. Though the workers at the airport had seemed happy enough to be getting a few more days in Fairbanks.

"Try Adeeb Azizi," the young man said. "Over there. Owns his own rig."

Adeeb didn't usually smoke, but there were times when the carcinogens were worth it for the nicotine hit. One rocky bump, an oil pan torn open, and a seven-hundred-dollar bill. His insurance only paid out in the event of a write-off. He'd hoped there were only six more runs for him to do to Deadhorse this winter; now there'd have to be another. It was a cliché, wasn't it, the dad saving for his kids' college fees so that they could leave him far behind? He wanted to be left behind. He wanted to see his sons disappearing over the horizon with not even a puff of exhaust from their hybrid cars as they entered a better world than his. What was it they said? First-generation corner shop owner (or in his case trucker—better wages, more dangerous), second-generation banker, third-generation poet? His grandchildren could be poets. A wonderful thought. The problem was that his boys would soon be teenagers and, at only forty-five, high blood pressure was giving him an old man's risk of a stroke. Clocks were ticking everywhere he turned. Seven hundred dollars.

He saw a graceful slender woman and a child coming towards him. She seemed composed but was surely aware of every mechanic and trucker staring at her. Halfway across the floor she bent down, so her face was level with the little girl, and said something to her. The little girl moved her hands in reply. Then they came closer and he saw that the graceful woman was afraid but combative, as if daring you to notice. He sensed that she wasn't afraid of the men, but of something larger.

"Can I help?" he asked her.

"I need to get to the Arctic Circle with my daughter, to see the northern lights. We're with a tour party, but we missed them. They'll wait for us at the visitors' center there."

Was there a visitors' center? Yasmin wondered. Surely there must be. Must be some kind of tourist thing. And even if tour parties didn't go in midwinter, maybe this driver didn't know that. And, once they got that far, she'd somehow persuade him to let them carry on with him.

Adeeb thought that this anxious woman was a terrible liar. But he wanted to help her. His older boy said he had a thing for "maidens in distress." "Damsels," his wife, Visha, had corrected. "They're called damsels, I believe," and she had smiled at him.

"There isn't a visitors' center at the Arctic Circle," he said. "But there's a truck stop with a cafeteria shortly before it. I think that's the place you must mean?"

"That must be it, yes," she said. "So will you take us, just to the Arctic Circle? It's what, a hundred miles?"

But knights didn't generally worry if their medication was still correct and the cost of a doctor to find out.

"I've been unwell," he said. "If something happens to me on the road, well . . ."

"Someone would stop, surely, and help?" she said, cutting right to it. What was it that made her so desperate to get a lift? Adeeb wondered. And yes, someone would stop and help. The camaraderie of the road had never included him, not in the usual run of things, but a driver would always help another trucker in distress, even him, and he'd have a woman and child with him. Someone would take them back to Fairbanks, should the worst happen. He looked at her again. They'd probably be lining up.

"Yes, they would," he said.

"So will you take us?" she asked.

He should turn her down. Alongside everything else, there was a possible storm forecast. But it was only a maybe and, even if it did hit, it wouldn't be till he was well past the Arctic Circle. And he saw how scared she was and desperate and trying so hard not to show it.

"I'll give you four thousand pounds," she said.

He'd have taken them without the money.

"I'll take you as far as that trucker stop, just before the Arctic Circle."

"Thank you," she said, and smiled at him, a womanly smile that brought Visha momentarily into this cold, oily place.


Mum and me are in the cab of Mr. Azizi's truck. Jimmy would love this truck; he'd call it *"AWESOME SAUCE!"* for definite. It's all shiny red with silver exhaust pipes like tusks and a big long snub nose with a silvery grille mouth, like a shark showing its teeth. We're really high, so we had to use steps up the side to get into it.

Our load is a ready-made house for oil workers. Mr. Azizi said we are like a tortoise with our house on our back, but hopefully faster. Or a speedy giant snail. He speaks very clearly and makes sure his face is pointing at me. Mum didn't even have to explain. I think he must have a friend who lip-reads. Our house weighs tons, which is good, Mr. Azizi said, because if you're heavy you stick to the road *like glue.* He put one hand on the other and mimed trying to pull them apart. He says pipes aren't a good load because they swing around like you're doing the Highland fling. And he mimed that too.

Now he's giving us his Grand Tour. There's loads of switches and dials, like in an aeroplane. There's a bed above our seats; Mr. Azizi's sleeping bag and our suitcases are on top of it. Mum and I have to squash up onto one seat, but it's pretty big, so we fit. There's only one seat belt, though, and Mum's made me wear it. There's a porta-potty. But we'll have to stop somewhere. There's no-way-José I'm using a potty. We've got a CB radio, which he says all the drivers use, because the road we're going to go on gets quite narrow and there aren't road lights so you have to let other drivers know where you are so you don't bump into each other.

Yasmin was glad they were with Adeeb, who was thoughtful and careful and would surely drive them safely. She studied the map he'd given her. He'd told her it was for trekkers in the summer, not drivers in the winter, as there was just one main road from Fairbanks to Deadhorse, the Elliott Highway, which led onto the Dalton Highway. She found Anaktue marked on his map: about four hundred and thirty miles from Fairbanks and thirty-five miles to the east of the Dalton Highway. She hoped there was a smaller road linking the Dalton Highway to Anaktue, but there was nothing, not even a hiking trail, so no way of getting there by vehicle. They'd have to go to Deadhorse and get a taxi plane to Matt, as she'd first planned. She'd be glad to get away from Fairbanks; the frontier town felt threatening to her, an outpost corroding into the wilderness surrounding it.

OMG! We have satellite reception in the truck! Mr. Azizi is linking up my laptop! I never ever say "OMG," even though it's really easy to finger-spell, because I don't like words you have to do with a ! I look really dorky when I pull a ! face. Dad says it's easier to do it with your voice; you just sound screechy when you say "OMG," like teenage girls, who use it the most. When he says "screechy," I say, "Like finger-nails dragging across a blackboard?" And he says, "Spot on." Even though I can't hear the screechy sound, I get the general ugghness. But the satellite is OMG in a coolio, not screechy way, because now Dad can email me back, even when we've gone past mobile reception and Wi-Fi.

Mr. Azizi says that when we leave Fairbanks it's going to be really dark. He shows me a little light I can use when Mum and me need to talk to each other, so we can see each other's hands and lips.

Did you know that the loudest bird in the world is called the superb lyrebird? Really! And I think some people—a very few—should have "superb" as part of their name too: *the Superb Mr. Azizi!*

I want Mum to say thank you to him for me, but she would tell me to say it myself, "USE YOUR WORDS, RUBY," so I give Mr. Azizi a "thank you" smile, and he understands because he smiles back and gives a little "you're welcome" shrug.

He's getting out of the truck to give it one final check, and then we're going to set off. Mum watches him through the windscreen. She's all tensed up like a greyhound; you know, at the start of a race? All their muscles tightened right up, ready to spring out and race at a hundred miles an hour after the pretend furry rabbit. I think she's worried Mr. Azizi will change his mind. But I'm sure he won't. He has something settled about him, like he says something and he'll do it. Mum's like that too, but in a less calm way. You'd have to know her for ages to know that about her.

In the yard's fiercely bright overhead lights, Adeeb saw a man walking around each truck, searching for something or someone. It was that man Silesian Stennet, not wearing a hat despite the cold, his blond hair glittering in the artificial glare. Silesian was carrying a crate, which Adeeb had seen him standing on so he could harangue truck-ers high up in their cabs. Silesian disturbed him, though he wasn't sure why, and he felt bad about it because really he should admire the man, coming here as he regularly did, and standing on his almost literal soapbox, to warn tanker drivers carrying heaven-knows-what to and from the fracking wells. The drivers invariably just gave him a load of abuse for his pains. Like Adeeb, they found him disturbing, which was maybe why they ridiculed him.

Adeeb turned away from Silesian Stennet and checked the satellite receiver mounted above the cab. The man who sold him the truck had installed it and claimed it was designed for ships and could get reception anyplace on the planet. He'd given Adeeb his sat phone. Adeeb hadn't wanted to keep the expensive contract going, but Visha had made him. There was no cell reception or Wi-Fi in northern Alaska, not for hundreds of miles. She said she had to know he was all right. Said she wasn't fussing. She'd stood there, long-fingered hands on her hips, daring him to disagree with her. He'd put an arm around her, awkward with those pretty hands still on her hips.

"I feel fit as a fiddle, no problems at all," he'd said. (His mother, who'd taught him English, enjoyed colloquialisms.)

"Then I want to know you feel fit as a fiddle, no problems at all, every day," Visha had said.

He phoned home on the sat phone every night, just long enough to reassure Visha and say good night to the boys. In the far north it helped him mark out night from day, reassured him that the diurnal rhythm still existed somewhere.

Before getting back into his cab he checked everything one more time—snow chains, spare tires, tire jack, tools to repair hoses and lines and filters. Today he was Amundsen triple-checking his airship before setting off over the North Pole, not a middle-aged refugee from Afghanistan with incipient OCD. He suspected that the special repair tools and the flares, the emergency medical kit, all of it, was totally inadequate against the enormity of what northern Alaska could throw at them. But he would be taking Yasmin and Ruby only as far as the Arctic Circle—whatever their real reason was for that—and no farther.

———

Mum is a bit turned away from me, like when she's playing twenty-one and is trying to hide her expression so Dad and I think she might have an ace and a king. I can't see her eyes, which are usually Mum's giveaway. I gently pat her arm to get her attention. Her eyes are all filmy.

"Dad told me a story about an Inupiaq hunter on sea ice," I say, because I think the story will cheer her up.

She says with her mouth-voice, "Can you tell me using your words?"

Normally, I'd turn away from her, so I can't read her lips anymore. Then she'd come in front of me again and we'd do a little maypole dance around each other. But we can't do that in Mr. Azizi's truck.

"I *am* using my words," I say to her, in my hand-voice. She just shakes her head, like I've made her sad.

The funny thing is that Mum understands everything else. She's kind and funny and wonderful; super-coolio-wonderful. Sometimes at school when I'm upset, I think of her and I feel hugged, just by the thought of her. But there's a hard bit, like a bit of gravel in a snowball. And it's awful because the only thing that's hard in her is something that I really really mind about.

It's a shame about the story because I think she might've really liked it.

I'm looking for Dad out of the windscreen, like suddenly there he'll be! I know it's stupid, we haven't even left Fairbanks yet, haven't even left the yard, so it's too early to be looking for him. And anyway, he's in Anaktue, waiting for us. I just really want to see him.

Mr. Azizi is trying to turn out of the yard onto the road, but there's loads of trucks coming in and we can't fit past them. Most of them have "AM-FUELS" or "F.B.F." on them, which the man at the airport said stands for "Frack Baby Frack," but Mum said he was only joking. Some of the trucks have houses on them, like the one we've got. Mum's asking Mr. Azizi questions, like how he stops fuel freezing. I'm not even trying to lip-read his answers because I'm pretty sure we won't have done that in science. Last week we put baby teeth in Coca-Cola to see what happens (borrowed from the Year Twos after the tooth fairy's visited as most of us Year Sixes have lost our baby teeth). So instead of trying to lip-read their conversation I look out for Dad again.

The slimeball man is next to me; BANG next to my window. He must be standing on something because his face is close to mine. I can see the top of his head; there's a horrible gray line either side of his parting, like a rat. I try to get further away from him, but I can't get very far away because I've got a seat belt on and Mum is next to me.

Mum hasn't seen him because she's turned away again, probably hiding her filmy eyes from me.

The slimeball man is taking off his big mittens, but it's so cold, why's he doing that? He opens his bare hand and puts two fingers against his palm, which means "Mummy"—MY sign for her.

Mr. Azizi hasn't seen him, because he's looking straight ahead, waiting to turn onto the road.

The slimeball man is moving his fingers slowly around his face, the sign for "beautiful."

His pudgy hands must be getting really cold because they're turning all mottled, like ugly blue and mauve jellyfish. He signs, "Get your mummy for me."

He's pointing one of his horrible fingers at Mum.

There's a gap for us to go and Mr. Azizi drives out of the yard and onto the road and slimeball man is running after us, but he'll never catch us.

I don't know if I should tell Mum about him. I pat her arm and she turns to me and her eyes are filmy, just like I thought they'd be. I don't want to make her more upset. And we'll never have to see him again. He's miles away from us already.

**Words Without Sounds** @Words_No_Sounds – 6m
*651 followers*
CREEPY: Looks like hands turning into jellyfish;
tastes like cakes that are alive; feels: too close.

## 5

It was inhumanly dark. Yasmin's eyes couldn't make sense of the blackness. They'd been driving for four hours and she'd stopped looking for glowing halos from far-off cities or towns because there were no cities or towns. Clouds made a barricade over the Earth, so there was no moonlight or starlight, nothing to pierce through the weighted darkness apart from the truck's headlights. Adeeb had told her that they shone for a quarter of a mile ahead, and to Yasmin they seemed like a search beam over an immense black ocean; a person disappeared in such a scale.

She remembered her terror of the dark as a child, how sometimes it had stopped her from even breathing, and it was linked to her being flung to the edge, a void in the center of her life, where once her mother had been.

Her brothers and father had thought her fearless; they'd enjoyed her fists in the air to settle an argument, her bruises and grazes; the kid's got balls. It was one way to try and fit into the all-male family. But being physically unafraid was easy, because after her mother died, what was there left to be scared of? Eight in the evening in February when they'd left the hospital. She'd tried to get out of the car but her father had put the child locks on—the metal handle digging into her fingers, the smell of old takeaways, stale cigarettes, her nine-year-old arms in the cheap fleece too weak to force the door open, and she couldn't rescue Mum. Couldn't stop them putting her into a dark box and nailing it shut.

Darkness was death and grief. But she'd hidden her fear from everyone, suffered her night terrors alone.

And then one night, ten months after her mother had died, she'd pulled up her bedroom blind and looked out of her window at the dark, confronting her demons, determined to face down her fear, and had seen stars, like thousands of tiny celestial nightlights.

Through the rest of her childhood the stars had comforted her, not only for their lights in the darkness but because as she looked at them she could imagine herself far away, as if the pain of grief was soldered into their flat and street and all the places she'd ever been with her mother, or seen on TV with her even, and that if she could only imagine herself far enough away, grief couldn't follow her there.

Her comfort from the stars had matured into an intellectual fascination, and they had become more, not less astonishing as she'd studied them.

This road was eerie, an endless strip of ice through the dark, but it hadn't been nearly as perilous as she'd feared.

She felt Ruby move closer to her, and she put her arm around her. Her determination to find Matt wasn't driven solely out of her love for him but out of her love for Ruby too. She couldn't bear for Ruby to suffer the appalling bereavement of losing a parent, the terrible violence of that grief.

She remembered putting on Matt's wedding ring at the police office and knowing that he had to be alive, not only because of her love for him but because of Ruby sitting next door.


The road is made of ice and we're driving on it! Cross-my-heart true! Our headlights show it all white with snow and mucky bits sticking on it. Around our headlights it's dark and it's like driving into a ghost train tunnel and never seeing the end.

Mr. Azizi said in winter they pour gazillions of gallons of water onto the old gravelly road and then it freezes. He said ice is the only thing that won't break with big trucks driving on it, because ice is very, very tough. I think he wanted to make me feel safe, but there was something in his face that meant he thinks this isn't a good thing. He told me about the ice before we left Fairbanks, when I could still read his lips.

Dad still hasn't emailed back. But it's really hard for him to check his emails. His satellite terminal is a lot more tricky to use than Mr. Azizi's because you can carry it around.

Mum and I are coming out here at Christmas, which is only four weeks away, and Dad and I are going to write a blog together—aweekinalaskablog.com—about all the animals and birds we see. Dad got me a special cover for my laptop so it will work in the cold, and I've just put it on because I think we should start our blog as soon as we're all together.


Adeeb checked his mirror. For the last fifteen miles or so, he'd seen blue headlights in the dark behind them, like two azure damselfish. HID lights were rare on the Dalton. The damselfish truck seemed to be following him, speeding up when he did, slowing when he did. He'd had a rookie follow him a couple of times, tailing him so he'd learn what to do, and so Adeeb would be there in case of any accident, but there was no rookie following him today. Nor could it be a friend, keeping mutually watchful eyes on each other. He had a reputation for keeping himself to himself, a reputation he felt had been created for him rather than earned. Marked as a loner, he'd felt acutely alone on his trips north.

In a few minutes they were coming to the first steep incline, and his hands gripped hold of the steering wheel in anticipation, as if he'd be holding on to it rather than using it to steer. He dreaded the hazardous driving ahead and feared the ice.

Before his friend Saaib's accident, he had thought that ice, like glass, was delicate, the very fact of its transparency making it not quite solidly formed. He'd wondered how ice could really take the weight of a truck.

When Saaib arrived in the UK he found work in the pouring room of a glass factory. It was a huge room, Saaib said, with a totally even floor, into which was poured—carefully, by special machine— molten glass, which then solidified into a perfectly even sheet on the even floor, before being cut. But one morning something went wrong with the careful special machine and the molten glass gushed into the room, too much and too fast, and the liquid glass forced its way out of windows and doors and set light to whatever it touched. Only the level room, made of marble, could withstand the heat; outbuildings and offices were destroyed in the fire. Saaib had been badly burned. Since then glass and ice had seemed not only tough to Adeeb, but also vicious, murderous even, and all the time their transparency belied their power.

Yasmin closed her mouth against a scream so that Ruby couldn't see her fear. They were plunging down a sheer drop into the darkness. She watched Adeeb locking the differential gearing in the rear axle, so that each wheel had all the torque it could, but it wasn't working because they were going too fast down this precipitous slope; surely this was too fast. They got to the bottom and the momentum sped them up the opposite slope. They reached the top. She was shaking from adrenaline.

She turned to Ruby, who smiled at her, showing no sign of being afraid, as if this were an adventure. She was excited about getting to her dad and excited about the road itself, not realizing how dangerous it was because how could a mother who makes you eat five portions of fruit and vegetables a day and has a homework schedule stuck to the fridge do something that puts you at risk?

"I'm sorry I frightened you," Adeeb said to Yasmin. "I had to drive fast enough for us to get up this side. Too slow is as dangerous as too fast. I should have warned you; should have warned you about the whole road before we left Fairbanks. It's just that sometimes I don't remember how bad it is until I'm driving it again."

"I asked you to take us," Yasmin said.

"Do you want to go back?" he said. "Because I'll take you."

The cab's thermometer measured the outside temperature as minus eleven Fahrenheit, already colder than Fairbanks. At Anaktue the average temperature in winter was minus twenty-two and could reach minus fifty-two, without the windchill. This road was dangerous, yes, she knew that now and wished to God that Ruby were somewhere safe, but if she left Matt there wasn't a risk that he would be hurt but a hundred-percent, no-margin-of-error certainty that he would die.

"I want to go on," she said.

I keep thinking we're going to skid and I grab hold of Mum, like you do on a roller coaster. In our headlights you can see this ginormous pipe running right next to the road. It looks like a huge metal vein in a white body, and inside there's all this slushy warm oil pumping along.

I'm squashed up next to Mum and she's got her arm around me and it feels really nice. Normally I don't do this, because I need to practice for being eleven and grown-up and at secondary school and everything. I wish she'd tell Mr. Azizi that we want to go all the way to Deadhorse because I'm sure he'll say yes and then she won't look so worried. I hope that if I go to sleep, when I wake up we'll be near to Dad.

As Adeeb navigated their truck around hairpin bends and down hills more like ski runs than a road, Yasmin focused on the drive axles and the air-actuated clutch and how power flowed to the tires without any differential action, giving each wheel all the torque the road permitted. She'd never enjoyed the engineering part of physics but out here, in this truck, she was glad she knew how Adeeb was keeping control because she understood why, for the moment, Ruby was safe.

Ruby had fallen asleep, tired out from the long flight, the trauma of their arrival, and the anxiety of trying to find a way to get to her dad. Of course she was exhausted. Ruby's head slipped a little and she juddered momentarily awake before settling into sleep. Yasmin stroked her hair and tried to stop her head from slipping down. If the danger to Ruby became too great, she knew she would have to ask Adeeb to turn around or get a lift in a truck going back to Fairbanks. But for now they would keep going.

As Ruby slept, Yasmin strained to see more of the landscape surrounding the ice-ribbon road.


The scale of Alaska frightened Adeeb; twice the size of Texas and the only sign of humanity through his windshield was the ice road itself and the Trans-Alaska Pipeline running alongside it. Technological marvels they might be, but Adeeb didn't think they felt either human or civilizing.

At the beginning of their journey, he and Yasmin had spoken about the mechanics of driving his truck. She said she'd studied a bit of engineering as part of her physics degree but hadn't specialized in it; she'd chosen astrophysics. Adeeb thought that a woman studying astrophysics was one definition of freedom.

But they hadn't actually talked—not about whatever it was that preoccupied her, had made her lie to him and bring a child to the Arctic Circle in winter. He guessed that she didn't want to talk to him about it, and it wasn't something he could ask her. He hoped he'd be able to help her, if she did volunteer it.

His headlights illuminated five spruce trees at the edge of the road, whitened by snow and ice. Although the trees were over a century old they were barely three feet high; it was a brutal place to grow. Farther north, there were no trees at all. He'd read about northern Alaska after his first journey to Deadhorse and the Prudhoe Bay oil wells, in the hope that knowing a place would tame it in some way, soften it a little, but the opposite had happened. He knew now that a landslide a hundred feet wide was moving towards the ice road, frozen soil and rocks and shrunken trees stealing closer inch by inch, gaining speed and destroying anything in their way, as if the land itself, like the cold, was not just passively hostile but actively aggressive.

Worse than the dangers of the road and the cold and the isolation was the absence of colors; just the white snow in his headlights and then the dark. In this monochromatic landscape he felt a craving for colors like a need for warmth. He thought of Leyla Sarahat Roshani and wondered if she had a lonely Afghan driver in mind, when she wrote her poetry:

> *"I plant my eyes / in the mirror / so that a sign / small and green / may emerge, proclaim / the eternity of Spring."*

But he'd never seen anything green, and spring when it came would be brief.

His love of poetry, like his knowledge of English, was a gift from his mother, a teacher in Zabul before the Taliban stopped her from teaching.

For the last thirty miles he'd seen Yasmin staring through the windshield, as if searching for something, more tense with every mile they covered, and he wanted to tell her that he'd never seen anything out there. Perhaps he'd been too focused on the road but he believed there was nothing to search for; nothing to see, just a sterile waste-land of snow and ice. Even the predatory packs of wolves, for which truckers carried loaded guns, were probably more myth than truth.

A truck passed him, going the other way towards Fairbanks. The glare of the truck's headlights momentarily flooded his cab, shining on Ruby and Yasmin.

He should never have brought them. He hadn't thought it through properly. He'd been too selfish to think it through properly. He realized now that he hadn't been motivated by chivalry but by a selfish yearning for company on the road. His headache, which had felt so mild in Fairbanks, bothered him more now.

Only a sliver of wilderness could be seen in the beam of the headlights but enough for Yasmin to see that it was relentlessly barren. Matt had told her he'd come back here to film animals. He'd told Ruby all about the winter wildlife. Yasmin had suspected that he was, at best, exaggerating so that Ruby wouldn't know the real reason he was staying away from home. She'd never challenged him because she'd thought it was a screen that protected both of them from a painful truth, not about Corazon—she didn't know about her then—but that he found home life stultifying, her stultifying, and needed to get away. Too decent to formally separate, too loving to cause Ruby anguish, he'd used winter wildlife in Alaska as a necessary fiction. For mile after bleak mile that fiction had stretched and broken.

She remembered the prolonged quiet during their phone call eight days ago, the time it had taken for her angry words to reach him and then his words traveling back to her across the globe—*"I kissed her because I missed you."*

It had made no sense. But the reason he'd returned to Alaska in wintertime had become clear.

She fervently hoped she was wrong—not because it would mean that Matt was, kiss apart, faithful to her. In the great scheme of him being alive or dead, that really, astonishingly, didn't matter to her now. But because if he'd told her the truth about coming here for the animals, there was a chance he'd been away filming when the village burned down, and that would mean he'd have his survival kit with him and not be out there in the killing cold and dark unprotected.

Two months after their knitting expedition, she'd asked him to meet her at Cambridge station. When he saw her on the platform, she was wearing wellies and carrying a large, oddly shaped holdall, and he later admitted he'd feared that loving her would not always be straightforward. At King's Lynn their train terminated and they got the last local bus of the evening, winding their way along the coast in the dark, the only passengers, until they reached the seaside village of Cley. He'd followed her over the wet shingle, the sea roaring-hushing alongside them.

"Look," she said, pointing up.

He looked at the enormous dome of the Norfolk seaside sky, an upended cosmic glitter jar knocked clumsily across it.

She took a telescope and tripod out of the holdall, digging the tripod into the shingle and calibrating the telescope.

"Now look."

He'd thought she was going to show him the moon up close, or a planet and he'd see rings or satellites or whatever planets had. He hadn't been prepared for it at all. The thousands of stars he'd seen with his naked eye had turned into hundreds of thousands, and all the time they had been there, these stars beyond stars.

They'd fallen asleep on a rug over bumpy shingles, the rhythmic thumping and sighing of the sea near to them. When she woke up, dawn was lightening the sky and had turned the stars invisible. Matt was already awake. He took her face in his hands.

"What . . . ?" she asked.

"I see you," he said, and she felt like landfall spotted by an explorer too long at sea.

I'm pressed against Mum and I can feel her heart beating really fast, like the little shrew Tripod caught (even though he's only got three legs, he still catches them). I know she's thinking about Dad. She hasn't seen that I'm awake, so I look at her for a bit and she's staring out of the windscreen and she's biting on her lip, like she wants to cry and is having to stop herself.

I feel like I'm spying so I wriggle a bit, so she knows that I'm awake. She gives me a squeeze-box hug.

I shouldn't have let myself fall asleep. I thought Mr. Azizi would look after her, but he has to drive this truck, and he doesn't know Mum well enough to see the signs of when she's upset, things she's never done before, like biting her lip and not crying.

I think she's worried that it's scenario one and Dad doesn't have anything with him. But I know that he'll be OK. His Inupiat friends showed him how to make an aputiak, which is a kind of iglu. Not the big sort, with rooms and everything, but the kind they make when they go on a hunting trip, just temporary, till Mum and me get there. So I'm sure he's built himself an aputiak and he's just waiting till we come and find him. He told me it's snug inside.

*"How can it be when it's made of SNOW?" I said.*

*"Snow's a brilliant insulator, lots of pockets of air, so it keeps the cold out. And your own body heat makes it cozy too."*

*"Cozy?"*

*"Cozy. And sometimes they use a qulliq, which is like a lamp and a heater all in one. It's a stone bowl and you burn blubber and that makes it toasty. Want to know something interesting?"*

*He knows that I always want to know something interesting.*

*"In late spring it just melts away. No skips or landfill or foundations left behind. Not even a wheelie-bin amount of rubbish or a wastepaper-basket amount. It all just disappears right back into the earth."*

We have our own signs for things. So for "aputiak" we make the letter A and then a curved shape like the roof with our hand. He learned signing when I was a baby. He said that he would learn a sign and it would take him ages and then he'd show it to me and it took me ten seconds flat to get it. He told me that instead of babbling with my mouth like other babies I babbled with my hands. He always has a super-big smile when he says that.

I pull away from Mum a little bit to free my hands up, and I tell her that Dad will have made an aputiak, which I finger-spell because Mum doesn't know my and Dad's sign for it. I show her the special sign and tell her that his friends showed him how to make one and it's really cozy. I think it's made her feel better because she smiles at me.

"Do you think Bosley is OK?" I ask. The sign for "Bosley" is a finger wagging like a tail, which everyone in our family knows is especially for Bosley.

"He'll be very happy. Mrs. F. spoils him," Mum says.

"Did you pack his bed?"

"Of course. And all his toys."

I don't need to worry about Tripod, because Mrs. Buxton is coming in to feed him every day. Mum says Tripod is like a teenager who can't wait to have the place to himself. I like thinking of everyone snug and asleep—Tripod on the sofa, where he's not allowed, and Bosley in his special bed and Dad in his aputiak.

Out of the window there's a giant wizard's black cloak, and hidden on the other side are animals and birds and fish and insects. There's caribou and moose and snowy owls and snowshoe hares and otters, all awake, and bears will be hibernating in their dens, but they still move around in their sleep, and under the ice on the rivers there's frogs sheltering at the bottom because that's the warmest place.

I know I'm weird liking caribou and musk oxes. Tanya and the girl gang like ponies most, then kittens and puppies. Hamsters and guinea pigs are OK to like too. Caribou and tundra bees would just be seen as weird like me. But they're super-coolio! You'd think a bee wouldn't survive a minute in the cold, but it shivers its tiny muscles to make heat and then traps warmth in its soft coat. My top favorite animals are river otters, and their babies are about five months old now. Dad's seen them playing tag and he's watched them playing hide and seek too. Cross-my-heart true!

I wouldn't be popular with Tanya and the girl gang even if I could hear and talk like them. I don't like glittery lip balm or fashion-design kits and I like river otters more than ponies.

Mum's still squeezing me, a little too tight, but I don't mind.

I look out of the windscreen, just to the edge of the road, rather than all the way ahead, trying to see what's out there. I think tundra bees are hibernating but maybe one is out there, flying along next to us. I must make some kind of sound because Mum and Mr. Azizi both look at me. I point and Mr. Azizi checks there's no one close behind us and stops the truck, right in the road because there's nowhere else to stop.

A little way ahead, on the very edge of the road, the snow and ice is all sparkly because no one has driven on it; in our lights it looks like diamond dust.

In the diamond-glittery snow is the shape of two wings, as if an angel has crashed and has got up and left her wing prints behind, or maybe just landed normally on her feet and then decided to lie down in the snow for a bit.

"What is it?" Mum asks.

I make two wing shapes with my hands, the sign for an angel, and it's like I'm making a mirror with my hands for the wing prints in the snow. I smile so she knows I'm only joking about the angel.

"I think they're wing prints made by a ptarmigan," I say, finger-spelling "ptarmigan." Dad showed me pictures, which is how I know.

A ptarmigan is as good as an angel, better even. But Mum doesn't know about ptarmigans.

"It's an amazing bird," I tell Mum. "Which stays in Alaska all winter. Its feathers turn white in winter so you can't see it in the snow."

Jimmy would say *"AWESOME SAUCE!"* and it is. It's BEAUTIFUL; these perfect wing prints in the diamond-glittery snow, with Mr. Azizi's headlights like a spotlight and then just darkness all around it.

Dad told me ptarmigans fly into snowbanks when they want to rest so a predator won't see their footprints.

**Words Without Sounds** @Words_No_Sounds – 1m

*651 followers*

AWESOME-SAUCE-BEAUTIFUL: Touching a black spot on a cheetah's fur; a lemonade sea w/ fizzing waves; a ptarmigan's wing prints in snow.

## 6

Four months after their first star-watching stay on Cley beach, she'd gone with Matt to the Insh Marshes at Speyside: damply cold in January, the rain dismal. She stood next to him in a bird hide that smelled of wet anoraks.

"So this is twitching?" she said.

"Or birding."

"That sounds kinky too. All this furtive hiding in hides and peering at things with binoculars."

He laughed, then showed her greylag geese and whooper swans, which wintered out there in the flooded marshes. She loved his passion and his knowledge and how it transformed the wet miserable place into something entirely different. She quizzed him, wanting to learn, to be fascinated too by snipe, wigeon, redshank, and curlew. They planned to come back in summer to watch the lapwings.

"Did your dad find you in the cabbage patch one night?" he asked. He'd already met—at his insistence—her father and brothers.

"A mulberry bush; cabbage patches only have dolls from America."

"Ah. Marry me?"


She saw a sign on the side of the road, illuminated by their headlights: SOAGIL ENERGY VEHICLES ONLY.

"Where does the road go?" she asked Adeeb.

"It's most probably an access road to a well," he said. "They're start-ing to frack the interior of Alaska now. Sometimes they make the road out of gravel; other times they link it to a river."

"And the river's frozen over?" she asked.

"Yes. A natural ice road. Though it can need reinforcing."

She checked Adeeb's map, holding it up to the small interior light. There was nothing on it to mark Soagil Energy's road. Perhaps there was a river road to Anaktue.

She found the River Alatnak, which started south in the Brooks Mountains and flowed north to the Arctic Ocean. Two hundred and ninety miles south of where they were now, the River Alatnak looped close to the Dalton and then went thirty or so miles all the way to Anaktue. Maybe it would be possible to drive on the river to Matt. But she couldn't ask Adeeb, not yet. She still hadn't told him their real destination. She didn't know how to convince him to take them and was afraid that he'd refuse—with kindness and sympathy, but still refuse—and she'd have no way of reaching Matt.


"Marry me?" he'd asked again, in case she hadn't heard the first time.

"Dad would have to give me away, me being his chattel and every-thing, before becoming your chattel."

"But he simply found you in a bush. Please?"

"Not yet," she'd said.


In his mirror, Adeeb caught a glimpse of the damselfish headlights still in the darkness behind them. He put on the radio, ostensibly to get the news and the hourly weather report, but in truth it was because the radio station played classical music. As he listened, Adeeb liked to imagine he was back in his childhood home of Zabul, looking at the field next to their house in springtime, the rows of pink flowering almond trees, like a blossoming corps de ballet.

Ruby was studying him and he realized that he was tapping his fingers on the steering wheel. "I'm thinking about blossom," he told her, slowly and carefully. "And I'm listening to Chopin." Then he looked back at the road, the windshield a pink-blossom lens created by the music.


Mr. Azizi just turned to me and said he was listening to Chopin, as if I'd understand; AND he doesn't ask me if I want him to turn it up REALLY LOUD and he doesn't ask if I play the drums. He is the Superb Mr. Azizi!

Most people think that I want LOUD and THUMPING so I can feel the vibrations, like I'll be grateful that sound has got through to me any old way it can. They're always putting percussion sticks into my hands and asking me to hit something (but not them!). And just because Evelyn Glennie is a musical genius doesn't mean that because I'm deaf I will be too. They think I'd love to learn the drums, or the cymbals or a rinky-dink plinkety-plink glockenspiel. (Jimmy said it sounds rinky-dink plinkety-plink.) But I'm terrible at them all. Our last school concert, in front of parents, I *air-glockenspieled*. Dad thought it was hilarious. Even Mum was trying not to smile, but I know she hoped I'd love a percussion instrument and join the orchestra and go on the orchestra trip and *be a part of something* (the hearing world with me thumping at something in time with everyone else). *"Hitting something isn't integrating, Mum,"* I said to her (I'd lip-read her saying "integrating" to Dad loads of times) and then I felt bad because it made her sad.

It was just after then that a harpist came to do a concert at school to "inspire future harpists," and because Mum was there I didn't make a fuss about putting my hand on the harp for a bit of the concert. I did mind, but I wanted to make Mum happy, so I stood there with my hand on it. Everyone else was bored. Feet shuffling, rows and rows of fidgeting, not a future harpist in the place, but it was lovely. It wasn't thumping vibrations, but like wings beating fast, like a hummingbird, so fast you can't even tell they're moving, or like when I picked up that shrew Tripod caught and it had these superfast little heartbeats and I could feel how fragile it was but also so alive. If I could choose a musical instrument to play it would be the harp. Not sure that you can go on an orchestra trip with one of those as it wouldn't fit in the coach.

Mum's and Mr. Azizi's faces have gone still. They're really concentrating on something and I don't think it's the music because Mum's never said anything about liking music.

The headline on the news was Anaktue. Although the radio was already loud enough, Yasmin leaned closer towards it.

"Here in the studio we have our governor of Alaska, Mary-Beth Jenston," the radio reporter said. "And on the line is Captain David Grayling, the state trooper who was in charge of the search-and-rescue mission at Anaktue."

The presenter's voice was neutral but the news should be done as drama, Yasmin thought, should recognize that it was about people's lives; that a wife was listening to this, that a child was in a truck on a dangerous road because there was nowhere safe her mother could leave her.

"Captain Grayling, coming to you first, can you give us an update on the situation at Anaktue?"

She'd done this while Mum was ill, her mind going into overdrive, creating a running commentary that she couldn't switch off as a kind of wordy shield against emotions, leaping cruel hope as well as anxiety.

"Unfortunately, I can only confirm that twenty-three Inupiat people died in the fire, including three children," Captain Grayling said. "There was also a British man, who was a wildlife filmmaker. All of the relatives have now been informed."

Yasmin saw Adeeb looking across at her and only then realized that her face and palms were damp with sweat.

———

It was clear to Adeeb that Yasmin was distressed and that she was trying to hide it. He turned down the heater.

"Isn't it odd, Captain Grayling, that a fire takes hold so fast?" the radio interviewer asked.

"A stockpile of snowmobile fuel and generator diesel caught fire and exploded," Captain Grayling replied. "A devastatingly intense fire would have been the result very quickly."

"But how did this fire begin? Surely fuel doesn't just catch light out there in the snow?"

"There was most likely an initial fire and small explosion inside a house," Captain Grayling replied. "We think gas for a heater or cooker caught fire, probably because of an electrical fault or careless-ness, and the fire then spread to the snowmobile fuel and generator diesel, causing the large explosion."

"But a village being wiped out by a fire in minus thirty is suspi-cious, surely?"

"No, as I just said, it can happen," Captain Grayling replied. "If you cook with gas canisters and there's a leak. If you stockpile fuel too close to houses. We have issued warnings to villagers and home-steaders throughout Alaska to store their fuel at least twenty yards from their homes. I'd urge your listeners to do the same."

"Thank you for joining us, Captain Grayling. Now if I could turn to you, Governor Jenston?"

"Good evening. I'd like to offer my heartfelt condolences to the families and friends of the victims of this terrible tragedy."

"Thank you for coming on our program."

"I'm glad to have the opportunity to be here."

"Perhaps you could help me with some facts on Anaktue?" the reporter asked, her tone neutral. "Is Anaktue—*was* Anaktue—sitting on hundreds of thousands of barrels of shale oil?"

"I really don't see the relevance of that," the governor replied.

"I've seen a geologist's report," the radio reporter continued. "The land under Anaktue has three layers of the rock that generated the huge volumes of oil and gas that migrated to Prudhoe Bay and Kuparuk."

"I am here to offer my condolences to fellow Alaskans, not to talk about geology."

"Didn't a number of hydraulic fracturing companies, including Soagil Energy Incorporated, want to frack the land under and around Anaktue?"

"That is wholly irrelevant to this terrible tragedy."

"Isn't it true that Soagil Energy wanted to put an initial twenty-two wells within a one-and-a-half-mile radius of the village?"

"That has nothing to do with—"

"And when the villagers refused to allow it, Soagil Energy tried to force them?" the radio interviewer continued.

"No one tried to force them," the governor replied. "We supported their decision, one hundred percent. We have huge respect for Inupiat people living here and we do our utmost to support their way of life. We are not like the rest of the USA, corralling First Nations peoples into reservations. We respect their right to live and hunt where they have always lived and hunted. We just do what we can to offer support. We were due to install new generators at Anaktue, and the villagers were given food coupons as well as unrestricted hunting rights."

"You are on the board of a hydraulic fracturing company?"

"I resigned my place on the board when I was elected governor. But I'm proud to have been involved and to still offer support to these companies. Mining companies, including hydraulic fracturing companies, are not villains, but employers. They offer jobs for Alaskans, which includes jobs for Inupiat people. And all resident Alaskans, including the Inupiat, benefit from the mineral wealth of our state through the Alaska Permanent Fund. We all get an annual dividend from investment earnings of mineral royalties. Energy companies are safeguarding our future. And they are helping to keep the lights on in American homes."

"That was under a thousand dollars."

"Excuse me?"

"The dividend last year. Nine hundred dollars. Not that much compared to the millions made by the energy companies. You said 'we' earlier, Governor. That, and I quote, 'we supported their decision, one hundred percent.' Did you mean you and the government of Alaska or you and the rest of the board of Soagil Energy?"

"As I said, I am no longer on the board. But as I have also said, the mining companies are good for Alaska and for the rest of America."

"So what happens now, Governor Jenston? Does Soagil Energy get to frack the villagers' land?"

"I've been informed that Soagil Energy is no longer going to pursue an interest in this area. Out of respect for the villagers."

"And the other fracking companies?"

"I don't have that information, but I imagine other hydraulic fracturing companies will follow Soagil Energy's lead on this. Look, if you want to find a villain, then you're looking in the wrong place. The only people who have behaved criminally in the energy business are the so-called eco-warriors. These people have deliberately sabotaged wells and condensate tanks, shot at the pipeline. And, by the way, that one shot resulted in a quarter of a million gallons of crude spewing out of the pipe and threatening an ecological disaster. One day I've no doubt they'll light a fire and try to blame it on hydraulic fracturing, though the truth is hydraulic fracturing hasn't caused a single fire, *not one,* even when the pad is right in someone's backyard, which certainly isn't the case in Alaska."

Mum and Mr. Azizi haven't opened their mouths, so they're not talking to each other, but Mr. Azizi keeps glancing at Mum. She isn't moving at all. Her whole body is concentrating, like even moving her chin might stop her from hearing whatever it is. I think it's something to do with Dad. I tug on her arm and she turns to me.

She doesn't say anything for a little while and I know she's thinking about whether to tell me and I want her to remember that we're a team, me and Mum, and she *has* to tell me.

After the news there'd been a local weather report; Yasmin had barely heard it.

"There's been a weather forecast on the radio," she told Ruby. "There's going to be a storm; they're not sure when yet."

She hated using Ruby's deafness to hide the truth from her. She and Matt had never done it, never turned their faces away from her so she couldn't read their lips. Better for her to lip-read hurtful words or for them to be silent with each other than use her deafness for some kind of advantage. But the forecast storm was the partial truth.

"We'll get to Dad before the storm, won't we?" Ruby asked.

"Yes. I'm sure we will."

"Have you told Mr. Azizi yet?" Ruby asked.

"Not yet."

Breakfast at the damp, flimsy-walled B&B in Speyside. Russell's girlfriend had phoned. He'd been sentenced to five years for dealing. Yasmin had swiftly packed, telling Matt not to come too; probably easiest and best if he didn't.

But Matt had come anyway. On the swaying train back to London, she'd looked out of the window, the brown rain-puddled fields turning into solid urban grays, and felt the warmth of him next to her.

He hadn't been her rock in a conventional way. He hadn't come with her to visit Russell that time, or the many visits afterwards, nor come with her to the care home to sit with her father. He hadn't given her advice or pep talks. But he'd wait outside for her, often with a telescope in the car, a bottle of wine in the boot, and sleeping bags for the beach. He showed her over and over again that her past didn't mean a future without happiness.

## 7

They were crossing the immense Yukon River, frozen over during winter, the bridge held up by concrete pillars, but in the blackness you couldn't see the bottom of the drop. Adeeb knew that there were dinosaur footprints along the banks of the Yukon, preserved and fossilized in the mud. He found it easier to imagine prehistoric creatures roaming unseen below them than any living animals.

Behind them, the damselfish headlights had fallen a little farther back.


I don't want Mum to hear something on the radio again or on Mr. Azizi's CB and for me not to know what's happening till later. So I'm going to use Voice Magic. That's what it's called, like, "Hey presto! I can hear and speak! Ta-da!" It's this program I have on my laptop that turns someone's mouth-voice into typed words on my screen. That's the magic part. And because the screen is lit up it's my secret weapon to hear even in the dark. Though it's not always convenient to be carrying a laptop around. And it doesn't work if there are lots of voices, because it scrambles them all up together. But if there's just one person you're OK, so I can just imagine me on a dark night with a boy wanting to whisper lovey-dovey things to me, and I make him wait while I pull my laptop out of my enormous handbag. That's a joke! I don't have a handbag. And I don't have a boyfriend. I AM

TEN and I think it's really silly that people in Year Six have boy-friends or handbags.

The not-magic part is that it turns my typing into a machine-voice. I like it much more if someone reads my type, so I'd only use the machine-voice if it was a big emergency. When I got it, I had to choose the voice I wanted, like Mum did when she got her satnav—so your language and then whether you want American or UK English, then man or woman, then young or older (which Mum doesn't have on her satnav). I knew that boys' voices get deep when they get older, but I thought girls stayed the same. Dad told me that a young voice sounds clear and a little tinkly, like tapping a metal kettle with a teaspoon. Years make your voice sound heavier, but an old person's voice sounds fragile and brittle, like it's made from very thin china. The Voice Magic people don't do a very old voice because they must think nobody wants to sound like a thin piece of china, but I think it might be coolio if you sound like a Ming vase.

When I was choosing I thought it would be funny to have my voice as an American man. As it's not *my* voice, I thought it would sort of point that out too, but Mum looked really upset when she heard it, which I didn't mean to do at all. So I changed it to "UK English girl."

I've known Jimmy since we were babies, and he learned a lot of sign without even realizing he was doing it. Anyway, me and Jimmy, when we were friends, had favorite words, like "tortoise"—weird word. And we'd just say "tortoise" to each other and then we'd laugh so much that Jimmy would fart and we called it fart-funny. One day our word was "vacuous." We spent all day saying everything was vacuous—people, bananas, loo rolls, pencil sharpeners. He said the word "vacuous" came from the inside of a vacuum cleaner, which is full of bits of fluff. I knew from Mum that it was because of the word "vacuum," meaning nothing there at all so sucking everything in, but I liked Jimmy's fluff-bag more. That was the same week I chose the UK English girl voice, and Jimmy, who was the ONLY person

I let listen to it, apart from Mum and Dad, said the girl sounded vacuous. So whenever I use this machine I know I sound like a fluffy vacuum bag.

But I want to thank Mr. Azizi for taking us, and I can't ask Mum to tell him for me because she'd say, "USE YOUR WORDS, RUBY," meaning my mouth, and that's even worse than using the Voice Magic voice. And—this is the big emergency part—I want to ask him to take us all the way to Deadhorse.


When Anaktue was on the radio news, Adeeb had felt Yasmin's tension in the confines of the cab. He didn't think it likely that she was a relative or friend of a villager, but the British wildlife filmmaker would make sense of things. He'd seen two wedding rings on her finger at the beginning of the journey and assumed that her husband was dead. He didn't know where Anaktue was but thought it must be near the Arctic Circle. Maybe she and Ruby were on a kind of pilgrimage to see the place where he died.

He heard a strange electronic voice—"Thank you for taking us." He glanced across at Ruby and saw that she was typing.

"I'm very glad I did," he said carefully, and saw his words appearing on her screen in type.

"And thank you for linking up your satellite receiver to my laptop."

He should learn sign language. The whole world should learn. There would be no foreign accent marking you as different, and if you wanted to block out abuse you could just turn away or shut your eyes. And if everyone could sign, if he could, then this great little girl wouldn't have some strange voice speaking for her but her own hands instead. Although he wouldn't be able to watch her sign or sign back and drive at the same time.

"It means Daddy can email me," the electronic voice said, and he saw Ruby smiling at him hard.

So her father must be alive and his guess about him being the

British filmmaker must be wrong. But Yasmin and Ruby were signing to each other, and the anxiety in both of them was clear, and Ruby was looking increasingly distressed.

The radio was playing classical music again. He tapped his finger on the steering wheel along to the music as a signal that he hadn't noticed their silent argument. After about ten bars, their signed conversation finished and Ruby looked unhappy and Yasmin more anxious. She also looked exhausted.

"Do you want to sleep awhile?" he asked her. "This stretch of road is not too bad and I'll wake you when we get near the cafeteria stop."

A look between mother and child, though they didn't sign anything to each other.

"Thank you," she said. He was pretty sure she closed her eyes so he couldn't ask her any questions.

"Shall I tell you something interesting about Alaska?" he asked Ruby, his words coming up on her screen in type.

"Yes," he heard back, in that peculiar voice.

"The Russians sold Alaska to the Americans."

"How much did it cost?"

"Around two cents an acre."

"That's not very much."

"No."

Don't give them a history lesson every dinner, Visha said to him, pleading. But the boys wanted him to; surely they weren't yet old enough yet to be humoring him.

"I think the Dalton Highway is a dull name for this road, don't you?" he said. "When you think about what they could have called it."

"Ghost Train Road?" she said.

"Ghost Train, Roller-coaster Road?"

"Ghost Train, Roller-coaster, Ice-rink Road."

"Exactly. So many very good names, but they called it after a man called James Dalton. And do you know what he did?"

"What?"

"He put spy satellites all the way around the Arctic Circle, so America would know if someone was invading. Probably the Russians, hoping to get their land back, I expect."

She smiled and he was glad. But he wondered if that was why northern Alaska felt hostile to him. It wasn't just the unholy cold and bleakness and darkness; this place was a frontier where people didn't circle their wagons but their spy satellites. The governor had spoken about eco-terrorists, though Adeeb had heard that the man who shot the pipeline was a regular drunken criminal, nothing more. But they were afraid of the usual type of terrorist attack too, by people who probably looked a lot like him. He'd heard there were plans to set up checkpoints along the Dalton Highway and a special antiterrorist task force to safeguard one of America's most valuable infrastructures. What would they make of him, an Afghan refugee, at one of their checkpoints? The only thing he'd ever blown up was a balloon, but would they trust him on that? He'd already learned not to go out and about with a backpack or wearing a puffy jacket.

"Do you know why the pipe's really high like that?" Ruby asked him on her machine. Running along next to them, the pipeline was raised high up on stilts. He saw her smile and knew she was enjoying the role of quizmaster with the answer in her pocket; his boys were the same.

"No, I don't. Do you?"

"It's so caribou can go underneath," she said, "when they migrate, so they can use the same path they always have for thousands of years."

No spy satellites or checkpoints for caribou, Adeeb thought.

"But Dad says that fracking can make some birds migrate the wrong way and they get lost. No one knows really why that happens yet."

"That's very sad."

"Yes."

She stared out of the window, her huge green eyes just visible from the little light in the cab, as if she were entranced.

"It's amazing out there, isn't it?" she said.

If he hadn't seen her eyes he would have thought she was joking.

"Truthfully, I'm not that keen on it," he said. If it were up to him he'd give it back to the Russians for nothing.

"There aren't enough colors for me here," he continued. "You know when I was listening to Chopin earlier?"

"Yes."

"It helps me to imagine I'm somewhere else."

"With blossom?"

"Yes. And other places too." He'd been training himself to find beautiful images in his new home of Oregon. "On sunny days we go to the park and there are oak trees, not like the short little trees out here, but giants. When the sun goes down in the summer the top leaves go from green to yellow, like they're turning to gold."

Mum said I can't tell Mr. Azizi where we really want to go. She promised me she'd tell him herself, soon. So I'll tell him about my trees, as he's told me about his.

"In the summer," I say on Voice Magic, "it's still light outside when I go to bed. There's these trees outside my window. I don't know what kind, but they're really high and their branches touch each other. You can't see the bottom of their trunks and you can't see their tops, just the middles. All these branches covered with leaves. Sometimes I imagine it's not air between their branches but water and I'm swimming through them, twisting and sliding through sunny passages of leaves."

I've never told anyone about tree-swimming before, but he told me about his oak trees and I think it might be the same kind of feeling. And it's nice to think of them, our summery green trees, because it's really weird being in darkness all the time.

There's new words on my screen: "What is your favorite music?"

No one has EVER asked me that question. Like it would be the stupidest question in the world. Maybe he means drum music, or the glockenspiel.

"Rachmaninov's second piano concerto," I say. "Brahms and the Beatles."

Voice Magic recognizes the names because I've said them before, but just to me, not anyone else.

Mr. Azizi nods. Like he's not one bit surprised.

"How about getting some sleep?" he asks me. "You look tired out."

I really, really want to go to sleep. Like sleep is right behind me, about to kidnap me by putting a big heavy blanket over my head and dragging me off.

"I'll take care of your mum for you," he says, so I nod and close my eyes, but I'm too jumpy to sleep, even though I'm being kidnapped with a heavy blanket. So I think of Brahms's first symphony because sometimes it helps.

Mrs. Branebury, the teacher who organized the harp concert, got me into him. We had a lesson, just the two of us, last term. She said she'd been learning some very basic sign language, so I didn't need to have a special assistant with me, which I really like as it's funny having two grown-ups to only one of me. Mrs. Branebury must have worked really hard at her signing. She wrote lots of things down, but she did a lot of signing too.

She said she could tell I didn't much like percussion instruments and that air-glockenspiel was (and she wrote this bit) *entertaining but not a good long-term musical option.* And then she told me that music isn't all about rhythm, in case I was worried about that. Which I was. She said it was about cadence and melody and harmonies and high notes and low ones. She said there were pictures and stories in the music and that everyone could imagine their own. She said she'd give me her picture story about Brahms's first symphony and then I could see if I'd like to give mine. She said it's a majestic piece of music, so she sees mountains with lots of thunder and lightning going on, beautiful and awe-inspiring. Did I want to have a go?

I said I'd choose a battleship in a storm, not mountains, because I think a battleship is more exciting. And she signed, "Thank you, Ruby; from now on that's how I'll see it too."

Mum sometimes says "big as a battleship." I don't know anyone else who says that.

So I'm thinking of Brahms's first symphony and I see that big battleship, gray and powerful, pushing through giant waves, and above are all these dark clouds, those ones that look like they're an army, mustering all their forces on the edge of the sky. I have a few seagulls too, doing that thing that seagulls do, kind of chasing after the ship, then dashing up into the sky. And the seagulls are the high notes, the ones a reed instrument makes, because birds sometimes live among reeds.

When we were still friends, I asked Jimmy what his favorite piece of music was, apart from pop, because he's really musical and is learning the piano and the cello too, and he said Rachmaninov's second piano concerto. He told me it sounded like catching the wind with silver lassos. And I think he must have loved me to tell me that.

## 8

Snow had drifted along the sides of the road, narrowing it to a single lane. Yasmin felt the darkness closing around them. Twice she'd almost fallen asleep but had forced herself back into consciousness again.

She'd heard Adeeb asking Ruby about music and she'd flinched, thinking it was insensitive. But Ruby had answered his question, on that awful machine, and Yasmin had felt the wind knocked out of her. Ruby was asleep now, so she couldn't ask her how she knew about this music.

Ruby hadn't let anyone hear her speak for two years now, point-blank refused to talk at all. Yasmin had tried everything and was constantly on her case, which she hated doing, and was furious that Matt took the easy soft option of "just let her be." Speech therapist after speech therapist had drawn the same silent blank. One of them had encouraged Ruby to sign up for Twitter, and every time she tweeted, Yasmin felt sadness pinch her that she was talking to strangers. If only she could speak with her mouth, Yasmin was sure she'd have friends.

When Ruby's hands had made the shape of wings for an angel, it had moved her. Driving through this dark night, she'd thought about the sign for "dawn"—a circle made between your thumb and finger coming up from your arm as the horizon.

She'd remembered vividly Ruby's excitement after an English lesson in her gifted-and-talented program.

*"We learned about onomatopoeia!"* Ruby had said, the moment Yasmin met her at the school gates. Yasmin hadn't understood why words that sound-like-the-thing-they-describe had lit up her face.

*"Sign language is onomatopoeia all the time, Mum. Visual onomatopoeia!"*

Yasmin had been struck by the truth of it.

But most of the world, almost everyone, didn't know sign language, so however beautiful and visually onomatopoeic the sign for "angel," Ruby must learn to say it with the roof of her mouth and her tongue and her lips.

It wasn't that Yasmin wanted Ruby to speak so much as she wanted her to be heard.

"Are you all right?" Adeeb said to her quietly, knowing she was awake.

Even though he needed to be concentrating on driving, she felt there was something deliberate in him looking so determinedly ahead and not at her.

"Your husband, he was at Anaktue?"

His voice was kind, and she felt the tension of her lies. "Yes," she said.

"The wildlife filmmaker?" Adeeb asked.

Ruby's gadget was still on, Adeeb's words coming up as type. Yasmin closed the laptop.

"He isn't dead."

Adeeb heard the frightened vehemence in her voice.

"But no one's looking for him," she continued. "Everything has burned down so he doesn't have any shelter, at best a tent but maybe not even that and he might be hurt. It's minus seven degrees Fahrenheit here, much colder where he is, and I don't know how long he can survive."

Adeeb didn't know the right thing to say or do. The police had said on the radio that the wildlife filmmaker was dead.

"The police—" he began.

"They're wrong," she interrupted. "Will you take us with you to Deadhorse? Then we can get a plane to Anaktue."

Deadhorse was over three hundred miles away.

"The road gets more dangerous the farther north you go," he said. "After the cafeteria place, which we'll get to soon, there's nothing else for sixty miles until you get to Coldfoot. There's a tiny village called Wiseman eight miles later, but it's three miles off the Dalton and the road's been closed for weeks. Then it's two hundred and fifty miles of nothing, worse than nothing. There's no hospitals or any kind of medical aid or help. If we break down, if the storm comes early, there's no one to call for help because no one can get to you."

"We love him."

Yasmin saw Adeeb look across at Ruby, who was sleeping.

"She and her father, they have this closeness. I can't explain it properly. She'd be lost without him."

Adeeb nodded, and she wondered if he also knew the pain a child feels when a beloved parent dies: the terror of it, shock waves rippling out and out and there's no perimeter to contain them.

"I wish I hadn't had to bring her," she said. "That I didn't need to be doing this, but I have no other choice."

Adeeb admired her hugely—her determination and her love for her husband and her courage. And she was fiercely loving and protective of her child, he could see that. He knew that she wasn't undertaking this journey lightly. But still.

"If it was your wife out there . . ." she said. "What would you do?"

And everything was clear. Because, yes, he'd get a lift with a stranger, however dangerous the road, his boys with him if they had to be, and he wouldn't stop till he reached her. Nothing would persuade him otherwise.

The forecast storm wasn't due to hit till after they'd reached

Deadhorse. The headache that had been bothering him hadn't got any worse and was caused by the worry he always felt when he was driving this road. He was one of the most experienced drivers, probably the most cautious because he had his own rig to look after, as well as being a natural neurotic. If anyone could get them there safely, he could.

"I'll get the next weather update," he said. "If we can definitely get to Deadhorse before the storm, then I'll take you."

"Thank you."

He smiled at her. "My mother would have loved to meet you," he said.

What would she have made of a woman who'd studied astrophysics? Who'd travel with her child across northern Alaska in winter out of love for her husband? She'd have thrown up her hands into the air, bangles jangling, her eyes widening, her whole being taken up with being amazed.

She had died three months before they left Afghanistan and came to the USA to seek asylum. His mother would have thought seeking asylum made him sound like a lunatic in one of her Dickens novels. And that was pretty much how he'd been treated, when people weren't afraid he was going to blow them up. His mother wouldn't have imagined that.


We've stopped and the bright light's on. I quickly open up Voice Magic. Mum is showing Mr. Azizi the map and they're talking about Anaktue. So Mum has told him and Mr. Azizi has said yes! I knew he would! And Mum looks different now.

Mum says there's a river, and in about two hundred and thirty miles it loops near to this road. She traces the river with her finger. "And then it goes north for about thirty-five miles all the way to Anaktue." Her finger touches Anaktue lightly, like it's precious. Mr. Azizi says someone needs to have built a road that joins the river to the Dalton. And the river road we passed was for a mining company, so they'd have checked that it was safe. It would be too risky for us to use a river road that no one had checked. And he keeps on saying "we" and "us," so I keep feeling happy because even though we can't drive on the river and take a shortcut, he'll still help us to get to Dad. He says we'll stop at the cafeteria and get some extra food and water.

I know it will be all right now, so I close my eyes and go back to sleep.

All Matt had to do was say "Will you . . . ?" for her to know the end of the sentence and say, "Not yet." He'd protest that he was simply asking, "Will you . . . pass the beer/not make such a racket/look at that beautiful sky up there/stop hogging the duvet/kiss me," but the locations gave him away and each time they had a picnic on the beach, or coffee in a bird hide, or looked at the night sky, blue skies, or skies of any other kind and almost every time they made love, she'd know he'd ask, "Will you . . . ?"

He wasn't crushed when she said "Not yet," or even disappointed. Made resilient by a loving past, he didn't perceive rejection. He thought she wanted to get to know him better first, and fair enough. She should know everything there was to know about the person she was marrying before committing the rest of her life to him, never realizing that it was the other way around.

She'd known she wanted to marry him from the time he held her face in his hands and said, *"I see you"*; she wanted him to look at her face and say that and fully know what he was seeing. But she'd feared that wasn't possible.

Adeeb pulled into the parking area by a portable building cafeteria; Ruby was still asleep. A young trucker had set the cafeteria up this winter, understanding drivers' need for a dose of company before the long lonely drive north and somewhere friends could swap war tales on the way home to Fairbanks. Adeeb had never stopped on the way home.

He was glad to have a break from driving. In the last five miles, his vision had occasionally blurred. He must be more tired than he realized. He wondered if he should get out, but the cold would make his headache worse; *"Brain freeze!"* his boys yelled when eating ice cream, clutching their heads. The cold was bad for a headache.

The parking area was occupied by two Soagil Energy trucks carrying pipes, an F.B.F. tanker, and three Am-Fuels trucks carrying prefab houses. Adeeb guessed the Am-Fuels trucks were headed south towards Fairbanks, because from the looks of the prefabs they'd been in Alaska awhile. As he parked, the Am-Fuels drivers got into their trucks and, as Adeeb had predicted, headed home towards Fairbanks.

He said he'd look after Ruby while Yasmin went to use the restroom and buy food.

Yasmin put on her Arctic parka and face mask and mittens before getting out of the truck. Even so, the cold shocked her; it was like plunging into a lake, not air. She smelled the cold and then realized that it was an absence of all odors. She wondered if it was because her airways were not functioning properly—she could feel the little hairs in her nose freezing—or if it was that in this degree of cold no molecules could permeate the air.

The cafeteria was warmer, with the tang of coffee and sweat. There were truckers sitting at two Formica tables, snow from their boots tracked onto the floor. She was aware of their stares as she bought drinks and sandwiches from a shy young man serving. As he packed them into a bag for her, she asked him about Anaktue. Maybe there'd been talk about it here.

"It was that place on the news, right?" he said. "That Inupiaq village that burned down? Stored their fuel right by their houses."

A trucker with a hugely fat belly turned from a table towards her. "Ain't that the place sittin' on a whole load of shale oil?"

A man at the other table turned so that the two tables were now in one conversation. "Heard they were given MacBook Air laptops and that was just to read Soagil's paperwork."

"Heard that too," another said. "And that they could have had a hundred K. Enough to buy a whole herd of fuckin' caribou."

"But they still wouldn't allow them to frack?" Yasmin asked.

"That's right," one of the men replied.

The shy young man talked to the truckers rather than Yasmin. "I met an Inupiaq guy, couple of months back, lived in Anaktue, but he'd bin workin' at Soagil's regular wells at Prudhoe? Said he'd be fired if his family didn't sign." He looked around, as if startled he'd said so much.

"They work at the Prudhoe oil wells to get cash?" Yasmin asked, wanting to keep the conversation going.

"Yeah, lot of 'em still doin' their own huntin' for food, pretty much self-sufficient some of 'em, but they need to buy snowmobiles and fuel and such. So durin' the winter that's what they do."

"The governor said that the fracking companies wouldn't try to frack Anaktue's land now," Yasmin said. "Out of respect for the villagers."

The man with the belly leaned forward. "Yeah, right. And tourists come to Alaska for the sunshine."

A door slammed and Yasmin turned. It was Ruby, in tears, her expression desperate, her parka not fastened. Ruby ran to her and started pulling her towards the door. Yasmin was aware of truckers coming with them; one of them was doing up Ruby's parka and pulling up her face mask to protect her from the cold. The only protection she'd been wearing properly was her mittens.

In the cab, Adeeb was hunched over the steering wheel, barely conscious.

Two of the truckers managed to get him out of the cab. Between them they got him inside the cafeteria.


The world had become blurred to Adeeb and wouldn't come back into focus, and then he'd lost his balance and couldn't swallow. He'd felt small arms around him, a child's arms, but his boys were two thousand miles away. He'd tried to open his mouth but couldn't speak.

He'd known then why he hated this ice road, truly feared it. Because this was how it ended, a bleak road to dark nothing; that was why he'd yearned for color.

And then stronger arms were around him and he was being pulled out of the warmth and into the cold. And then it was warmer again. A woman was talking to him. He hoped it was Visha. She was telling him that he was being taken to the hospital in Fairbanks, that a driver was taking him. But Fairbanks was the wrong way. And then he remembered the slender, graceful woman and her child and he knew what she would do. He had to warn her about the shrieking winds and the killing cold and tell her that avalanches could bury a truck even as it was moving and that even inside a forty-ton eighteen-wheeler a person was nothing more than a poor, bare, forked animal, that it was too dangerous for her and the little girl, but he couldn't open his mouth to say the words.

He heard her saying that she was putting a check into his jacket pocket and if anything happened to the truck she'd make sure it was paid for. Then he felt, or thought he felt, her lips on his forehead as she kissed him.

He thought of his gentle, intelligent, brave mother; his mother of excited bangle-jangling and tenderness and poetry, beaten from her classroom by the Taliban. He'd grown up with a hatred of the Taliban as fierce as his love of poetry; natural for him to become a translator

for the American army. But he should have thought about the consequences. They'd had to leave so quickly. Relieved that his mother had
died so he didn't have to leave her. Terrible to be relieved. There were
men around him, concern on tough faces, being kind to him, offering
him sanctuary after all.


I woke up because Mr. Azizi had kind of fallen across me. He was
so white and his eyes were closed. I typed on Voice Magic and told
him to wake up, but he didn't hear and I couldn't make Voice Magic
go louder. I tried to talk to him loudly, feeling for the sound vibrations in my throat, like my speech therapist tries to make me, but it
didn't do any good and I don't know if it was me not being able to
mouth-talk loudly or because he just couldn't hear me. Then I kind of
hugged him, trying to get him to sit up, trying to make him better,
but I couldn't. I quickly put on my parka and my mittens, but then I
couldn't zip up my parka. I opened the door, which was really heavy,
and then I ran to find Mum.

Two men are carrying Mr. Azizi into a truck and another man's
got a blanket and has wrapped it around him. It feels like we've been
alone for ages, me and Mum and Mr. Azizi, and now we aren't and
people you might think would be rough, because they look like that,
aren't one bit.

The truck with Mr. Azizi in it is leaving now, going back to Fairbanks. Mum says he'll be OK once he gets to hospital. She thinks he's
had a small stroke, but he's getting better. I think she's right because
just before he left he lifted his arm like a little wave, and he couldn't
do that when he was in the truck with me before, so I think he must
be getting a bit better.

There's no lights out here in the car park. It's so so cold, like an ice
rink has wrapped its way all around you in a jumbo ice sheet. Mum
told me to wait in the cafeteria, but I want to make sure that Mr. Azizi
is all right. The lights on the back of the truck with him inside are red

and I follow the little red lights till I can't see them anymore and now it's just dark.

I haven't thought about Dad.

I've been thinking about Mr. Azizi, not Dad.

I should have been thinking about Dad too.

Dad more because Mr. Azizi will be all right now; he's going to hospital and he's in a nice warm cab and people have put a woolly blanket around him, but Dad might not have anyone with him. And I don't know if he has a blanket. And we have to get to him. But how are we going to do that without Mr. Azizi?

The other drivers and Mum and me go into the cafeteria place to warm up, and I'm waiting for Mum to ask someone to take us to Dad. I stand so I can watch her lips. She tells them that we are waiting for our tour party to get to the Arctic Circle.

But why's she said that? One of them looks like he doesn't believe her, he's asking her something, and then she says something back and he looks like he believes her now.

The truck drivers leave and I run out after them into the cold, because one of them has to take us to Dad.

Mum is coming after me. She holds on to me, stopping me going any further.


With her arms around Ruby, Yasmin watched a truck, driven by the man with the huge belly, pull out of the parking area and back onto the road heading south. Other drivers were turning on their lights before leaving. They'd told her that they were all heading home. She had to somehow go on to Matt, but should she ask one of these drivers returning to Fairbanks to take Ruby with him? Rhetorical questions answered as a loop in her mind, because how could she put Ruby in the care of a strange man? When Ruby couldn't ask anyone for help? Couldn't phone her mother if she needed to? When Yasmin couldn't talk to Ruby and check she was safe? She had to keep Ruby with her.


All the trucks are driving away; pairs and pairs of little red lights, all going back the way we've just come. So that's why Mum didn't ask them to take us to Dad. There's just Mr. Azizi's truck left. It feels even colder now that all their lights have gone. The man in the cafeteria has just stayed there and we're alone out here.

Mum goes up the steps to Mr. Azizi's cab and holds out her hand to help me up. His cab isn't locked or anything, so Mum gets inside and I do too, and we shut the door. Mr. Azizi's left the keys and she takes off her mittens and turns the engine on. Warm air puffs at our faces.

I take off my big mittens too so I can type. My laptop is open on Voice Magic, from when I was trying to get Mr. Azizi to wake up.

"How are we going to get to Dad?"

Mum is sitting in Mr. Azizi's seat and she's pulling at a lever and her seat shoots forward.

"I am going to drive us," Mum says.

I think she must be joking, but now she's turning on the headlights.

At home she drives a Toyota Auris, which is quite small and there's only just room for the supermarket shop, and now she says she'll drive this DREADNAUTUS MEGATRON truck with a whole house.

It's so different from how she usually is. Normal Mum is a bit per-nickety about things, like my uniform being ironed and getting my homework done on time and keeping everything tidy.

There's something on her face that I've never seen before, like she's not just Mum anymore.

She's moving the gear stick and I laugh because we're going to find Dad, right now!

Maybe we can drive all the way to Anaktue and Dad will see Mum driving and he'll think she's amazing! The Superb Mum!

"Dad will never ever believe this," I say, with my face doing a ! expression because you can't do expressions on Voice Magic.

"Will Mr. Azizi mind we took his truck?" I ask.

"I think he'll understand," Mum says.


She checked that Ruby's seat belt was done up, then put her foot down on the pedal, a stretch even with the seat as far forward as it would go. She drove out of the parking area and onto the Dalton, going north.

This was a road. It was just over three hundred miles to Deadhorse. And she could do this. She was in a specially adapted truck with heated fuel and alcohol in the pressurized air to the brakes and specialized filters and she understood the mechanics of driving it. She knew that Adeeb had filled up in Fairbanks with enough diesel to reach Deadhorse. They didn't have a phone—Adeeb had his sat phone with him—but they did still have his satellite receiver so Ruby's laptop was connected to the Internet, and they had the CB radio.

The cafeteria owner was the only person who might have seen her take the truck, and she was pretty sure he hadn't been looking out of his window at the parking area, not when he didn't even come out to watch the drama with Adeeb. Adeeb owned the rig himself, so there wasn't a transportation company who'd want to know where it was. Maybe she could even get the prefab load to its destination at Deadhorse before the people who owned it realized she had inadvertently taken it when she took the truck—if you could inadvertently take a whole prefabricated house, which she now knew that you could.

She needed to be realistic. It was just a matter of time till someone noticed and reported her. The police would arrest her for stealing the rig or the load or for driving without the right license, or for whatever other laws she'd broken and she was sure she was breaking many. She just couldn't let that happen. Not until she reached Matt. Then the police could arrest her, imprison her, do whatever they liked, once she got to him.

They'd become engaged almost two years after his first proposal. The day before, she'd been staying with him in his flat by the river, which his parents had helped him buy. They were practical, sensible, middle-class solicitors, and Yasmin thought they were great, but had teased Matt,

*"So you were found under a mulberry bush too?"*

*"It was a bumper year for mulberry bushes."*

That Saturday morning, they'd walked along the leafy pavements— no graffiti on the walls, no police signs up appealing for witnesses, the only intrusive noise the flight path to Heathrow.

They'd bought lunch in the deli and were walking towards the newsagent for the papers when a car, the wrong kind of car, cheap, dented, careened down the narrow road, sirens caterwauling behind it. The car mounted the pavement, coming towards Yasmin, and Matt pushed her out of the way, his body between her and the car. A lamp-post had taken most of the impact, and Matt was lucky to escape with a broken shoulder and cracked ribs.

The next day, she found the much-traveled ring in his jacket pocket, which smelled of mints and cigarettes and oddly of biros, and put it on.

Everyone assumed that Matt's heroic act was the reason for his ring on her finger, like Albert taking the bullet for Victoria and winning a place for his desk next to hers.

That first year of marriage, she'd gone with him on his first filming assignment and he'd come with her to observatories and shared her enthusiasm and tried hard to understand her doctorate. Living together in the riverside flat was a time of late nights with

Matt and friends and making love and early mornings working and a new job and then she'd become pregnant and it had felt as if life was expanding to its edges. During that time together, Yasmin felt their love for each other becoming larger and denser, a metal ball at the core of the Earth, she'd imagined, four thousand miles beneath the pavements and beaches and marshes they walked on, anchoring her.

And she'd no longer been weightless with loneliness.

## 9

For the first few miles, adrenaline and sheer bold-faced nerve and a kind of spirit of adventure had kept Yasmin going, but as she drove further north, the vastness of the Arctic wilderness became more intimidating, their isolation more disturbing. She had to maneuver this huge vehicle for another three hundred miles over the ice.

She went around a tight bend and headlights—sudden and dazzling in the blackness—glared into her eyes. A truck was heading straight towards them on the single lane. On the right-hand side of the road was a sheer drop. She heard Ruby make some kind of sound, like a scream. There was a sharp scrape, metal on metal, and the rig juddered, but somehow the truck passed them. Her heartbeats were furiously fast. Next to her Ruby had vomited.

The truck driver came on the CB, his voice tight with anger.

"Who the fuck are you? Why didn't you give your fuckin' position on the road? That's what the goddam CB is for."

Yasmin had heard Adeeb give his position on the CB but hadn't thought to do the same. She turned to Ruby.

"I'm sorry, sweetheart. We'll pull in as soon as we can and get you changed."

I thought this ginormous truck was going to hit us and I was sick and now it's smelly in here. I open the window just a tiny bit and the freezing-cold air dashes in like wasps. There's a big space on the side of the road. Mum pulls into it and puts the light on in our cab so we can see each other properly. She gets my case, which is on Mr. Azizi's bed above where we sit.

"I'm really sorry," she says. "That was all my fault. Let's get you changed."

The heater is puffing out warm air. I keep my under layers on because they're OK, but I'm going to put on a new all-in-one Arctic fleece, which Dad calls a "woolly bear." It's lucky Mum thought to bring a spare woolly bear. She always thinks about things like that.

"If you want to use the porta-potty, now's the time," Mum says.

And even though it's just Mum, it's kind of embarrassing. She's putting on ski trousers and her parka over her other layers.

"I think we should ask the police to get Dad," I say, because if the ginormous truck had crashed into us, Daddy wouldn't have anyone coming to get him.

I didn't say anything about the police finding him before because I thought if Mum went to find Dad, he'd see how much she loves him, because I know that she does, but he might not know that because she's been so cross with him.

But we can still tell him she tried to. It's not her fault Mr. Azizi got ill so we had to ask the police. And Dad will still know that she loves him.

Mum's never driven a truck like this, I know she's super-clever, but I think it's a really hard thing to do.

"We can't ask the police to get Dad," Mum says.

"But they'll be quicker, they might have a helicopter or a plane and—"

"They think that Daddy died in the fire."

Outside it's black. All black. Like somebody's putting a black plastic bag over my face.

"The police are wrong, Ruby."

I want Dad to hug me and chat to me and read me a story and tell me one day I'll have loads of friends because they'll get to know me.

*"Life is a little bit like a ship and sometimes it feels like you're sailing solo, but you're not because I'm with you. And so is Mum. And one day you'll have a full crew of friends and a family of your own. You'll be an ocean liner, like the 'Queen Mary.'"*

But I just want Dad.

"Dad isn't dead," Mum signs, and I sign, "Dad isn't dead!" at the same time. The sign for "dead" is pointing your fingers out like they're a gun, and it's like we're firing at each other.

I'm crying now. Trying not to. It wasn't true, what I said about signing at the same time; she did it a little tiny bit before me.

"We will get to him, won't we, Mum?"


Yasmin saw Ruby's terror of losing her father naked in her face.

"Yes," Yasmin said to her. "We will get to Daddy. And I will be much more careful and use the CB."

She put on her goggles, then pulled her big Arctic mittens over her glove liners and went out, hurriedly shutting the door to keep Ruby warm.

How could she have been so bloody stupid, so reckless? She'd put Ruby in unnecessary danger. From now on, she would keep the CB on and use it and follow what Adeeb had done to the letter.


Mum's gone to throw away my smelly clothes and I'm emailing Dad.

To: Matthew.Alfredson@mac.com
Subject: EMAIL US!
From: Ruby.Alfredson@hotmail.co.uk


Dear Dad,
Please please email us. Just anything. So we know
you're ok. Mum and me are coming to get you in a
lorry.


Love you megatonnes
Puggle


Yasmin had left the headlights on, which lit up this rudimentary car park, bizarre in the snowy wilderness. She saw a sign, THE ARCTIC CIRCLE. It must be a parking place for tourists in summertime, though she doubted even then that there were many visitors. She hadn't thought about space for many years, but it was impossible not to here, at this famous circle of latitude around the globe; they were entering the very top of the planet.

She put Ruby's vomit-stained clothes in a bin; her fault for terrifying her. Ruby's vulnerability stripped Yasmin raw, and she remembered when Ruby had been born how helpless she'd seemed; how terrified Yasmin was that she couldn't look after her properly; that she was entirely inadequate; more fearful still when they said her baby was deaf.

A memory played out in front of her, vivid in the darkness. She hadn't thought of it for a decade, but it was as if it had happened only minutes ago. She'd had this sense before that time was not linear, but bending back on itself, with current emotions finding a twin of themselves in the past.

Late at night in their bedroom, feeding two-week-old Ruby, her hair soft as thistledown, her body still a comma not yet stretched out.

Matt was asleep in bed a few feet away. She'd pulled back the curtains and looked out of the window. The stars were dim through the light pollution above the city, and she'd strained to see them. Suddenly, her grief for her mother was felt again so sharply that she'd juddered, causing Ruby to startle, her tiny arms and legs flinging out like a starfish.

She held the weight of Ruby's body against her, watched miniature fingers curling and uncurling around her thumb, wrapped her dressing gown around both of them as long-ago anguish scythed its way back into her present and she was powerless against it.

In the winter darkness and subzero cold at the Arctic Circle, she remembered the soft wool of her dressing gown, the drop of milk on Ruby's chin as her head tipped back in sleep, the rhythmic sound of Matt's breathing and how she had felt like she was floating far away from everything that was good and secure, unmoored and adrift, and Matt could no longer tether her to happiness and safety.


I touch Mum's parka and it's like touching ice cubes.

"OK?" she asks, and I nod, but I don't feel OK because Dad hasn't emailed back.

"My brave girl," Mum says to me. Then she takes off her mittens and liners and puts her hand across and gives my hand a little squeeze. It's like her fingers saying something really nice to me without turning it into words. Normally, it makes me feel a bit better. Even when horrible things are happening at school, like people faking talking to see if I know that they're not really talking, Mum picks me up from school and on the way home she holds my hand and it makes me feel better. Not totally better, but just OK, like we're going home now so I don't need to think about it for a bit.

I can feel the little dent of her rings in my palm.

———

Yasmin put on the CB and steeled herself to start driving again into the blackness. She pulled out of the Arctic Circle car park, heading north.

"Can I check your email, Mum?" Ruby asked on Voice Magic. "In case Dad's emailed you."

"He won't have done, sweetie."

"But he'll probably have borrowed someone's laptop. And he lets all his friends use his terminal so it'll have the right software. And he'll definitely have his terminal."

"I checked my emails before we set off."

While they'd waited for Adeeb's truck to be ready in Fairbanks, she'd looked through her inbox, but of course none of the emails were from Matt. She'd moved the whole lot into the junk folder. She hadn't realized before how much time she wasted on things that were basically junk.

"But that was hours and hours ago, Mum. Please?"

"It won't do any good."

"Please?"

"OK."

Because Ruby would only believe there was no email when she saw for herself there was no email.

They were at the top of a steep incline; she didn't know how far it went down because it was too dark to see the bottom. She started the icy descent, wanting to inch her way down, using the brake all the time, but she needed to get up enough speed so they'd make it up the opposite side and not slide backward. Going backward out of control would be more dangerous.

As she drove down the steep incline, forcing herself to go faster than felt safe, she remembered catching Matt once, watching her as she ironed napkins, the irritation and sadness on his face, before he abruptly turned away, because he thought these domestic chores were absurd and unnecessary, not understanding that it wasn't about ironing, washing up, two types of vegetables; it was about creating order and stability, that security was built on tiny details like a striped ironed napkin.

To start with, he'd teased her about her new Martha-Stewart-meets-Mrs.-Tiggy-Winkle kick, this new domestic-goddess camouflage; then he'd become serious and concerned. He'd offered to take care of Ruby himself so she could return to her job as a research fellow in astrophysics, but Yasmin wanted to take care of Ruby herself and no longer looked at the stars.

He'd suggested once that it was because Ruby was deaf and that she was trying to compensate in some way. But that hadn't been true at all and she was angry he could think that.

She heard their arguments woven into the darkness, a mass of small-scale disagreements, separated with silences.

She'd been cross so much of the time and often about small things. Looking back at herself, she thought that her crossness was like a shapeless overcoat, covering loneliness, and it wasn't the old loneliness she'd felt after her mother died, or even an adult version of it, but something different and more punishing.

They were still going down the steep incline and she thought she'd reached about the right speed now, a little fast if anything, so she braked. But the truck didn't slow and it felt now like they were falling down the slope. She pushed the brake pedal harder and still they didn't slow and the forty-ton truck was gaining momentum, the killing law of physics making them go faster. She stood up, putting all her weight on the brake pedal, but there was no response and the truck was out of control, and she was aware of the accelerating weight of it and soon they'd go over or crash. She grabbed the CB radio and yelled into it, "I can't brake!"

A calm slow voice came on the CB. "Pump 'em. Pump the brakes."

She pushed the brake pedal, then let her foot come up, then down again and up, and again. The truck slowed. She could taste dried fear in her mouth. With control of the vehicle, she managed to get up the opposite side of the slope.

Ruby was still logging into her email account and was barely aware that there'd been any danger.

The slow calm voice was back on the CB. "You OK out there, lady?"

"Yes. Thank you." Her voice was strung tight.

"You have to dry the brakes out, or they don't work."

"Thank you," she said again. She'd go on saying thank you to whoever this was.

"No problem."

She thought she recognized the slow calm voice as a trucker who'd turned her down, slowly, at one of the yards. She understood now why truckers and dispatchers had virtually laughed in her face at the idea of her and Ruby coming on this road, and that was an absolutely fair and pretty moderate response. They hadn't been cruel or unhelpful, just realistic.

"You take care of yourself out there, OK?"

"Thank you. Yes."

Then another voice came on the CB. "Who you chattin' to, Coby?"

"Not yet been introduced," said the trucker called Coby in his measured sympathetic voice. "But from her accent, she's gotta be English and I'm guessin' she's the same lady wantin' a ride to Deadhorse this afternoon . . . ?"

Yasmin didn't say anything.

"Someone let you rent a rig?" Coby said, and chuckled. "Who'd have thought it."

"She's got a license, right?" asked the other trucker.

"Must have," Coby said.

Yasmin didn't know what to say and, as she said nothing, the truth became clear.

"Jesus Christ," said the other driver. "If you ain't trained to drive a truck, then you gotta stop, pull over someplace safe. You got that, lady?" She imagined him with fiery red hair and freckles, alarmed and cross, but not aggressive.

"I have to get to Deadhorse. My husband's missing and I have to find him."

"Ain't that somethin' for the state troopers?" Coby asked.

Yasmin didn't reply.

"The road will kill you," said the fiery redheaded driver. "Or you'll kill someone else. You gotta pull over."

"No," said Yasmin. "Not till I've found my husband."

"You don't get it, ma'am," the red-haired driver said. "It's not safe to have you out here. Not safe for you, but not for us either. You'll cause an accident. Or you'll break down and we all get held up and there's a likely storm blowin' in and that ain't safe either."

"I'm sorry, really. But someone has to get to my husband and at the moment that's me."

"Reckon you're one helluva lady," Coby said in his kind voice. "Least we can do is get you to Deadhorse in one piece. What's your position?"

Yasmin checked the road marker on the side of the road, which marked off the miles from the beginning of the Dalton Highway. "MP 117," she said.

"You'd best learn some rules of the road," Coby said. "First off, big trucks have right of way. What you drivin'?"

She didn't want to tell him that it was Adeeb's rig; that she hadn't actually hired a rig, which presumably would have some kind of paperwork and insurance on it, but just taken one.

"Eighteen-wheeler, forty tons," she said, remembering Adeeb telling her this.

"OK, that's big, but there may be bigger than that on the road and you give way to 'em. Other than that, it's your right of way goin' north. Keep your headlights and taillights clean. You'll have to stop and clean the muck off 'em once in a while. What am I missin'?"

"Never stop where you can't be seen," the red-haired trucker said. "Bridges, bends, hills. Keep watchin' your rearview mirror and if anyone's behind you don't go brakin' too sudden."

"If you break down, get off the road and set flares."

A third voice came on the CB. "You got a gun?"

She thought she recognized the voice but couldn't place it. American accents were too new to her to make subtle distinctions and match to a face.

"No."

"OK, so if you break down and there's wolves, which I ain't never seen myself, you stay in the cab," he said.

"You gotta listen in to the weather reports," Coby said. "Our dispatcher is updatin' us all the time and I'll put it out on CB, OK? There's a blow headin' our way—that's a storm, right?—possibly a big one. So keep listenin'."

"Thank you. Yes."

She put down the CB, glad of friendly voices in the dark, no longer feeling so isolated or afraid. Company of some kind felt like daylight.

She'd used the word "husband," emphasized it, as if it were married love that was making her risk so much to get to him, each year adding legitimacy to this journey, the vows and commitment of marriage condoning the danger. She'd tried to persuade herself of that too. But she knew that it was only one of their twelve years, and that it was winter sun slanting through a window, a flock of geese on marshland, her face held in his hands, that was driving her.

Ruby's hand was tapping on her leg; her face was lit up.

"There's an email!"

She was jolted by hope. But it wasn't from Matt; of course it wasn't. She checked her mirror; just blue headlights a long way behind them. She stopped the truck on a straight stretch of road, leaving her headlights on so they'd still be visible, and took the laptop from Ruby.

## 10

A photo of a large animal, savagely killed, filled the screen. One of its eyes was missing; a leg had been ripped from its body; a bone gleamed nakedly white. Yasmin's body reacted instinctively, leaning across Ruby to protect her from the violent attacker out there somewhere in the dark. The sender was Akiak@alaska.account.com.

"It's a musk ox," Ruby said, finger-spelling "musk ox."

Who was this Akiak? How did he get her email address? Why did he send her this? She'd given the cards Ruby had written to anyone who'd take one, never pausing to think that it might not be safe.

"We can tell the police that Dad is alive."

"This isn't from Dad."

"It is! Dad must have a friend called Akiak and borrowed his computer, just like I thought he would."

"Dad would never send us this."

She looked out at the darkness. She'd felt a sense of being watched, hadn't wanted to give way to it, thought she'd been tilting at black-shrouded windmills, but the feeling had persisted.

Akiak sounded like an Inupiaq name. Perhaps Matt knew him. But she'd never asked Matt about the people here. Angry and hurt about the time he'd chosen to spend in Alaska—another three months after his first assignment finished—she'd tried to be uninterested, not to endorse this other life of his with questions; maybe hoping that her lack of interest would be catching, a kind of emotional and intellectual osmosis, and he wouldn't want to return.

The subject was DSC_10023; 68950119 149994621 was just underneath the photo. None of it made sense to her.

"Did Dad ever mention Akiak to you?" she asked Ruby.

"I don't think so," Ruby replied. "But Dad's borrowed his computer, so they must be friends."

Surely Ruby didn't believe Matt would send her a picture like this?

"I think Dad wanted to send this to work," Ruby said. "But he's using Akiak's laptop so he won't have his contacts. But he knows your email address off by heart."

Ruby was trying so hard to make it plausible the photo was from Matt, and Yasmin realized that Ruby no longer took what she told her on trust. She'd said that Matt was alive, but it wasn't enough for Ruby, so she was creating her own evidence.

Yasmin studied the photo, hoping to find some clue as to Akiak's identity and where he was. The mutilated musk ox was lying on the snow, lit by the beam of a torch, she thought, darkness around it. She clicked the cursor on the photo, enlarging it. She couldn't see any blood, but it could be hidden in the animal's thick fur, or the animal had been mutilated after it was dead. Perhaps this man, Akiak, had just found the musk ox, but would that make it better? It still didn't explain why he'd photographed it, why he'd sent it to her.

She tried to see a landmark in the photograph, but there was nothing apart from the butchered animal on the featureless snow. The email had been sent five minutes ago.


Mum doesn't think the email is from Dad. And it is a horrible picture. But sometimes horrible things happen in the wild. And Dad says you have to look at animals as they are, not Disney-fy them. This musk ox is strange, which is probably why Daddy wants it for work.

"Wolves kill musk oxes," I tell Mum. "It's really hard to find food in the winter, so they eat every little bit of what they catch. They wouldn't leave an ox like this. That's what's so horrible and weird. It hasn't been killed to be eaten. And there's another funny thing too. Least I think so. It looks like a big adult male because its horns are really big and wide."

Yasmin saw Ruby mastering her horror at the photo, trying to be every inch her father's daughter as she responded to wildlife with an open mind, not city-girl squeamishness.

"When wolves kill a musk ox, the whole wolf pack has to do it," Ruby continued. "Because musk oxes are so big. The wolves surround them and then try to get one away. They choose the weakest, which means a young one or a baby. So I think that's why Daddy's taken the photo, because wolves have killed an adult and just left it after they've killed it."

What could Yasmin say to her? Better to let her think it was wolves behaving in a strange way than a sadistically violent human.

If Akiak was out in the dark wilderness, he'd be using a snowmobile or sled and huskies; there were no other options over the terrain.

She opened the window, the cold air numbing her cheek, and listened, but could hear only the wind. How close would a snowmobile have to be before she could hear it or see its lights? A sled would be quiet and invisible.

Akiak probably wasn't his real name, because whoever sent her this photo would surely want to hide his identity. She couldn't think why anyone would want to threaten her. Maybe there was a reason and she was just too tired to see it. She longed for mental clarity. If she could sequence things together, perhaps something important would reveal itself, but her thoughts frayed around the points where they should connect. She hadn't slept for over twenty-four hours.

After her instinctive physical reflex to protect Ruby, her next instinct, or perhaps deeply ingrained belief, was that she must tell the police. But then they would know that she was out here in Adeeb's truck, and they'd come and arrest her, or come and protect them; whichever it was, they would stop her from getting to Matt.

Behind them the blue headlights had stayed the same size, static in the darkness. So he had stopped too. Maybe the driver and the man calling himself Akiak were one and the same person, but the idea didn't bear logical scrutiny. No one could kill and butcher a musk ox, take a photo, and email it while also driving on an ice road.

She'd told herself before that if the danger became too great she'd ask Adeeb to turn around or get a lift with a trucker going back to Fairbanks. Now it would be up to her to turn around. She wouldn't do that, not yet, but she felt the time when she may be forced to make a choice was getting closer and that she would have to choose Ruby's safety.

She couldn't think about what it would mean for Matt if she turned around, but the consequence haunted the edges of her mind, a dark shape in the shadows.

She started driving again. The light from their headlights was becoming dimmer, hardly penetrating the darkness, as if a lid were closing on them.


I know it was Daddy who sent us the email. But the police would probably be like Mum and go, "It's from someone called Akiak." Maybe Dad wants to start our blog early too.

I like thinking of Dad in his Inupiaq furry parka sending the email to us. But Dad in his furry parka sort of turns into Dad in a Superman T-shirt, with his eyes all crinkled up against the sun. It's such a warm bright memory that I want to step right inside it.

We were trekking up Mount Cairngorm with Mum saying that in a previous life I must've been a mountain goat and Dad said a short-haired one, because I was just wearing shorts and a T-shirt but that was because we walked really fast so I got hot. At breakfast, Dad said he wanted us to practice posting the blog we were going to do together at Christmastime. He gave me a special cover for my laptop and downloaded the software for his satellite terminal, like I was his proper partner. He said in Alaska we'd have to climb a hill to get a satellite link, so it would be good to practice that too.

We got to the top of Cairngorm and he showed me how to connect the laptop to the satellite terminal.

"Then you turn it on," Dad said.

"Well, duh," I said, and Dad said with technology you need to be pedantic, and Mum said the word "pedant" comes from the Greek, meaning "the slave who escorts children to school," and that it was no fun being a pedant so I shouldn't be too hard on Dad. And they both laughed. And I could see how much they liked each other, just for a little bit, like best friends laughing at the same thing; like me and Jimmy and the word "tortoise."

"Did you know that a group of satellites is called a constellation?" Mum said, and I said, "I love that!" But Dad isn't that interested in satellites. He says he's just glad when "it does what it says on the tin."

Dad had bought us all special Arctic work gloves, which are meant for people who do tricky jobs in really cold places. He says mittens are warmer than gloves because your fingers are like ten little radiators, but you can't sign in mittens. He wanted us to practice in the gloves like a dress rehearsal. We could sign in the special gloves, but we couldn't type in them so we had to take them off.

He showed me how to upload a photo onto our blog page. He was really excited about it too. But Mum wasn't smiling anymore. She didn't know about our blog. She'd thought he was just showing me his satellite terminal. She hadn't been there at breakfast. I lip-read bits of what she was saying; there was a lot of "reals"—". . . real friends . . ." And ". . . I don't want a virtual world for our daughter but the real world," for another example. And she said something about being lonely and isolated, but I didn't watch her mouth anymore.

Mum left and I was worried Dad would tell me we couldn't do

it, but he kept showing me what to do. When you get a connection, there's a little picture of a satellite that flashes. In Scotland it only took a minute; Dad said there are so many satellites above Europe they'll need to get traffic lights and lollypop ladies up there. But in space above Alaska there's hardly any, so when he saw the flashing satellite he'd have yelled "Hoorah!" which he yells in American sign—fists beating once on your chest then going up in the air HOORAH— even though I wasn't there, I know he yelled it in sign because he really likes that sign—then he put Mum's email address, and his little box sent his photo up into space and then to us.

In Scotland I didn't get how super-coolio a satellite terminal is, but it's a wonder of the world. Because in this huge dark cold place, with no houses or wires or anything, Dad's little box connects up to space and he's sent us an email. It's like that mollusk that was 507 years old and was alive at the same time as Henry VIII. A Tudor mollusk! Some things are just catch-your-breath amazing.

We've stopped in a pulling-over place because Mum has to clean the lights. She's putting on her Arctic clothes, which takes ages because there's so many layers, and while she's doing that I email Dad again: "Please tell us it's you! PLEASE!!" I just clicked reply, so it'll go into Akiak's inbox. Dad isn't nosy, so he might not even look at his friend's inbox. He hasn't got my other emails, because he'd have to log in to his own account, which is fiddly so he'd have to take his gloves off for ages and just have liners on and he might get frostbite. So he won't do that. If he loses his fingers he won't be able to talk to me.

I'm sure the photo is for Dad's work, not our blog. But just in case I'll upload it. I won't publish anything yet, not till Dad's here; it's our blog *together*.

Mum was really upset by Dad's photo. I shouldn't have told her how weird it is. But I know lots of great things about musk oxes.

"Musk oxes look fierce with their big horns," I tell her. "But they're not at all, they're gentle vegetarians. They've got long hair that looks like a beard—"

"Can you use your words, please, Ruby?"

I am! I am signing my words.

Yasmin waited and Ruby turned away from her, as she always did. But Yasmin wasn't going to stop asking her. Her determination that Ruby would speak, that one day her daughter would be heard, was undiminished. She refused to be intimidated by an email. She was going to find Matt and he was going to be OK and Ruby was going to speak with her own voice and if the man who sent the email was watching them out there in the darkness, then he would just have to watch her as she made that future happen.

Wearing all her Arctic clothing, she put on the work gloves Matt had bought them all. Mittens wouldn't give enough dexterity to grip the scraper. She got out of the cab, closing the door quickly to keep Ruby warm.

She took a breath and the freezing air went into her lungs and she felt them going into spasm. She gasped and more cold air went into her lungs and it was as if she was drowning.

She pulled her balaclava down over her mouth. She took a breath and this time the air warmed between the balaclava and her skin before she breathed it in and the air reached her lungs.

Breathing carefully, she started cleaning the huge taillights with a scraper; the air from her exhaled breath, trapped within her face mask, froze against her skin.

Cold felt like it was a hunter and she was warm prey. Behind her the desolate winter landscape was reddened by the glow from the taillights.

As she crouched, trying to scrape off the ice and dirt, she looked for the blue headlights, hoping to see them. There was no sign of them in the darkness.

She'd dismissed the idea that the driver and the man who'd sent the email were the same person because it wasn't practically possible.

Instead, she saw the blue-lights driver as their protector because with him behind them, the man calling himself Akiak wouldn't risk an attack.

The cold was freezing her eyebrows and eyelashes, but it had also forced her awake and sharpened her thoughts.

If this man wanted to attack them, why would he bother to first frighten her with an email?

Fear must be the point.

He wanted her to turn around.

Her thoughts were staccato, bullet-point thinking, as if in this sub-zero temperature mental processes, like physical ones, had to be done with the utmost economy.

Why would anyone want to prevent her from getting to Matt? He had no enemies or dark hinterland. He was a wildlife cameraman and the worst thing he'd ever done was kiss a woman who wasn't his wife.

Maybe the man who'd sent the threatening email wanted to stop her from going to Anaktue, rather than to Matt, but it was hardly likely that she'd find something the police had missed.

The only thing that made sense was that Matt knew something, most likely about Anaktue, and this man didn't want her to rescue him because then the secret, whatever it was, would get out.

The scraper fell onto the ground and she picked it up. She hadn't done up the glove on her left hand securely and ice came inside the glove, burning like acid against her skin.

What could Matt have discovered?

Ever since the airport, when he hadn't been there to meet them, she'd absorbed what everyone had said, seizing on anything as potentially vital. Now, as she cleaned the red taillights encrusted with snow and ice and dirt, she thought back.

*"All the hydraulic fracturing companies know where Anaktue is. They'll have source rock samples and drilling data for Anaktue."*

*"Anaktue is sitting on hundreds of thousands of barrels of shale oil."*

*"I met an Inupiaq guy, couple of months back, lived in Anaktue, but*

*he'd bin workin' at Soagil's regular wells at Prudhoe? Said he'd be fired if his family didn't sign."*

*"No longer going to pursue an interest in this area. Out of respect for the villagers."*

*"Yeah, right. And tourists come to Alaska for the sunshine."*

Their voices in different places and times threaded together into a common theme.

Surely to God the police would have found out if the fire was a murderous land grab. Surely they'd have discovered it was arson.

But now that she was outside in this degree of cold, when it was a struggle simply to clean the truck's lights, she realized how hard it would be to investigate a crime. She was working at the lights in minus eighteen Fahrenheit, and the cold was predatory and remorseless. Arctic clothes protected her now, but Anaktue, miles further north, would be colder still.

And the unutterable darkness. They'd have needed to work with artificial lights, positioning them, choosing what they lit and not knowing what they had left in the dark. What kind of conditions were those to get to the truth, when you didn't suspect anything other than catastrophic human error?

She thought about Akiak. Perhaps the name wasn't an alias but his true identity. He could have wanted to allow the fracking company to drill. The man in the cafeteria said they'd been offered a hundred thousand dollars.

The subzero temperature had welded dirt onto the taillights, and she had to turn the scraper around and use the handle to chip at it, her knees aching from crouching, her left hand stinging with pain.

Could she convince the police that the fire was a land grab; that she thought Matt knew about it; that someone was trying to scare her off?

But it was just guesswork and conjecture and she had nothing to substantiate it. Again, she faced the risk that the police would simply prevent her from getting to him and they wouldn't be convinced to go in her place. Now that she was out in this killing cold she was more afraid for him. Even if he had his emergency supplies with him, she didn't know how long he could survive.

Ruby joined her outside. Yasmin was alarmed but saw that Ruby was properly dressed, with all her Arctic clothes, and that she'd remembered to pull her balaclava down over her mouth and her gloves were correctly fastened.

Light from the cab spilled down enough for them to see sign.

"Did Dad say anything about an oil company wanting to frack Anaktue's land?" she asked.

Ruby nodded, and Yasmin was startled.

"They didn't want them to," Ruby continued. "Corazon organized everybody." In the light from the cab Ruby finger-spelled "Corazon."

Snowflakes started falling, twisting in the amber light.

"He told you about Corazon?" Yasmin asked.

Ruby nodded. "She's super-clever, Dad said."


I can't believe Mum and me are chatting out here in the freezing dark. It's like we're teeny people talking at the bottom of a deep freeze, with just a little yellow pilot light on, and the lid shut. But I know why. It's because out here you think about the big things. And I think that this is big for Mum, because Corazon and her twin brother, Kaiyuk, are Dad's best friends out here. A best friend is what stops you being lonely.

As we're chatting at the bottom of a deep freeze, I want to tell her that I'm sad that she didn't ask Dad about his friends, because when he was home she never really asked him anything about Anaktue or Corazon and Kaiyuk and I know he'd have been super-pleased if she had.

Mum signs to me that she has to turn the headlights off before she can clean them. They're so bright that she wouldn't be able to see afterwards. She tells me to get back in the cab, but I just pick up the torch that she's left wedged in the snow and shine it so that she can see to get back into the cab, because the steps are covered in ice.

She turns the headlights off and you can't see the road ahead anymore and it's like this little patch of light from the cab where I'm standing is all there is in the whole world.

I keep holding the torch so she can see her way back down again. She shakes her head because I didn't do what she said and get in the truck, but I can tell that she's smiling at me too, even though she's got her face mask on.

I go with her to the front of the truck and hold the torch while she bends down and scrapes at the huge headlights.

It's horrible having the balaclava pulled over my mouth because my breath turns damp inside it and then gets icy. Dad said that Inupiat parkas have big furry hoods so that the freezing air warms up before it gets to your nose and mouth, like there's a warm cushion of air against your face, and when you breathe out your breath doesn't freeze against your skin. Though he says it doesn't work on snowmobiles because the cold air comes at you too quickly. My parka is only from an outdoors shop.

I hope Dad's with Corazon and Kaiyuk. He said he was friends with Kaiyuk first, and then he met Corazon and it was like meeting a woman version of Kaiyuk. Dad wishes he has a twin sometimes, and asked me if I did. I said no, because truthfully one of me was probably enough for everybody, and he laughed and said it absolutely wasn't, but there could never be two of me.

Corazon and Kaiyuk know this old lady, I think she's their great-great-aunt, and when she was young she helped stop the government testing a nuclear bomb right by where her village fished. The government man said the village should be grateful for a harbor, and they were so good at nuclear bombs they could make a harbor in the shape of a polar bear. Their great-great-aunt said that for one, they didn't need a harbor, and for two, she'd rather have a real polar bear. Dad and I think that she's super-coolio.

Mum hasn't been saying anything, just cleaning the lights, and then she turns to me and I can see her face in the torchlight and also her hands.

"Did Dad say anything else?" Mum asks me. "About the oil company?"

She takes the torch so that she can see my hands.

"He said oil is made by plants and animals that died in ancient seas," I say. "It takes millions and millions of years and we are looters and hooligans, thieves from the future."

He was upset and cross. "They drill two miles down—two miles!—and then they go out sideways and crack the rock with poisons into bits so we can force out the gas or oil, and do you know what we do with the gas and oil that has taken millions of years to make, deep under the Earth?"

"Run a tumble dryer on a sunny breezy day?" I said, knowing it would be something like this. Dad really doesn't like tumble dryers.

"Exactly. Or accelerate a car down a clear stretch of road. Millions of years . . ." He waved his hands up in the air. "Gone in forty seconds."

Mum holds the torch for me so I can see my way back up to the cab.


As Yasmin climbed the steps, she checked again for the blue headlights. There was still no sign of them. He must have turned around.

She joined Ruby in the cab, the fabric of their clothes stiff with cold. They changed out of them, the warm air painful on their skin, the ice on their clothes melting. Yasmin found a towel, a swimming one of Ruby's that had incongruous suns all over it, and wiped up the icy water. Her hands were still stiff and awkward from scraping the lights, and the skin on her left hand looked scalded. Ruby had to help her take off her jacket. Her face mask had stuck to her skin with a layer of ice and she had to rip it away, leaving her face raw.

The heater was puffing out warmed air, the interior light was bright, and the cab felt like a sanctuary. But with the warmth came tiredness again. At some point she would have to stop and sleep a little while, but not yet.

She put on the CB, checked there were no vehicles coming in either direction, then pulled out onto the road to the north. The headlights shone further and more brightly, illuminating a light tunnel a quarter of a mile long of tumbling snowflakes.

## 11

The wind had strengthened; gusts of snow billowed across the road like chiffon veils. Yasmin moved her head from side to side, trying to ease the tension in her neck. She checked her mirror again but there was still no one behind them.

She was so proud of Ruby, holding a torch in the freezing cold and not complaining once. Hardly anyone knew about Ruby's courage, nor how bright and funny she was, because she didn't speak to them. But one day she would, and then everyone would know her too.

She and Matt had argued incessantly about allowing Ruby to sign or making her use her oral voice, and about the laptop and the Internet, and for the last year the huge decision about where Ruby would go to school in September. The mainstream secondary school had an excellent learning support department, but Matt didn't trust it. "She'll be special," he said. "You know that's how they tease each other? You're 'special.'" Yes, Yasmin did know that. And it wasn't each other, it was Ruby. She nodded and their eyes didn't meet because they had failed as parents in protecting their child. Yasmin thought that secondary school would be better than primary school; they'd talked to the head teacher, who'd given reassurances, but Matt hadn't been swayed.

"She has to learn to survive in the real world," Yasmin had said. Why didn't he understand that? "If she does that now, the tough part now, while we're there with her, helping her, then—"

Matt had interrupted her, "It's not working at the moment."

"Not now, maybe, but—"

"The real world thing, it's bollocks. The world is a million different places and Ruby will find the place she wants to be."

Then Ruby had come downstairs and interrupted them, but their argument had continued, in disrupted fragments, with nothing gained or conceded on either side because when you argued about your child there was no compromise or turning away from what you believed was right.

Secretly, Yasmin yearned to be kind to Ruby; to stop trying to make her speak with her mouth and to let her sign and to spring her, right now, out of the mainstream school where she was so unhappy. But if she did that she'd be a coward. She had to find the courage to look down the road at eighteen-year-old Ruby, twenty-five-year-old Ruby, Ruby the age she herself was now; when her parents wouldn't be there to help her, not every day like Yasmin was now. She had to do the right thing for Ruby and risk Ruby hating her, because she was doing it out of love.

She checked her mirror again. There were blue headlights behind them.

There had been no sign of him when she'd been cleaning the taillights. Or when she'd turned out of the passing place. She'd been sure that he must have turned around. Instead, he had turned his lights off and waited, hidden in the darkness, to follow her again.

She thought of the man with the dyed blond hair at the airport—Silesian Stennet—and his unnerving refusal to break eye contact with her, following her down the corridor, taking hold of her arm.

She didn't think that an obsession so extreme could be formed in minutes, but she remembered his pale dyed hair streaked with sweat, offering to look after Ruby, wanting her to owe him even as he professed otherwise, *"You wouldn't be beholden."* And there'd been other men, ostensibly sensible men, who'd claimed coups de foudre upon seeing her; lightning bolts landing all around her, jolting her, but only later when she learned of them.

The voice who'd asked her if she had a gun, was it Silesian Stennet? She couldn't remember his voice at the airport clearly enough to do a match with confidence, but it could well be the same man. She knew she'd heard it before.

But she hadn't seen Silesian Stennet since the airport, so he didn't know she was out on this road.

She checked the blue lights again; they were keeping an exact distance behind her.

She took hold of the CB mouthpiece. "MP 150 heading northbound. Can the truck heading north behind me tell me who you are?"

There was nothing.

The silence on the CB was broken by Coby's warm slow voice. "Gutsy lady, did I just hear you on the CB again?"

"Is it you behind me?" she asked Coby, desperately hoping that it was.

"I'm at MP 170. Can't see anyone in front of me right now," he said.

So he was twenty miles north of her.

"Just got the latest on the storm," Coby said. "Anyone else out there gotten this?"

"Big blow," someone said. "Massive fuckin' blow."

"They're sayin' hurricane-force winds, negative fifty. They don't know for definite."

"Bin told there's a risk of avalanches at the Atigun Pass," another trucker said. "Ain't had the time to clear the snow from yesterday."

"Fuckin' hell," a trucker said, and other drivers were swearing too.

"Avalanche buried a truck three weeks back," Coby said, explaining the oaths to her.

"A north wind blows in, only takes an hour to load a slope," another driver said.

"Ain't no one settin' out now from Fairbanks or Deadhorse," came another voice. "Leastways not from Northern Haulage and I reckon other companies will be the same. Too damn expensive to risk losin' a rig in a blow."

"You gettin' this, gutsy lady?" Coby asked in his unhurried voice.

"Yes."

"Reckon we should be on first-name terms."

"Yasmin."

She saw that next to her Ruby had turned on Voice Magic and was following this.

"You're at MP 150, you said?" Coby asked.

"Yes."

"OK. Too far from Fairbanks to turn around. Best thing, go on to Coldfoot, twenty-five miles from you; hard drivin' but nothin' worse than you've already done. Hole up there and wait this thing out. I'll be there first. Have your coffee waitin'."

"Reckon you'll be linin' up for that," another driver said. "Anyone can't get back to Deadhorse or Fairbanks'll be waitin' there."

Was the driver with blue lights behind her listening in? She was pretty sure he would be. Adeeb had said all the truckers listened in to the CB.

"See you there," she said. "If they have a motel, I may stay over."

She hung up the CB.

"We can't stop," Ruby said. Voice Magic gave her words the same techno-impersonal tone as ever, but Yasmin felt Ruby's body shaking.

"We're not going to stop," Yasmin replied. They had eight hours, maybe a little more, to get to Deadhorse, and while the drivers had been speaking on the CB she'd calculated their average speed and the distance to travel and they could make it.

"We're still going to Daddy?"

"Yes."

Once they got to Deadhorse, she'd persuade a taxi plane to fly to Matt. Minus fifty. Hurricane winds. She had to reach him.

She was afraid of the risks to Ruby, of course she was, but perhaps she'd been conjuring up additional dangers where none existed. The blue lights were still behind them, but it didn't mean the driver was following them. Dozens of truckers must be driving this route. He could have simply pulled over for a rest break and turned his lights off. Or perhaps he'd been cleaning his lights too and had turned them off as she had. There had been no more emails, thank God. Maybe it was just some kind of one-off weird spam. Exhaustion could have been making her paranoid, and in this landscape it was easy to be afraid.

As she drove on, she thought about her and Matt's first meeting, no coup de foudre involved. He later told her that he'd seen her around the university, but he'd been unfairly dubious about a person so unreasonably beautiful. Or possibly, he'd said, it was some kind of Darwinian self-preservation thing about the competition being too fierce and him keeping his tusks or horns or antlers safe.

And then he'd spoken to her and got to know her and had fallen in love with her and had been afraid, he'd admitted, of these feelings he had for her. But there it was. There he was. Slain. No help for it. And she'd felt they were kindred spirits even in their fear of love. As a physicist, she knew the kinematic equations for an object plummeting from a height, but there had been nothing logical about her falling and no equations for the consequences.

While obsession was about ownership, a narcissism reflecting on the person who felt it, she knew now that passion was love, at its most extreme edge, that made you cross an Arctic wilderness in winter; and this, here and now, was where it could lead you.

Suddenly the blackness lightened. The clouds, blown by the harsh wind, had separated and illuminated the mountains. In the half light, she saw how high they were and the sheer drop down a precipice, barely three feet from the left side of the road. She wished it had remained dark so that she didn't have to see the violent terrain, a scene from a gothic tale, nothing soft or hospitable, which dwarfed her into nothing.

She looked up at the night sky, a long-forgotten reflex from child-hood when she'd felt small and afraid.

She saw three moons. She felt reality tilting.

She realized that two of the moons were paraselenae. They were rare and beautiful; she'd never seen them before.

She pointed at the sky for Ruby.

"There are three moons!" Ruby said on Voice Magic.

"They're called 'moon dogs.'"

"Why are they there? Why don't we have moon dogs at home?"

"They're not real. They're made by moonlight."

"How? Tell me!"

She stopped the truck. "Up there, really high in the clouds, are ice crystals. The moonlight bounces against the crystals and makes the moon dogs. Their proper name is paraselenae." She finger-spelled "paraselenae." It occurred to her that the only thing she ever taught Ruby that really mattered to her was to try to talk; more surprising was her realization that the paraselenae mattered to her.

"Paraselenae," Ruby finger-spelled back to her.

Then the clouds covered the moon and the paraselenae and it was dark once more. She continued driving.

The illuminated clock on the dashboard showed it was three a.m. The black heart of the night, Yasmin thought, but there was no heart to this night because there was no daylight coming to end it. It was snowing again, the flakes only appearing when they were in the headlights, as if they'd been suddenly formed in the darkness. Her limbs were heavy with tiredness. Outside the cab it was minus twenty-two Fahrenheit.

Ruby tapped on her arm.

There was another email.

She wanted to prevent Ruby from looking at the photo, but Ruby had already scrolled down. She checked her mirror—the blue headlights were still a long distance behind them—and stopped the truck.

A blackly shining dead bird filled the screen, even its beak and feet black, the feathers with a metallic glint, its ghastly eyes protruding. Yasmin found it demonic and recoiled.

A school trip to the Tower of London, recalled in ugly detail. Ravens devouring biscuits soaked in blood and a whole rabbit, tearing it up. Other girls screaming, Yasmin silently appalled.

Through centuries of Western literature, ravens were associated with death, carrion birds, feeding off corpses on the battlefields.

She studied the photo, searching for a clue about the man who'd taken it and where he was. The dead bird was lit by a torch but too faintly to see how it had been killed. She couldn't see any blood on the white snow around it. No landmark was visible. The subject was DSC_10021; 69051605 150116989 was under the photograph.

Behind her, she saw that the blue-lights driver had also stopped. She could no longer explain away either man as the product of her own exhausted paranoia.

Surely she could go to the police now. Someone didn't want her to reach Matt and Anaktue—therefore he had to be alive. But what did she have? Macabre photos of dead creatures from a man who might, or might not, be called Akiak. The police could well dismiss the emails, as she had done the first time, as a crank or spam. And this road was northern Alaska's only highway, so how could she prove the lights behind her were malevolent without sounding like she was neurotic and deluded? But Ruby and she were under threat; she felt that acutely now.

Unless she could find a way to convince the police Matt was alive, and to rescue him, her terrible choice was coming closer. She felt the terror of abandoning him, which had first haunted her mind, become a presence somewhere on the dark road ahead.

"You can tell the police that Dad's alive!" Ruby said on Voice Magic. "Now Dad's sent us two emails."

"Ruby—"

"Dad loves ravens. They're super-coolio."

Had she not realized that the raven was dead?

"There's an amazing Inupiaq story about a raven."

Yasmin, afraid and exhausted, couldn't stand the machine-voice anymore. Couldn't stand it that Ruby wasn't trying to use her own voice; couldn't stand it that Ruby's future sounded so lonely.

"Please, Lovely Girl, please use your proper voice. Just try to. Please."

Ruby turned away from her.

Mum still doesn't think it's Daddy sending us the emails. And so the police wouldn't think so either. But I KNOW it's him. I'm going to write about ravens on our blog, because it will feel a bit like Daddy is with me. I think he'll be pleased I've started already, then when he's with me we can publish it together. So I'm uploading the photo and all the numbers, because they must be important if Dad sent them.

We decided to do a blog just before we went on holiday to Scotland, because after Scotland Dad was going straight off again to Alaska.

I was crying on my bed and Bosley was trying his wagging-tail thing but it wasn't really working and I was just making his fur all damp, then Dad came in.

"School?" he asked, and he sat down next to me.

I nodded.

"Not so great starting Year Six?"

"No."

"Friends or foes?"

Dad knows it's worse when friends are mean than foes are.

"Friend," I said. "Jimmy."

"Has he been mean to you?" Dad asked, and he looked really surprised, because Jimmy had been my best friend since always.

"Not really," I said. "A bit."

"Why don't you tell me?" he said. And when I just kept stroking Bosley, kind of tugging at his ears, which he really likes, Dad said, "Better out than in," which is this joke, because he first said it when I was sick with food poisoning and I thought it was gross, and funny too, and ever since then he says it when he thinks I'm bottling something up and he wants to make me smile.

I stopped stroking Bosley, though Bosley kept lying with his head on my lap, and I told Dad that people were teasing Jimmy about me being his girlfriend. So he didn't want to be seen with me anymore.

"Does Jimmy want a girlfriend?" Dad asked.

"Don't think so. We don't talk about that kind of thing."

"Would he be embarrassed if people thought he had a girlfriend?"

"Maybe."

"I think he just doesn't like being teased. Most people don't," Dad said, and I could tell he was thinking about it really carefully. "Especially about having a girlfriend. Any girlfriend. It's nothing to do with you."

I started stroking Bosley again because even if it's nothing to do with me, it is, because Jimmy was my friend and now he isn't. And because I love him, in a friend way, but now I can't anymore but I still do. And because I don't know how to tell him that you can love someone without being their boyfriend or girlfriend, because we don't talk about things like that.

"Isn't it a bit young to be starting boyfriends and girlfriends?" Dad said. "Ten?"

"Ten and a half and lots of people do," I said.

"Sorry. I'm out of touch."

The thing with Dad is that he waits for you to talk again. Bosley's tail was wagging really fast, but it still couldn't make me happy.

"I don't have any other friends, Dad."

I didn't look at him when I said that; it's a fail thing to say.

"You know you're coming to Alaska for Christmas?" he said.

I nodded. It was me that had wanted to go and be with Dad in Alaska rather than him coming home, but it was ages and ages away.

"We don't have to stay put in Fairbanks; we can go off and do some proper exploring. And you and I can do a blog together about all the animals we see."

It was a super-coolio idea and Dad could tell that's what I thought.

"We can take photos and post them on our blog and we'll write it together. You can tweet a link to it. We'll be trending."

Since I started Twitter, Dad knows all about it, so he knows it's silly to say we'd be trending, only pop stars and film stars and people like that trend, but it was funny to think we could.

Then we started designing our blog and Dad showed me all these animals and birds on his iPad that we could put in. And then when we went to Scotland we practiced together.

And I know the emails are from him. I know they are.

When I close my eyes, I can see Dad in Scotland really clearly: his Superman T-shirt and his smile and he hadn't shaved so his face was all stubbly. But I can't see him sending the photos here. I imagine his Inupiaq parka with the furry hood, but when I look at his face I can't see him. It's hard because he'll be wearing goggles. But it's not really that. Because inside the big hood, under the goggles, it's not Dad's face, but a frightening one. It's that creepy slimeball's face, the one with the blond hair and gray parting and jellyfish hands.

Mum says that horrible thoughts sneak up on you when you're too tired to fight them off. She says that on school nights. And I think she's right. Because even if I can't imagine his face properly I know it's *Daddy* sending us the pictures.

There's little blue lights behind us, like they're following us in the dark.

Outside the temperature had dropped to minus twenty-seven and the snowfall was getting heavier. Yasmin longed to sleep, just for a few minutes to close her eyes and give way. She'd be useless at being tortured; two nights without sleep and the sensory deprivation of light and she'd tell everything. A bright bulb as an instrument of torture seemed rather attractive to her.

"Gutsy lady," Coby had called her. It had been a long time since anyone had thought her gutsy. But she'd felt the change in herself, had heard it in her voice as she spoke to Coby and the other drivers. It wasn't new, this voice, this self, that was the thing: it was deeply familiar to her. And she recognized that it was herself as she used to be—determined, stubborn, brave even, more than a little mad.

It shocked her to realize that for years she'd felt bland, dull even to herself. Around her, everyone else's characters were clearly defined, the borders of their personalities etched sharply, but not hers. She'd had tasks and chores and love for Ruby, huge love for her, but how would she have described who she was? Somewhere along the line she'd lost the idea of herself.

She saw herself back in the kitchen on the other side of the world, and the contrast between the woman in the kitchen and where she was now was giddying. Out here in the immense Alaskan wilderness, she saw the claustrophobia of their house, the claustrophobia of herself. And she knew she had been lonely not because of long-ago but still-felt grief for her mother, or because of the distance between her and Matt, either literally or figuratively, but because she had been missing herself as she used to be.

It was only now, in this monochromatic land at the very top of the planet, that she could start to understand herself, as if the distance and difference to her life on the other side of the world allowed her to see her story.

And she wanted to tell Matt; she wanted to explain.

*I kissed her because I missed you.*

She pushed her foot harder down on the accelerator. She would reach him.

## 12

The blue lights are still behind us. Mum looks at them in her mirror. She's done that quite a lot. I'm worried that it's the slimeball man behind us and it's all my fault. He found Mum at the truck place in Fairbanks, but she doesn't know. I should have told her, because when we were still in Fairbanks Mr. Azizi was with us, and lots of other people too, but now we're all on our own.

His face was really close to mine, just glass between us.

I put on Voice Magic.

"The blue lights behind us," I say, and I can tell she's a bit surprised that I know about the blue lights. "Do you know who it is?" I ask.

I'm really hoping that she does. Or that she doesn't mind who it is behind us.

She shakes her head and I can tell she's worried, even though she's trying to hide it. I have to tell her.

"It might be the slimeball man," I say, and I do the gross finger-up-the-nose sign so she'll know who I mean.

"I agree he was creepy," she says, "but it's not him behind us. It's nothing to worry about, only a driver."

But she's just trying to make me not worry.

"When we were at the truck place with Mr. Azizi," I say, "the slimeball man was there too."

"He was at the truck place?" she says.

"Yes."

"Do you think he saw us leave?" she asks.

"Yes. He did. He wanted to talk to you. But I didn't want you to worry. As well as worrying about Dad."

"That was very, very kind of you," she says.

But she's the one being kind. She wishes I'd told her.

"He's just a slimeball," Mum says, doing the gross sign to cheer me up. "And we don't need to worry about slimeballs. Go to sleep now."

She really does want me to go to sleep, so I close my eyes. I think about Scotland and all of us safe and warm and happy. I can see the hummocky grass that was springy as a trampoline and loads of purple heather, like someone had flicked purple paint all over the place, and Mum and Dad smiling.

Yasmin had wondered about Silesian Stennet before, but the idea that he could be following her out of some kind of menacing obsession had become more far-fetched the further she'd driven along this treacherous road.

Maybe, however, he had a link to the fire.

If Matt knew something about the fire at Anaktue it could be Silesian Stennet, rather than a fracking company, who wanted to stop her from reaching him; Silesian Stennet who had something to hide.

Right away he had known where Anaktue was. And yes, he'd given a rationale for that, but even so. He'd blamed fracking for the fire, not realizing how absurd that was—fire leaping across miles of snow and ice in freezing winds; now that she was here herself that idea seemed even more ridiculous.

But Silesian Stennet was frightening, not ridiculous.

*"Better a small village in Alaska has everyone die, than a highly populated area. So yes, if wiping out a village is what it takes to stop this madness, then yes."*

And he'd looked stimulated by it; that's what had repulsed her. Perhaps he had started the fire, thinking idealistic ends justified terrible means. And it hadn't worked out as he'd hoped. No one had believed him that it was fracking that had burned down the village. If he'd gone to the police or the media, they'd have laughed at him as the men at the airport had done. But perhaps he hadn't foreseen that. And the police investigating in the literal dark might not have seen the signs of arson, so wouldn't have known it was murder or why.

He had worked for an oil company, been a director. He must still have contacts; he could have got a lift in a truck, or even be driving one himself.

She remembered his offer to take care of Ruby—*"I'll look after the girl. Keep her safe for you."* Was that so he'd have Ruby as some kind of collateral?

Ruby had fallen asleep beside her. She felt her body rhythmically rising and falling.

Exhaustion was battering at her in waves. She thought of all those English seaside towns with their stalwart Victorian seawalls, and hoped her defenses were as robust because she couldn't sleep, not yet. She longed for dawn, at least for the knowledge that it was coming, not driving into an endless night.

She couldn't see the blue lights; he must have fallen a distance behind them, but she was sure he was still following them.

She drove up a steep incline, her right leg aching, unable to sustain the unnatural angle of reaching for the pedal for much longer. Ruby's hand brushed against her as she signed in her sleep. It was only adrenaline that was keeping her awake.

At the top of the incline she saw a halo of light as if the sun was rising. She knew it couldn't be true, that it was like a mirage of water in the desert; that she was hallucinating the sunrise out of exhaustion and primal need for light. She reached the top of the hill and beneath her was a collection of buildings, with orange sodium lights and floodlights and flickering neon. Coldfoot.

She drove into Coldfoot, Ruby still asleep. It was a tiny place; basic low-rise buildings lined the road. She slowed to a crawl as she passed them. Through windows, honey light filtered out onto the snow. The pull towards company and safety was physical, each lit building exerting its own drag.

There was a gas station, flooded with bright lights, showing pumps purpose-built for trucks, and beside it was a rudimentary large truck park. There was a ranch-style café and a motel, built out of the same type of modular unit as the house on her rig. She'd lived in one of the most metropolitan cities in the world, but she'd never before felt civilization so acutely.

Perhaps she could leave Ruby here. Perhaps she would be safe. But the blue-lights driver would arrive, looking for her. She imagined him hunting for her in the café, the motel, and instead finding Ruby.

Coby would look after Ruby, she was sure. And there'd be other decent men here to protect her. But she'd need to ask Coby, check that the other men were trustworthy, and as soon as they clapped eyes on her they'd stop her from leaving again. She was sure of that. And she couldn't ask Ruby to find Coby herself while she drove off again, because how would Ruby find him? Who the hell would understand sign language out here in the middle of nowhere? She'd be utterly vulnerable.

She drove towards the parking area. The two-way road was poorly lit, with dark shadows between the streetlights. There were about fifteen trucks already parked, and another truck driving in ahead of her. Presumably all of them were waiting out the storm.

She drove around the parking area, then back towards the highway. In the shadowy space between two lights she pulled over and stopped. From here she'd see him arrive. And once he'd driven past them, they'd slip away. Hopefully, he'd spend a long time searching for her and they could get a distance ahead of him.

She turned off all the lights, including the interior one in the cab, just leaving the heater on. Snowflakes tapped noiselessly and relentlessly against the side window, soft battalions pressing at the huge windscreen in front of her. In the dark and the warmth, her face slackened with tiredness. She opened the window a crack and the narrow band of icy air kept her awake.

Eight minutes later, blue headlights came towards the truck park on the other side of the road. She'd made a terrible mistake; headlights coming towards them would flood the cab with light. She bent down, lying across Ruby, in a futile effort to hide.

Moments before his lights reached them, the driver turned them off. He must have wanted to hide their distinctive color.

She was still lying across Ruby, so didn't see him in his cab as he passed them just a foot or so away; she just made out that he was driving a tanker.

She turned on the engine and drove away, only putting on her lights when she reached the road. She checked her driver's mirror: no blue headlights from the tanker, just the receding lights of Coldfoot.

Adeeb had told her Coldfoot got its name from gold prospectors who'd get this far north, then lose their nerve and turn around. She understood the loss of nerve. Driving away from Coldfoot felt like you were pulling against a rope that tethered you to safety, and any further it would break and you'd be away from the shallows and into the deep ocean. The people who built Coldfoot knew that this was as far north as a person could reasonably go. She felt the diminishing lights tugging her back to warmth and shelter. She drove on. The lights of Coldfoot dwindled and then she went round a bend and they disappeared.

When she looked in her driver's mirror there was just darkness behind her. She knew the tanker driver would only be at Coldfoot until he realized she wasn't there, and then he'd come after her. She listened to the CB, but there was nothing about her; anyone who'd heard her earlier conversation with Coby would assume that she was heading towards Coldfoot or had already arrived there and was waiting out the storm.

A truck came round a bend towards them, its headlights fuzzy through the falling snow and darkness but still bright in the cab as it passed them, and then it was gone again, hurrying towards Coldfoot, and they were alone once more.

It was six a.m. Yasmin's body and mind, calibrated for a circadian rhythm, felt trapped in the darkness of night, as if in a fold of time. There would be no more lights from a human habitation to provide a man-made sunrise.

She passed a milepost; they had two hundred and thirty-four miles to go until Deadhorse, with no kind of services along the route.

She drove as fast as she dared, dark mile after dark mile, imagining the tanker in that darkness behind them and closing in. Next to her, Ruby stirred.

"Is it morning yet?" Ruby asked.

"Yes."

"Are we nearly at Dad?"

"Still a long way to go."

She drove on through this dawnless day, keeping watch on the il-luminated milometer as the single miles turned into ten, then twenty. The snow was getting heavier and the wind fiercer, outriders of the storm to come. She felt sleep deprivation dulling her reflexes and drag-ging on her limbs. For the last ten miles the numbers on the milom-eter blurred as her eye muscles lost the strength to focus. Around the light tunnels made by her headlights she thought she saw the darkness move, a thing with sinews and a pulse. And then abruptly it liquefied, black water surrounding them.

She saw a passing place a few yards ahead. She managed to maneu-ver the truck into it. She hadn't factored in a stop in their journey to Matt, but she couldn't physically drive any further. She asked Ruby to wake her up in fifteen minutes.

She closed her eyes. In the dark and the quiet, she remembered back to her first visit to Cley with Matt, the sound of the sea thump-ing and hushing next to them. They'd undressed in the dark and she realized that she loved the smell of him and the sound of his voice as much as the way he looked and his ease with talking about things that mattered.

He'd said it was incredible that they'd met each other, both in a lecture of a subject neither was taking. What were the chances? She said that four and a half billion years ago, give or take, comets bombarded the Earth, bringing with them ice, which melted into water. "You have proof of that?" he asked.

"Crashing a satellite into a comet and measuring the amount of water," she replied.

"And?"

"A billion-liter water bomb in space," she told him. "The comets crashed and volcanoes erupted, blowing out steam that turned to cloud and it rained for thousands of years. People quibble about the exact amount of water and from where but however it got here, voilà . . ." She pointed at the sea. She said the chance of a planet with water to sustain life was trillions and trillions to one, so remote as to be unimaginable. That was the miracle. Them meeting each other four billion or so years later, not doing the same course, wasn't so much of a long shot.

She remembered the warmth of him next to her and the bumpy shingle under their blanket, and then she felt she was falling into the solid core of the Earth and Matt.

## 13

Ruby was asleep next to her. She switched on the cab's light and saw her own face as a chiaroscuro in the windscreen against the darkness outside.

She put on the truck's headlights, but there were no light beams. The blackness outside was solid. Her old terror of being trapped in a coffin under the Earth slithered around her. Her breathing shallow, she flicked at switches. The wipers pushed snow clear of the windscreen like snowplows.

In the beam of the headlights, she saw heavy snow, with gusting winds blowing it violently fast across the road in front of them. She looked at the clock in the cab. She'd been asleep for two hours. She hurriedly checked her driver's mirror, but there was no sign of the blue headlights. A delineator post showed that a foot of snow had fallen while she'd slept. The thermometer read minus thirty-five outside.

She put on the CB. Drivers were talking to one another from depots at Fairbanks and Deadhorse and the truck stop at Coldfoot. No one else on the CB was out on the road.

There was another email on Ruby's laptop. He had sent it while she slept.

All she could see in the photo was snow, and she felt relief. The torchlight was weaker than the previous photos, the white of the snow bleeding quickly into the dark around it. She reluctantly clicked the cursor to zoom further in and saw black marks. There were animals partially buried under the snow, their white coats indistinguishable from it; just black lines of fur, like kohl around their dead eyes, and the black tips of their noses giving them away. There were five animals in all, but there could be others. She tried to see how they had been killed but couldn't see any blood or injury; maybe the torchlight was too poor.

Was he warning her that this was what would happen to them— buried without trace under the snow?

The subject was DSC_10025; 68945304 149992659 under the photo.

She turned up the brightness on the laptop screen to maximum. In the bottom right-hand corner of the photo, she could just make out the shadowy image of a husky dog, with a part of the harness, a buckle perhaps, glinting faintly in the torchlight. So whoever this man was he was traveling by sled, silent and invisible in the dark. How close was he to them?

The light had woken up Ruby. She was about to shut the laptop, but Ruby had seen the photo.

"Arctic wolves," Ruby said.


I think Dad's sent the photo to show what poachers have done. Because it's only people who kill wolves.

But they still have their beautiful thick white coats, and a poacher would take their fur.

They must have got caught in a blizzard and buried. Probably a bank of snow fell on them, or an avalanche even.

"We have to tell the police that Dad's alive," I say, because surely now we've had THREE emails from him Mum'll realize they're from Dad.

But Mum doesn't say anything and I know she *still* doesn't believe me, so the police wouldn't either, and I don't know how to make anyone believe me. In our headlights there's huge sheets of snow, like shape-shifting ghosts haunting the road.

Yasmin was driving again. The snow came thick and fast towards the windscreen, the wipers on maximum speed.

Abruptly, their headlights were extinguished and they were driving in total darkness. She slowed quickly, trying not to skid, praying they would keep on the road. And then the snow fell away from the windscreen, a fat sheet of it. The snow had accumulated on the roof while she'd slept and then fallen onto the windscreen like a blindfold.

She heard Coby's voice come onto the CB, less calm than usual. "Anyone yet seen that crazy woman?"

So she'd gone from gutsy to crazy; she thought that fair.

"I'm here," she said.

"Jeez. Yasmin. I've bin real worried about you."

"I fell asleep."

"You're in your cab? I just been looking in all the trucks."

She wanted to tell him the truth, but the tanker driver might still be looking for them in Coldfoot, and might hear this.

"Yasmin?"

But surely he'd have discovered by now they weren't at Coldfoot and would already be coming after them. As she debated about what to say, Coby must have guessed the truth.

"You went past?" he asked.

She was silent.

"Jesus. The storm's goin' to hit in three hours."

Three hours. It was impossible for her to get to Matt, even halfway to Deadhorse.

"Are you sure?" she said.

"Comin' in real fast. You've gotta turn around."

"My husband's out there. He won't survive."

"I'm real sorry about this, lady," another driver said. "But you won't get to Deadhorse and there's no safe place to stop on the way. Once you cross the mountains, you're on the north slope Arctic plain; ain't no trees to stop the wind. Storms blow across there like it's turned into hell. Eighty-eight thousand square miles of nothin'. Do you know how big that is? State of Utah. Bigger even."

"It just ain't an option," another voice said. "The winds will knock you clean over, the snow can bury you, you can't get out of your truck for anythin', so you can't fix your brakes, your lines, nothin'. If your engine goes you freeze inside your cab."

Then came Coby's voice, slow and kind. "There just ain't the time for you to reach Deadhorse, Yasmin. Not even if your truck were a turbo and it was July, OK? You gotta wait it out in Coldfoot. Your husband's just gonna have to wait for you."

In a storm like this without protection? When even experienced drivers in their nice warm cabs in massive trucks were taking shelter? Through the closed windows of the cab she could hear the wind.

"You turn around now, you hear me?" Coby said. "But first, you're goin' to need to put on snow chains. It's comin' down real fast now and'll be gettin' slippy."

Slippy. Something a little girl would say of a polished wooden floor in her socks. She momentarily loved Coby for his understatement.

"So you need those chains; even if you wanna kill yourself and keep drivin' you need those chains. Do you know how to put them on?"

She understood that he'd get her to put on the chains and then he'd persuade her to turn around. He was doing this one step at a time with her, patiently and kind.

"No."

"OK, they're stored by the wheels, under the truck. You lay 'em in front of the wheels, then roll over them, then hook 'em closed."

"OK."

"Then you look for a turning place."

"Thank you."

She hung up the CB and checked her driver's mirror. No one

behind her. She stopped the truck. Ruby had put on Voice Magic and had been listening in.

"We are still going to Dad," Ruby said. "You told the people before that we'd stop at Coldfoot but we didn't, so we are still going to Dad."

A statement, not a question, because it was unthinkable for them to leave him in an Arctic storm. Yasmin's terror of abandoning him, which had first haunted her mind and then become a presence on the road ahead, was right in front of her in the darkness.

For now, she had to focus on putting on snow chains, because whatever she did they needed snow chains.

As she pulled on her Arctic clothes, she saw herself, so many years ago, walking along the sunny leafy pavement from the deli towards the newsagent; the beaten-up car mounting the pavement and Matt pushing her out of the way. Through the sound of the Arctic wind, she heard the reverberating clang as the car hit the lamppost; the horn blaring senselessly loud and urgent as the driver slumped forward, just sixteen years old.

That night she and Matt had talked and she had known why they could marry. It wasn't because he'd put himself between her and the car, but because they talked about the boy—what made him do it; what kind of home and family and education; what kind of hopelessness—because Matt used his full intellect to try to understand what had happened.

And because while their leafy neighbors exchanged outraged emails about the joyriding delinquent getting what was coming to him and "Thank God nobody innocent was badly hurt," Matt had felt grief for the boy. Because the following day he'd found the mother by the lamppost with her cellophaned carnations and bought parcel tape from the newsagent, and tied the flowers onto it with her.

"You are my prince's kiss," she said to him. "And good-night kiss and shoes that fit and a glass slipper and with you there's no such thing as a vacuum in nature, nor in me anymore, and I love you."

The snow is like thick net curtains, from the sky to the ground, layers and layers of them. Mum is putting on all her Arctic clothes, because we have to put on snow chains.

"I can help," I say.

She shakes her head.

"I can shine a torch again," I say. "And if I get too cold, then I'll get back in here."

"Thank you," she says. "But I really don't want you to come outside, OK?"

"OK."

"Promise?"

"OK."

Mum's still looking at me, waiting.

"OK, I promise."

She wouldn't let Ruby go outside again; a child would become hypothermic faster than an adult. She tugged her Arctic work gloves on over her liners and went out, closing the door as quickly as she could.

The cold was shocking in its violence. She'd thought the color of cold was white, like snow, or blue perhaps, like on a cold tap, but cold like this was conceived in a place without daylight and was black, the absence of all light and color.

She heard a piercing scream, then realized it was the sound of the wind gusting newly fallen snow across the hard-packed snow beneath, white wraiths crossing the road and barren terrain.

She shone Adeeb's torch and found the chains. She tried to unhook them but couldn't hold the torch at the same time. She wedged the torch into snow and shone it under the truck. The chains seemed welded by cold into the hooks that supported them. It was hard to get a grip. After three attempts, she managed to get purchase on the chains and, using all her strength, tugged them free.

She had to move the torch again to shine it at the wheels. Then she laid the chains in front of them.

The snow around the wheels turned pale blue. There were head-lights in the darkness behind her.

He'd realized they weren't at Coldfoot and come after them. Her conversation with Coby on the CB would have just confirmed it. She couldn't tell how close he was.

She felt that the tanker behind her and the man sending the vio-lent photos were working together and they were closing in.

The wind became a caterwauling siren, getting louder; the boy's terrified face in the darkness. He'd died before they got there.

Her goggles had fogged in the extreme cold. She felt for the steps to the cab and managed to climb up and get inside but couldn't find the handle to pull the door closed.

I put on my gloves, and then I lean across Mum and reach out for the door and tug it shut. I can't see Mum's eyes in her goggles, which means she can't see out. I help her to take them off and I wipe them clear for her. She drives very slowly, just a tiny way. She puts on her mask and goggles and goes outside again. I watch her out of the win-dow in case she does need my help after all.

Crouched by the truck, Yasmin studied the tanker's lights. They weren't getting any bigger, so he'd stopped too. It was as if he was biding his time. The screaming of the wind in the dark changed into a low-pitched moan as it eddied around the truck. She'd left the torch wedged in snow, pointing at the wheels, but it had become buried. She scraped around in the snow with her hands to feel for it, but her gloves were too thick. She took them off and just wore liners as she felt for the torch. After two minutes, she found it and hurriedly put on her gloves, then turned it on. In the torchlight she saw that the tires had missed the chains by a few centimeters. She'd have to do this all over again. And she needed to do it quickly, but there was no way to do it quickly.

She felt time falling away from her in the gusting snow.

She would never get to Matt in time to beat the storm.

The low moaning of the wind and the tanker behind them pressed her fear hard and tight.

She looked up at the cab, the amber light illuminating Ruby's small face at the window.

She looked out into the blackness and saw the mutilated musk ox and the raven and the buried wolves and heard the storm building.

There was horrifying clarity: the choice she had to make sharply focused, right bang up in front of her. She had to turn around. There was no longer any other option. It's what Matt would want her to do, and she felt that without needing to articulate it as a thought. Ruby's life trumped everything.

She would think about Matt when Ruby was safe.

If she thought about him now, she wouldn't be able to put on the snow chains and get back in the cab and drive; she wouldn't be able to breathe or blink or swallow.

Twice more during a dark frozen hour she failed to get the chains on and had to do it all over again. The tanker's lights remained the same size: parked and waiting.

When she'd tried to find the torch in the snow she'd felt the metal of her wedding ring and Matt's becoming colder in the subzero Arctic temperature, and then the soft skin of her finger was sticking to the metal, like lips to a frozen iron railing. Matt had told her the truth about needing to take off his wedding ring when he was working.

She thought back to holding his ring at the police station, the touch-warmed metal in her fingers.

## 14

The temperature had dropped three degrees in the last fifteen minutes. Yasmin finally had the chains on. She went back up the steps to the cab. Through the window she saw Ruby shaking, her face pale. She hurried in.

The laptop was open on a new email.

The photo was a dead Arctic fox with gently rounded ears and big eyes in soft white fur. Yasmin wanted to see it as being like a plush toy you could buy, impossibly fluffy and appealing, not a once-living creature, but the fox's childlike vulnerability and soft beauty reminded her so strongly of Ruby that she caught her breath. The man's torch lit only the cub's face. Blood was smeared around its mouth.

The subject was DSC_10027; 68733615 149695998 under the photo.

He'd sent it four minutes ago.

Ruby looked devastated, but there wasn't time to comfort her; she must get her to safety. She hurriedly started driving, looking for a place to turn.

I was crying with Bosley and Dad came in and we talked about school and Jimmy, and he said we could do a blog together. He showed me photos on his iPad of beautiful animals and birds. There was a photo of an Arctic fox cub. Dad said every time he saw an Arctic fox cub and looked at its pretty face he'd be able to see me really clearly. Just like Mum and the peridot in the ring.

The fox cub in the photo is dead.

Dad would never send Mum that photo.

The emails aren't from him.

When I thought Daddy was emailing us, I thought that he was safe because he had a laptop and a terminal with him and he was OK enough to type things and send them.

There is so much snow falling, like it's an army of siafu ants. One little ant-flake can't hurt you, but millions and millions of them kill everything, even people. Dad might not have anything with him. Not a laptop or a blanket or a knife even. What if the snow attacks him and he can't hide?

The sign for Daddy is making a D shape with your fingers, and the shape makes me cry, but I'm trying hard not to. And it's no good because Mum can't see me sign because she's driving, so I put on Voice Magic.

"Dad needs a knife to make an aputiak," I say. "He might not have one."

"I think he has his survival kit with him," Mum says. "And he'll have all the tools he needs."

I read her words on Voice Magic, over and over again. I wish I was a little Reception child again and could believe her and think that Dad is safe.

But I'm in Year Six. And in September I'll be in secondary school.

I look out of my window at the siafu-ants-snow, like if I stare at it enough, I can make it go away, but it looks like there's even more. Mum's said something because there's more type on Voice Magic:

"We have to go back to Coldfoot and wait there till the storm's over."

She can't mean that.

"We'll set off as soon as the storm's over, I promise, go straight to find Daddy then."

"No! We can't leave him!"

I'm trying to shout, but Voice Magic won't shout.

"He might die! Mum, please!"

It isn't my voice, it's a stupid fluffy vacuum bag voice.

"I'll be alone!"

I type something for her to read in my own voice and I push my laptop onto her. She's driving us into this big lay-by and I know it's where she's going to turn around and leave Dad.

She stops the truck, but the engine's still running because I can feel the humming of it under me.

"Daddy is all right," she says. "He'll have made a shelter."

It makes me feel sick to shake my head.

"It's scenario two, Ruby. Daddy went off on a trip and took his survival things with him."

But she doesn't really believe there's a scenario two. She just wants to believe there is. It was like that even at the airport, the very first time she said it. I didn't think it in words, just felt it. But I didn't mind because for ages I thought Dad had important things with him, like his terminal and a friend's laptop and a knife.

"I was just pretending that I believed Dad went off on filming trips," Mum says, and I'm so surprised I do a little flip-jump inside. "I pretended to the police, to you, to me even. But now I've seen pictures of a musk ox and Arctic wolves and an Arctic fox and a raven and the wing prints of a ptarmigan and Lord knows how many other creatures there are out here too."

"There's river otters," I say. "And snowy owls and snowshoe hares. Loads and loads of things."

"Exactly," Mum says. "And Daddy came out here to film them. And I think he was away on a filming trip when the village caught fire. So he's got his survival kit with him, with everything he needs."

She's smiling at me and I know she really believes it.

"He told me an aputiak is a good shape in a storm," I say. "Because it's curved and the wind just blows over the top."

"That's true, I hadn't thought of that. Well then, his emergency kit will have the tools to make an aputiak and he's snug inside it."

When her wedding ring and Matt's had frozen to her finger, the Matt she knew and loved had come crashing into her memory, his decency and honesty assailing her. He hadn't lied about his wedding ring. And he hadn't lied about coming here for the animals.

The threatening emails and the tanker driver chasing them frightened her, yes, but also gave weight to her belief that he was alive, because someone didn't want her to reach him. She would get Ruby to Coldfoot and ask Coby to look after her, and then she would go on alone to find him. If the men there tried to prevent her from leaving, then she'd just have to fight her way out.

She put the truck into gear and checked her driving mirror before attempting to turn the truck around. Glaring headlights behind them dazzled her, momentarily blinding her. The tanker was right behind them, headlights on full beam, about to ram into them. She was forced to accelerate out of the turning place and they were still going north.

She just needed to get far enough ahead of him to turn, because surely there would be another place that would be wide enough.

But even if she did turn around, she'd have to pass him going the other way. He was dangerously violent towards them, she knew that now. He'd force them off the side of the road, and they were in the mountains, a sheer drop on one side.

She quickly took Ruby's hand and squeezed it before reaching for the CB.

"Coby, are you there?"

"Yasmin, good hearin' your voice. You headin' to Coldfoot now?"

"I couldn't turn around. A tanker tried to ram the truck when I slowed to turn around."

"Jesus."

"He's been following me for miles. Can you get the police?"

"Sure. You just hold on, OK? The police'll come through on this channel."

She looked in her driver's mirror. The tanker had dimmed his bright lights and stopped. He must be listening in to this. He wouldn't want the police to find him so close to her.

It meant that she too could stop the truck, and for a moment the relief of not driving was overwhelming.

"I'm sorry, Mummy," Ruby said. "I didn't mean it."

Yasmin knew that Ruby had been terrified by the tanker, and marveled at the strength she had still to be kind. She also knew that Ruby had meant it.

She remembered telling Adeeb that Ruby would be lost without her father, and it had startled her when she'd said it, the truth of it hitting her as if this knowledge had come from someone else, not there inside her all the time. Lost without her father, yes. Devastated. Bereft. Yes to all of those terrible things. But not alone.

A man's voice came onto the CB. "Mrs. Alfredson? It's Lieutenant Reeve."

She remembered him from Fairbanks. As soon as Coby mentioned her, the call must have gone to him.

"You're out on the Dalton?" he asked, sounding appalled.

"Yes."

"Where's your child, Mrs. Alfredson?"

"She's with me."

The tanker driver would be listening. If it was Silesian Stennet, he already knew Ruby was with her, but another man might not. Would it stop him being violent? Or maybe he'd exploit their vulnerability.

There was silence on the CB. She imagined people listening to this and their horror towards her, and she felt it towards herself. What kind of mother endangered her child like this?

"I have been told that someone tried to ram you?" Lieutenant Reeve said.

"He was trying to stop us turning around. He's been following us for at least a hundred miles, maybe all the way from Fairbanks."

"Are you drivin' Azizi's rig?" another voice said, that she thought she recognized.

"Yes. He—"

The man interrupted. "I'm at MP 181, headin' south? Passed Azizi's rig 'bout twenty miles back. There's nobody behind this lady."

She was sure he was the same man who'd asked her if she had a gun.

"Drove another twenty minutes before I saw another rig headin' north," the man continued. "And that was a truck, not a tanker. Like I said, there ain't nobody behind her."

"You're lying," she said. "It's you, isn't it? Driving the tanker with blue headlights. Going north, not south. Right behind me."

"Hey, don't go gettin' delusional with me, lady."

Lieutenant Reeve came on again. "Here's what we're going to do, Mrs. Alfredson. You are going to try to find someplace safe to stop while we send a rescue helicopter to come and get you both. OK?"

He was talking to her very calmly, self-consciously reasonable, like you would try to talk someone down from a ledge, she imagined.

"Yes."

She wanted to tell him about the emails and the possible land grab and Silesian Stennet, but at the moment she had no credibility—a bereaved madwoman who'd stolen a truck, endangered her child, and imagined a tanker chasing her down.

But when their helicopter flew over the Dalton, they'd see there was a tanker behind her. Then they would know that he'd lied. They'd have to listen to her. And she would convince them that Matt was alive, that he most probably knew something about Anaktue, which was why someone was trying to prevent her from reaching him.

Behind them, the blue lights were getting larger as he moved closer. The road ahead was two lanes and straight for a few hundred meters, not wide enough to turn a massive tanker but wide enough for him to overtake. And if he did that, he'd say he'd never been behind her.

She started driving again, keeping ahead of him through the squalling snow.

She just had to keep ahead until the police arrived. The huge wipers were scraping the thick swarms of flakes off the windscreen as they hit it but only just giving her space to see.

They reached a narrow steep stretch of road, winding round the mountainside. There wasn't room for the tanker to pass them here, so she slowed down and stopped. The tanker driver was forced to stop behind them. This was how she'd wait it out till the police came. In front of them, she saw two small spruce trees, bent sideways by the wind.

"It's all my fault," Ruby said. "I went to sleep."

"Nothing's your fault."

"But if I'd woken you up we would have got away from the man behind us, we'd have got nearer to Daddy."

"It made no difference."

Ruby shook her head.

"I promise you. No difference at all."

Yasmin hadn't realized till this appalling journey how generous Ruby was to her, and now here Ruby was taking the blame on herself when all of it—everything—was entirely Yasmin's fault.

Lieutenant Reeve came onto the CB. "I've spoken to our rescue team. I'm sorry but it's impossible for a helicopter to fly in these weather conditions."

Yasmin immediately started driving, knowing that the tanker driver, listening to this, would come after them now.

"Even if they could get to you, and that's doubtful," Lieutenant Reeve continued, "we couldn't risk having you and your daughter in a helicopter in these winds. They're gusting up to fifty miles an hour and look set to get worse. Hurricane force."

"There's a tanker, with blue headlights, right behind us. Trying to ram us off the road."

"We checked. None of the haulage companies have anyone out there. Their drivers are waiting it out at Deadhorse, Fairbanks, or Coldfoot. No one else is driving in these conditions."

"Please, you need to believe me."

"We'll come and get you as soon as it's possible."

"A helicopter went out to look for survivors of Anaktue. Even though there was a storm—"

"The winds weren't as strong. It was risky to fly but not suicidal. That's simply not the case today. You'll be safer waiting out the storm in your cab."

Behind her, the blue lights remained the same size in the darkness, so he was keeping pace with them. Maybe she could try and outrun him. But the road was steep and windy and treacherous, and the snow was getting heavier.


We're going very very slowly because it's hard to see through the snow and the man behind us is going very very slowly too. Like he's hunting us in slow motion, but he's still hunting us.

There's a sign: FARTHEST NORTH SPRUCE TREE—DO NOT CUT. Next to it is a dead tree, all white with snow and ice, like it's made of tiny bones. The furthest-north alive tree was probably miles and miles ago.


In her mirror, Yasmin saw the tanker's blue lights move suddenly to one side before becoming centered again. He must have skidded. Perhaps he hadn't stopped to put on snow chains. Perhaps he would just skid over the goddam mountainside and be gone. Or, not as good, he'd have to stop and put on snow chains and would be as ham-fisted at it as she'd been and would take an hour and they'd get far ahead of him.

Through the snow she glimpsed the road marker MP 242. She

knew from Adeeb's map that they would soon be approaching the Atigun Pass, the highest mountain pass in Alaska. On the other side of it lay the immense north slope coastal tundra.

The dense darkness and snow were punctured only by her headlights and behind them the blue lights of the tanker. But she felt her guilt following her in the darkness too, for putting Ruby in such danger, and behind that guilt another quieter culpability: *"I'll be alone."*

## 15

The wind was blowing the snow horizontally at the windscreen, their truck pummeling its way through. Yasmin couldn't see the sides of the road, relying on the delineators reflecting a brief orange flash to guide her. She felt their huge truck tilt in the building wind.

She had turned off the CB after her conversation with Lieutenant Reeve and didn't put it on again; she didn't want to hear the tanker driver's voice, though she longed to hear Coby's, a man she'd never met and most likely never would.

The visibility was so bad that she didn't know how close the tanker was behind them. It had been half an hour since she'd been able to see his headlights.

The tanker man is hiding in the snow and dark behind us, but we don't know where.

Mum stops the truck. She asks me to get Mr. Azizi's bright orange tunic-thing, which is in a compartment in my door. It's like the one she makes me wear on my bicycle. Mr. Azizi wore it when he was sorting out the truck in Fairbanks.

She drives us towards the edge of the road, right by the drop, and opens the window. The truck sways, like the wind's got its fingers through the open window, and snow blows in, loads and loads of it, and lands on Mum's lap, really fast, like if she left the window open for too long she'd be covered in snow and turned into a snow-woman.

Mum throws the bright orange tunic out of the window, and the wind grabs it from her and whirls it away and then she asks me to get clothes out of Mr. Azizi's suitcase and I do and she throws them out too. But she doesn't throw out his parka, probably because Arctic parkas are super-expensive, and then she quickly closes the windows. We've been looking out for the blue lights but we still can't see him.

Mum reverses us away from the edge of the mountain and then we go forward again, right up to the drop. Then she does it again and I feel a bit sick. She says she needs our tracks to be really deep so that the snow won't fill them in.

She was a mother who'd changed fairy tales, editing out psychotic stepmothers; who didn't allow Ruby to watch anything above a PG; and now here she was telling Ruby how the tanker man would see the clothes and their tracks and think that they'd gone over the edge. And the terrible thing was that this was the only comfort she could offer her.

"But he'll see our tracks when we drive away," Ruby said.

"No, because they won't be so deep and the snow will soon fill them up."

"But the wind might blow the orange thing and the clothes down the mountain."

"That would be OK."

Because then the man would think they were dead and that was a good thing. Whatever happened to them, she knew that this journey would always mark for her the end of Ruby's childhood.

The road is so steep; sometimes on one side you can see mountains like giant horses rearing up, right next to you, like they're going to smash their hooves into you. On the other side, there's just black, and that's even scarier because we could drop right off the edge of the mountain.

Mr. Azizi told me that the Atigun Pass is a quarter of a mile high. He told me that when he didn't know we'd be driving on it. Or that there would be a snowstorm and a man chasing us. I don't think he'd have told me that if he'd known. There are barriers at the sides of the road, which Mum says are to stop you going over the edge, but I just caught a glimpse of one and it looks a bit flimsy. I don't think it would stop a truck like ours with a whole house on it.

Sometimes you see a small sign in our headlights, and it's just an arrow pointing right or pointing left and that means Mum knows to turn the steering wheel, otherwise we might just drive off into the sky and we'd fall for a quarter of a mile. I don't know how long that would take.

There was so much snow falling on them that it felt like it was smothering them. Yasmin could only just catch glimpses of the delineator posts on the edge of the road and panicked that the delineator glinting on her right should be on her left and she was driving them off the road and the barrier would give way and they'd go over the edge. Unsure what was ground or sky, left or right, not knowing if it was night or day, her physical disorientation in the darkness and snow crept into her mind, so there were moments when she no longer knew who or what she was running from. Perhaps the blue lights following them unseen in the dark were a phantom, her terror for Matt hunting her down. But that couldn't be right, because it was her guilt and failure as Ruby's mother that was stalking her. And she couldn't turn around and face either, not yet, not till she'd got Ruby safely over the mountain.

I don't know how Mum knows where to drive. If I had to, I wouldn't know where the road is. There are little orange flashes when our lights hit a stick, but they're teeny. I think it must be like this for aeroplane pilots at night, you know when they come down from a black sky and all they see are little lights to guide them? But as they get closer the lights get bigger, and they're straight and these ones stay really small and twist around the mountain.

My bracelet vibrates and the truck is vibrating too and the vibrations get into my bones, like we're harps, Mum and me, and I like thinking of us this way, but I know it's a bad noise because Mum looks so frightened.

At first Yasmin thought it was an explosion, but the noise carried for too long, as if the solid earth and rocks and ice of the mountains had turned into thunder. She heard the avalanche roaring behind them, but she didn't know how close it was, didn't know if it was widening to include them in its path. She drove as fast as she dared away from it. And then the noise weakened and stopped. The only sound now was the violent wind, as if at any moment it could start another lava flow of snow.

Mum tells me there's been an avalanche. She says that there is good news and not-so-good news. The not-so-good news is that the avalanche will have blocked the road behind us, so we can't get back to Coldfoot and no one from Coldfoot can get to us. I don't think that's bad at all because I want to go nearer to where Dad is.

"What's the good news?" I ask.

"I think the tanker might be on the other side of the avalanche."

"Or it landed on top of him!"

We both sort of laugh because although the road is high and twisty and it's really hard to see, the main frightening thing was the tanker man and he might not even be there anymore.

We aren't speaking very much because Mum needs every speck of concentrating for driving. So we haven't talked about the man who sent the emails, not since I knew it wasn't Daddy. I think he's the tanker man, or they're friends.

Mum's taken off her seat belt so she can lean forward. Her face is super-close to the windscreen. Her fingers are gripping round the steering wheel, like she can hold us on the road.


The wind was at hurricane force, the snow slamming against the windscreen, as if she were ramming this truck through the core of it. She feared the tanker had also made it through before the avalanche and was close behind them.

She'd thought about going on Ruby's laptop and emailing for help or asking for help on the CB, but she'd already spoken to the police and they couldn't get to them till after the storm.

She longed to talk to Coby or other drivers on the CB but worried that the tanker driver, if he'd made it, would hear her. She still had a hope, slight but tenacious, that her decoy plan might have worked and he'd thought they'd gone over the edge of the mountain.

She felt their cab tipping forward and realized they must have reached the top and were starting the descent. If there was another avalanche she wouldn't be able to accelerate away from it because they'd skid and go over the edge.

Twice the tires slipped and for a few feet they went forward out of control and she had to pump the brakes to slow the truck. She could only just see the delineators and sometimes thought her eyes were imagining the orange glints; that they were like Sirens, luring her out into the void and the rocks thousands of feet below.

She could hear Ruby's rapid shallow breathing and knew how

frightened she was, but she couldn't reassure her, concentrating solely on driving.

Finally, they reached the bottom of the mountain.

In their headlights, she saw a tidal wave of snow accelerating across the Arctic tundra.

At their back were mountains, bisecting Alaska in a seven-hundred-mile-wide barrier, impossible to go back over or around. In front of them, a hundred and seventy miles away, was Deadhorse and the Arctic Ocean.

She remembered the driver's voice—". . . *no trees to stop the wind. Storms blow across there like it's turned into hell. Eighty-eight thousand square miles of nothin'.*"

The wind's MEGATRON strong. It's snowing even more now, like there's a ceiling of snow and it's collapsing on top of us.

We start juddering and I think it's the wind shaking us, but Mum says it's not the wind doing the juddering. She says we've got ice in our wheels so they're not turning properly and she needs to chip the ice out. She doesn't say "otherwise the man might catch us," but I know that's what she means. We don't know if the avalanche stopped him. And Mum's plan with Mr. Azizi's clothes might not have worked either.

You know that outdoor theater they had in Rome? The one where they had a slave and let the lion out? It's like we're in this huge cold dark theater, but it's not a lion who'll be let out to hurt us but a person who kills a musk ox and a raven and wolves and an Arctic fox cub when they've done nothing to him at all.

Yasmin was hurriedly putting on her Arctic clothes, frustrated at the amount of time it took—the base layers and midlayers and outer layers, her fingers struggling to go faster with the zips and Velcro.

All the time the tanker could be getting closer. But the outside temperature was minus forty-two, far lower with the windchill, and she'd
need all that protection or she'd get hypothermia and frostbite and
there would be no one to keep Ruby safe. Her ice-scalded left hand
was painful as she dressed, but she was glad because she was pretty
sure pain meant she didn't have nerve damage. She wedged a hammer
from Adeeb's toolbox into her parka pocket; in her right hand she
held his torch. She wanted to wear thick mittens, but she wouldn't be
able to grip the hammer, so she put on liners and Arctic work gloves.

She left the heater running and got out of the cab. She'd made
Ruby put on extra clothing to protect her from the subzero blast of air
when she opened the door.

She climbed down onto the first step and was slammed against
the side of the truck, hitting her face, and then she was flung to the
ground. Lying on the snow, winded with pain, she turned to face her
attacker, the tanker driver surely, but no one was there. It was the
wind at hurricane force that had attacked her. The noise was like nothing she'd heard in the natural world, a jet engine screaming across
the tundra. Her right hand was still holding tightly to the torch; the
instinct for self-preservation had been to hold on to light rather than
save herself. She was grateful for the layers of clothing that had cush-
ioned her fall.

Snow was falling so thickly it appeared solid. She crawled on her
hands and knees and then flat on her tummy and arms, pulling herself
towards the underside of the truck.

Her eyes were stinging as if she were blinking hot ash; there was a
burning in the skin underneath her eyes. When she fell, her goggles
had got dislodged. Blinking was getting hard, as if her eyelashes were
sticking together.

She felt the cold surrounding her, a predator made of darkness.

She crawled over the hammer, which pressed hard into her. She
picked it up, then slid underneath the truck, where there was shelter
from the Arctic hurricane. Her eyes had frozen shut, the lashes glued

together, and she couldn't open them. She wiped her face hard against the sleeve of her parka, over and over, but it didn't work. The only warm thing she had was her own breath. She pulled her balaclava up, stretching it over her eyes, so that her eyes and mouth were in the same micro-environment, and gradually her exhaled breath warmed her eyelids until they unfroze and she could see again. She pulled her goggles back onto her eyes, but ice had formed around the rims and the fit wasn't as tight against her skin as it should be.

She shone the torch at the wheels; as she'd feared, ice was wedged into them. She hit the ice with the hammer but it was hard as metal and wouldn't give way. She tried again and again. Each time it was harder to hold the hammer. She thought about the coastal bus journey to Cley that she and Matt had gone on so many times years ago. First stop Holme-next-the-Sea, then Thornham, Titchwell, Brancaster, Brancaster Staithe. Each time she hit the ice she thought of the next seaside stop. Burnham Deepdale, Burnham Market, Burnham Overy, Holkham, Wells, Cley.

When she hit at the ice for the twentieth time she could no longer remember which seaside village came next, or even their names, and she couldn't keep hold of the hammer. Loss of memory and poor grip were early signs of hypothermia. She had to get back into the truck.

She shone her torch away from the wheels and into the darkness. Sky, land, and snow had fused together into one alien infinite totality. She thought that this was what grief looked like; this was her mind when her mother had died; the endless bleak aloneness of it.

Somewhere out there was Matt.

She yelled his name into the dark as loudly as she could. But although her mouth formed the shapes to make the sound and her lungs forced his name into a scream, the sound was obliterated by the wind so that she didn't know if she'd made any sound at all. It was as if she'd created a void around herself and she could no longer be sure of her presence in this place.

She climbed the steps back towards the cab, the wind trying to tear her away, her feet numb.

She'd left the headlights on and from the top step she could see a rocky outcrop, a little higher than the truck, about ten meters ahead of them, with the road cutting through on one side. It was shelter of a kind where they could wait out the storm.

She looked back to see if she could see the tanker, but the darkness and dense snow would hide him; nor would she be able to hear him above the sound of the wind. But he wouldn't be able to see them or hear them either. And it was impossible for either of them to drive in this. He would have to wait it out, like they would.

Mum is getting back inside. Her face has got sore red marks on it and the part of her face next to her goggles is bleeding, like the cold has been biting her. I'm taking off her gloves, which are all icy, and the heater is puffing full blast.

She starts driving, with only her right hand on the steering wheel because I think her left one hurts too much. There's so much snow. It's like we're inside it.

Our truck's still juddering really badly, jumping me out of my seat with my seat belt digging into me.

Mum stops and I can see teeny gaps in the snow.

"This is a good spot to wait out the storm," Mum says.

The wind can't push us over here. It just rocks us, like it can't get its hands around us properly.

Mum smiles at me. "Even if tanker man made it over the mountain, he won't be able to find us in this."

I've been frightened of the storm and the tanker man and the big dark theater with the man who sent the emails; too afraid to be frightened for Daddy too.

I make the D shape.

Mum hugs me. She's still got her parka on and her sleeves

are covered in ice. She takes off her parka so she won't make me shiver.

"He's in his aputiak," she says. "And he'll be OK. Inupiat people must have weathered storms like this for centuries."

I can tell that she really believes it. An aputiak's much better than a tent, because a tent would just blow away.


Yasmin knew now that Matt had told her the truth about his wedding ring and about coming out here in winter to film wildlife, and he'd told Ruby that he could make an aputiak. She believed him now about all of it. Trusting Matt meant that he had a chance of being safe.

She felt terror for him, as if fear were a living thing inside her, but she couldn't allow herself to think about him, not now, not yet. Her priority, and the only practical thing she could do, was to get Ruby through the storm unharmed.

## 16

Mum's getting everything out of our suitcases and we're putting on all our clothes. We started with the tightest things and we're putting baggier things over the top. Arms are the hardest and Mum's helping me tug sleeves over other sleeves, though she can't use her left hand properly because the ice burned it. She helps me put on Mr. Azizi's parka over the top of everything else and it has a lemony soap smell, which is what Mr. Azizi smelled like, only I didn't know that till I smelled lemony-soap and thought of him. I want Mum to wear the parka but she won't.

Our headlights are off so we can't see anything outside. It sometimes feels like we're moving, but it's the wind blowing us. Mum must hear things, because she keeps going stiff, like she's playing a five-second go of "statues."

Mum says that when the police come and get us in their helicopter she'll make them believe Dad is alive and MAKE them go and look for him at Anaktue. She says she'll hijack their goddam helicopter if she has to. I have never lip-read her saying "goddam" before but Daddy says it quite a lot, about any old thing, like traffic jams. I like the shape her mouth makes when she says it, her lips closing at the end of it—goddaM—like she's really determined.

She's tucking Mr. Azizi's sleeping bag around me and it has the lemony smell too. She says I should go to sleep because time goes more quickly when you sleep. When I was little she told me that sleeping is like space travel, you just go away for a little while, but when you get back again to Earth it's been much much longer there. So I close my eyes.


Yasmin was glad Ruby couldn't hear the wind's violence: the polar vortex high above them in the stratosphere descending down to Earth as a hurricane, rocking the truck and sending horizontal avalanches of snow across the tundra.

The truck's thermometer showed that it was minus forty-three outside, colder still with the windchill. The thermometer inside the cab read fifty. They were dressed in as many layers of clothing as they had, but she didn't know how long they'd survive if the engine cut out.

She put on the CB in the hope that she'd discover the police were braving the hurricane and storm and coming to get them after all, knowing even as she thought it that it would be insane. But the only voices on the CB were truckers stuck at Deadhorse, Coldfoot, and Fairbanks, complaining about delayed trips and lost pay. Their voices were nonetheless comforting, so she left the CB on.

Beside her, Ruby had fallen asleep. Yasmin remembered her pale face and shaking body when she saw the email of the Arctic fox cub and knew that the emails weren't from her father. Ruby had thought then that he didn't have any survival tools or shelter.

She remembered looking for a place to turn around.

*"No! We can't leave him!"*

She saw a place ahead they could turn.

*"He might die! Mum, please!"*

Ruby was pushing her laptop at her as she pulled into the turning place.

*"I'll be alone!"*

And the tanker was right behind her, headlights blinding her, and she'd had to drive on, the road steep and windy and treacherous and she hadn't been able to think about what Ruby had said or read what she'd written on her computer; but she'd felt her failure as Ruby's mother following her in the darkness.

She opened the last document on Ruby's laptop.

These are my words Mummy. This is me talking.

This is me

# SHOUTING!

This is my voice.

This is me.

———

Matt had understood that. And she loved him more for it.

She stroked the fleece of Ruby's face mask, as if she could smooth away the crease of tiredness and anxiety on her face beneath.

She opened Ruby's blog.

> **aweekinalaskablog.com**
> Hi, this is a blog about our time in Alaska by Matt Alfredson, who's a wildlife cameraman, and Ruby Alfredson.
>
> *(Do you think that's OK, Dad? You'll probably write something much better and I don't mind AT ALL if you change it. I'm not going to publish anything till you're here too. I'm putting the musk ox photo in first for now. We'll delete these bits before we publish it!)*

Ruby had uploaded the photo of the mutilated musk ox and had meticulously copied down all the numbers.

> *(Is this for your work, Daddy? Hope so because people reading our blog might feel sick if they see it. I think that you took a photo because it's a big musk ox, and wolves don't usually kill big ones. Was he ill or hurt? But we'll see a musk ox who's alive, won't we? So I'll write about musk oxes and then we can put a different photo and you can add everything I've left out.)*

Yasmin remembered Ruby's face as she'd tried so hard to make this grotesque image something that was a part of the natural world, something her father would have sent. She'd realized that Ruby no longer took on trust what she told her; that Ruby had to create evidence for herself that her father was alive. She felt fury now and anguish that Ruby had been tricked, however willingly, into think-ing these photos were from her father, that she'd so carefully blogged what this man had sent her.

> Musk Oxes look really big and frightening but they're gentle
> vegetarians and they only have big hooves so they can crack
> the ice and get water and walk around on the snow without
> sinking. Inupiat people call a musk ox *umingmak,* which
> means "The bearded one."

Yasmin remembered Ruby telling her about musk oxen, but she had interrupted, telling her to use her words, focused only on wanting Ruby to talk with her mouth. And Ruby must have sensed her lack of interest—did she even try to disguise it? She read what Ruby would have told her, had she allowed her to speak.

> Musk oxes are very brave. Wolf packs hunt musk oxes and
> they always kill the smallest ones (nearly always). So when
> they see a wolf pack, all the grown-up musk oxes make
> a circle around the babies and children. They put their
> bottoms inward to the circle and their horns out, to look
> fierce. About a hundred years ago, people hunted them and
> the musk oxes did their circle around the babies and didn't
> move and the hunters just shot them and shot them. And
> when one of them was injured they surrounded the injured
> one and tried to protect him or her too. Hunters thought
> they were stupid, but really they were brave.

Yasmin was moved by Ruby's description of the musk oxen and by her knowledge. She clicked on the next page of the blog.

Ruby had uploaded the photo of the dead raven and scrupulously copied down the numbers.

*(You've told me lots about ravens, so I'm going to write what I know and then you can put in all the things I've left out.)*

Ravens are the largest of all the songbirds and sing lots of different songs. They sing when they're frightened, or sometimes when they're just talking to each other. They do croaking sounds and knocking sounds, but mainly they like to sing.

Ravens choose a husband or wife and stay together all their lives. They're very loyal. Sometimes they get as old as thirty together.

When they fly, they like doing somersaults and barrel rolls. Sometimes they carry sticks when they're flying, or feathers, and they pass them to each other, like playing catch in the sky.

Yasmin could hear Matt chatting to Ruby about ravens and Ruby's delight in it; she could feel the warmth between the two of them.

After baby ravens are born, they stay with their parents for a year. Sometimes there's a third raven, like a godparent raven, helping the parents get food for the young ones and helping to teach them. Ravens are super-coolio copycats and play jokes; they can imitate other animals and even humans.

Ravens stay in Alaska all winter. If there's a snowy hill, they love sliding down it, like they're tobogganing, and they take turns, going one at a time. And they don't just play with each other, they play with animals too, even animals like wolves and bears. Isn't that amazing?

Yes, thought Yasmin, it is. She looked again at the photo and instead of seeing the demonic bird of Western literature and the ugly captive symbol-laden birds at the Tower of London, she saw birds who sang and tobogganed and kept a mate for life. No wonder Ruby liked ravens so much; no wonder Matt did. She'd already realized that there was wildlife here for Matt to film, but now she had a glimpse of why he might want to.

Ruby had wanted to tell her an Inupiaq story about a raven. But she had told Ruby to use her proper voice. And then, when Ruby didn't speak with her mouth, she'd thought that there probably wasn't any story.

She clicked onto the next page of the blog.

The photo of dead wolves, almost buried in snow, filled the screen. She saw again the glint from a harness in the bottom right-hand corner, a husky dog just visible.

Ruby hadn't told her anything about wolves. Not one single fact. She hadn't even attempted to.

How often did she silence Ruby, without even being aware of it?

*(Why did you take this photo, Dad? Was it because the poor wolves had got trapped in the snow? I thought animals in Alaska were really good at not getting trapped in the snow. I think that these photos aren't for our blog, but work. And you'll tell me all about it when you see me.*

*But I really want to write our blog anyway, because when I do it's like you're with me.*

*And we'll see wolves, won't we? Ones that are alive, with their thick white coats? So I'll write about those now, the wolves you and I are going to see.)*

Yasmin heard the sound of her name on the CB.

"OK, Yasmin, I'm bankin' on you listenin' into the CB."

She'd put on the CB fifteen minutes ago to have the company of voices. Now she turned it up. It was Coby.

"If you've heard me before, like a dozen times, then I apologize for gettin' repetitive. And anyone ANYONE who interrupts me on the CB because they're gettin' sick of this stuff has me to answer to in Coldfoot."

It was as if the raging storm had a calm, answering voice.

"Right. So you have a child with you," Coby continued, and surely he must despise her for that, but his tone was kind. "We need to look after her, right? Keep her and you warm so that the both of you get through this storm OK. Bin askin' the fellas here at Coldfoot and we've put together a cheat sheet on the best things to do."

She thought how when this was over she'd enjoy the idea of a cheat sheet on how to survive a polar storm in the middle of the Arctic tundra. With Coby talking to her, she believed that there would be a time when this was over.

"So first thing you gotta do is put on every single piece of clothin' you have with you. If you've got three hats then you put on three hats, got that? Sleepin' bags, towels, anythin' like that, get 'em wrapped around you."

She felt like he'd give her a gold sticker at the end and wanted to boast that she had indeed done exactly that.

"You probably got that nice warm heater goin' full blast, right? But we need to make sure your exhaust ain't leakin' carbon monoxide."

Yasmin knew that people who got stranded in cars sometimes got poisoned by carbon monoxide because of snow blocking the exhaust outlet. But the outlet in a truck was very high, so she'd thought that wasn't a danger.

"Can you see what's comin' out of your exhaust?" Coby asked. "If you can, does it look funny, like thick and billowin'? That's a sign that you've got some damage."

So it was damage that would be the problem, not a blockage. But it was impossible to see the exhaust in the dark and snow. Even if she could, the turbulence from the wind would disperse it immediately.

"Now I'm guessin' the wind's roarin' its head off, but before the wind started yowlin' at you, did you hear any noises from the bottom of the truck? Like a loud rumblin'? The holes can make a rumblin' noise."

Yasmin hadn't noticed a strange noise, but there was so much else she was focused on she probably wouldn't have done. She had seen ice wedged in the wheels, iron hard and destructive; it could have caused holes in the exhaust system. And if it was in the section running under their cab, carbon monoxide could leak in.

She'd left the heater on before, when she'd fallen asleep after Coldfoot, but the truck had taken much more of a battering since then.

She pulled the sleeping bag up over Ruby, then turned off the engine; the heater and the light went out immediately.

Coby's voice continued in the dark.

"Let's go assumin' a worst-case situation and you've got yourself damage. So when you're runnin' the engine keep the windows open a little bit, both sides, keep good air comin' in so the poison can't build up. Brady here says to run the engine for ten minutes each hour, so I'm guessin' it would be OK to run it for five minutes every half an hour."

She looked at the clock on Ruby's laptop, which was backlit and fully charged. She'd time half an hour before putting the engine on again.

"Adeeb'll have a tool compartment in the cab," Coby continued, calmly and slowly. "Most likely the middle compartment, if his cab's like mine. In there, he's sure to have a knife. You need to cut into the seat covers and get out the insulation. Then pad yourselves out with it. Your heads too."

Yasmin looked in the middle compartment and found a Stanley knife, thick tape, screwdrivers, and a small ice pick. She took out the Stanley knife.

"Not sure if you've been hearin' the police puttin' out messages to you?" Coby continued. "But they've been tellin' you, you mustn't get out of the cab. Not till this thing's blown over. Not for any reason. Hold on here, other people are tellin' me what I'm missin'."

She imagined these drivers around a table in the café in Coldfoot, hot coffees in front of them, stamping their feet perhaps to keep warm because she imagined it was cold even inside. They didn't know if she was alive, let alone listening to this, and it moved her that even so they were trying to help.

"OK, so listen up, Yasmin. This is real important. You've gotta stay awake, because you need to remember to turn the heater off. If you start gettin' cold, then move your arms and legs as much as you can, keep the circulation goin'. I know the cab ain't that big, but move as much as you can."

She was cutting her seat open with the Stanley knife. There was wadding inside. If she made a long enough cut she'd be able to take a sheet of it out and wrap it around Ruby as an extra layer.

"Gabe here says to tie something colorful to the radio antenna, once you're safe to go out. But I reckon a chopper'll be able to see you pretty clearly, only thing out on the road, so don't worry too much 'bout that." He paused a moment, and Yasmin was worried he'd gone.

"I know you can't answer on the CB," Coby continued. "You think there's some psycho on your tail. And I don't know 'bout that, but let's say there is—and you think there is, so I'm goin' with that—you're not goin' to answer back and give anythin' away, right? So I'll just keep comin' on and doin' my little routine till the storm's let up. Got that? Good."

She wished she could say thank you.

Outside it was minus forty-five. Inside it was still fifty. She didn't know how quickly the temperature would drop inside the cab. When it got to freezing she'd wake Ruby and make her move around and keep her circulation going.

In the dark cab, with Ruby pressed up close to her, she carried on reading her blog.

> I know lots of people are scared of wolves because they think
> they're like the wolves in "Little Red Riding Hood"; nasty
> animals that like killing things. Or because they make a
> frightening noise. But wolves aren't like that at all, especially
> Arctic wolves. They're really beautiful, with thick white fur

that's specially designed to keep the cold out. And Arctic
wolves aren't very big. I think the main thing people don't like
about wolves is that they are in a pack, and they surround an
animal, like a herd of musk oxes, and then they get one little
musk ox away and kill it. But wolves are much smaller than
musk oxes so they need to do it as a pack. And they need to
eat otherwise they'd die. And they don't have much energy for
chasing things, because staying warm in Alaska is a full-time
job, and so they go after the animal that will take the littlest
amount of energy.

Anyway, we eat lamb, don't we? Nobody wants to eat
mutton. Though I don't think a wolf minds much about what
the musk ox tastes like.

Yasmin could imagine Matt smiling at that, enjoying Ruby's
chatty blog. And she related to the wolves; putting what energy you
have towards survival made sense to her.

She'd thought that when Ruby was on her laptop she was lonely,
leaving the real world to enter cyberspace, peopled by strangers, not
realizing that there could be intimate worlds inside it.

She remembered back to Scotland, her fury that Ruby would be
doing a blog, not understanding that it was about Matt and Ruby,
that it was a place for them to meet and be close. One of many
places. And she could have—should have—found places to join
Ruby too.

There was another page of the blog. She'd thought that when Ruby
saw the dead Arctic fox cub, its pretty face smeared in blood, she'd
known, finally, these photos weren't from her father and had stopped
blogging.

The temperature in the cab was dropping quickly. She took off the
glove on her right hand and felt Ruby's face, as she'd done countless
times when she'd been ill. Her forehead was warm; she'd let her sleep
awhile longer. Then she read the final page.

*(I saw something super-coolio today, Dad! And I want this to be about all the amazing things in Alaska, and I hope that's OK. I don't have a picture but maybe we'll be able to take one when you're with us.)*

I saw three moons!

Cross-my-heart true!

It was the usual one, and two other moons, one on either side of it, which are called moondogs. Mum told me all about them. Paraselenae is their proper name. They're made by moonlight bouncing off ice crystals. They're beautiful. The three moons looked like they'd shared out the sky.

It was now twenty-eight Fahrenheit inside the cab, minus forty-six outside. There was still fifteen more minutes before she could run the heater again.

She opened a new document on Ruby's laptop and typed

## 17

Y ou can see our breath like smoke. There's no lemony smell of Mr. Azizi anymore, no smell of anything; the cold has killed it.

The wind is rocking our truck, like we're a battleship in a stormy sea.

Mum's being sergeant-major-Mum, saying we need to put on all our things—"ALL of them, Ruby." So we're even getting out flannels and putting them inside our hats to make another layer and when it gets warm again my hair's going to smell of toothpaste. School only let me leave during term time if I brought homework, and I'm ripping pages out of my books to put as another layer. It'll be the best excuse ever—"I HAD to tear up my homework otherwise I might have got hypothermia!"

I have put Mr. Azizi's map, folded out, inside my fleece, really carefully, because it has Anaktue on it, and that's where Dad is, and so we don't want to tear it.

Mum checks the thermometer. It's twenty-one in here and minus forty-eight outside. We've got the little light to the cab on, and Voice Magic. And Mum and me are wearing the special gloves Dad got us so we can still sign too. I'd be frightened if we couldn't talk to each other.

Mum says she thinks we're in the eye of the storm. I look out of the windscreen to see if there's an evil eye watching us, like Sauron in *The Lord of the Rings,* but there's just the reflection of our faces.

They don't look like our faces because we have goggles and face masks on and lots of hats.

Now we're stamping our feet and waving our arms around, and Mum says we also need to keep ALERT. She says our job, each of us, is to keep the other one awake. So we'll tell each other an interesting thing. I have to go first, but I don't know what to say to Mum. I think she must see that I don't know.

"Can you tell me the story about the Inupiaq hunter on sea ice?" she asks.

I wanted to tell her ages ago, when we were still with Mr. Azizi, because it's a really happy kind of story and I thought it would cheer her up. But she didn't think it was interesting then.

"Are you sure?" I ask.

"Absolutely," she says, and I can tell she's doing a big beamy mum smile under her face mask.

"OK. A hunter was sitting all alone by a breathing hole in the sea ice," I say. "The ice seemed like part of the land because it was so, so thick."

She nods at me to go on, like she's really interested.

"He had to sit really still. For hours and hours and hours. The wind got stronger and stronger, like it is now I think. It tore the ice away from the land and the ice floated off into the sea. To start with, the hunter didn't even know the ice he was sitting on had broken off. He didn't know there was deep deep sea between him and the shore. And the poor hunter got carried further and further out to sea on the ice. Dad said sometimes a hunter drowned or froze to death. But their families always held out hope."

That's what Dad said—*"held out hope."* But I think it should be "held ON to hope," because hope is a warm thing you want to keep close to you.

"Ruby? You said the family held out hope?"

She's worried I'm not ALERT, but I'm just thinking about hope.

"Yes. Because this man was isiqsuruk"—I finger-spell *"isiqsuruk"*—

"which means 'a strong and enduring hunter,' and he got all the way to Siberia on his bit of ice. And the next winter he came home to his family back over the frozen sea."

Mum's smiling at me, but I can see tears in her eyes through her goggles, and I think the tears hurt because her eyes look redder.

"That's a great story, Ruby."

I think so too but I wish Dad had told her, because he tells it much better than me.

We're stamping our feet now in our big boots, which are tight because we have so many socks on, and we're pretending we're marching on parade, in front of Buckingham Palace with tourists taking our picture, and I imagine that Buckingham Palace has snow in front of it and the soldiers with bearskin hats stop marching and have a snowball fight, so I run on the spot and wave my arms and pretend I'm throwing. Mum says I'm doing brilliantly. It's harder for her than me because she has to stoop while she does the pretend marching and snowball fighting.

Mr. Azizi's thermometer says it's seventeen in here and minus forty-nine outside.

Now I'm jumping and so is Mum, though a crouched kind of jump, and we're waving our arms like someone we know is winning a race and we're cheering them on and we decide it's Bosley in a dog race, though Bosley would just run to the crowd, wagging his tail, and ask to be stroked. Our arms keep bumping into each other so we can't do really big arm waves.

Mum says I'm one of those people at airports with the flags telling the planes where to park and I have a jumbo jet with a shortsighted pilot so I have to make super-big arm movements.

"You told Mr. Azizi you liked music?" she says, and then she finger-spells "Brahms."

I didn't know she'd listened to me talking to Mr. Azizi.

"His symphony has a battleship in a storm in it," I say, and Mum smiles. I think Mum might feel like we're inside the music too.

"What other music do you like?" Mum asks.

But it's her turn to tell me an interesting thing.

"Please, Ruby, I'd love to know."

"I like pop too," I say. "The Beatles most of all because of the pictures in their songs."

"'Yellow Submarine'?" Mum asks. "I love that one."

"Yes, and 'Octopus's Garden.' I like 'Lucy in the Sky with Diamonds' the most. And I do quite like Rihanna's diamonds-and-star song too."

It's tiring signing, like my hands have just run a long race. You can't see our faces in the windscreen anymore. There's ice on the inside of it, in swirly patterns; in some places it's much thicker than other places.

"Ruby? We're talking about music?"

"Sometimes I like dancing to it," I say. "If the music's on loud enough."

I use the American sign for dancing, making a dance floor with my left hand and dancing two fingers on my right hand.

I look at Mum and I can see from her eyes, behind the goggles, that she's happy about this, and I wish I'd told her before.

"I can sort of feel the music on the floor, if there isn't a carpet, and then through the rest of me. And I can copy the other person dancing and if they sign the words that's really good too."

Jimmy said I was an awesome-sauce groovy dancer. ("Groovy" was our word that week, and we thought it's a hippie-in-purple-bell-bottoms word.)

"Where do you dance?" Mum asks. She really wanted me to do ballet at school, but I don't like ballet.

"At Jimmy's," I say. "His mother always yells at him to turn the music down but he won't."

She said the music was *deafening!* which Jimmy and I thought was pretty hilarious.

"Good for Jimmy," Mum says. "I've got a great idea. We can dance!"

The air stings when you breathe, like you're breathing in siafu ants with their sharp pincers. I think if you touched the door handle without gloves your skin would stick to it.

"I will sing," Mum says. "Rihanna!"

I pull a face at her, though she can't really see it because I'm wearing a face mask. But she knows and I can tell she's laughing at me.

"I'll be John Lennon, not Rihanna, then," she says, and her eyes are still smiley behind her goggles.

She pulls down her face mask so I can lip-read her singing "Lucy in the Sky with Diamonds," and she signs at the same time. Dad says that singing is lovely for the sound it makes, even if you don't understand the words. And I think signing is like that too. Like it's beautiful just for itself.

You make "singing" and "signing" with the same letters.

Mum is signing and singing about tangerine trees and marmalade skies. And it's good thinking about them because it stops you thinking about the cold and being frightened.

Mum's words are little puffs of white and it's funny that words look like that, like you can see that they're made of breath. I wonder if each word has its own special shape. Speech therapists have told me about breath sounds and now I can see them. Maybe if we lived somewhere this cold I'd learn to read word-shapes in the air.

Mum's singing Rihanna's diamonds-star song now. We both want to giggle when she signs "a shooting star." And I haven't told anyone this, but last term Mum told me about sex, as I'm going to go to secondary school next year and I need to know grown-up things. She told me that the sign for "star" looks very like the sign for "vagina" so you really have to watch out when you sign "star." Then we both giggled for ages and ages, and she said she thought that a star was a nice name for it. So when she signs "star" in the Rihanna song we laugh, but it hurts to laugh because the siafu ants sting you all the way down inside.

Mum says that there's no such thing as a shooting star. It's really little bits of dust and rock falling into the Earth's atmosphere and burning up, and I think that would be an even better song because it's really exciting and also you wouldn't have to worry about the vagina/shooting star thing.

We're not doing proper dancing, we're just kind of moving as much as we can and pretending it's dancing. Then she stops signing and dancing, and under her goggles her eyes aren't crinkly with a smile.

"You don't spend so much time with Jimmy nowadays?" Mum says.

There's a song they used to sing:

> Jimmy and Ruby,
> Sitting in a tree,
> K-I-S-S-I-N **G**

The tree and G rhyme, they said.

We don't have a tree in our playground. Even if we did I'd CLIMB it with Jimmy, or make a camp.

It's a fail, rinky-dink song.

"Ruby . . . ?" Mum says.

Yasmin waited for Ruby to sign to her, but she didn't. Matt had told her Jimmy and Ruby weren't close anymore, and she'd been upset for Ruby but thought it might encourage her to make new friends.

Next to her Ruby was so still. And Yasmin could feel in Ruby's stiff unmoving body her terrible loneliness.

"Right then, my Ruby, let's carry on dancing!"

She shouldn't have asked her about Jimmy. She had to keep her moving. If only they could walk, run, jump up and down properly, but they were caged in this small freezing cab until the storm abated. She'd got her face mask still pulled down so that Ruby could see her lips clearly, as well as her fingers signing, anything that would help Ruby to focus and stay awake.

The thermometer read ten in the cab now, minus fifty outside. She was meant to wait another eight minutes to put on the engine but wasn't sure Ruby could wait that long.

It's getting so hard to breathe; my lungs are filling up with ants and there isn't room for air anymore. There's a monster made of cold, hard as the edge of a pavement, coming towards us in the dark and it's cutting through the windscreen and doors and windows and the only weapon against it is heat, but we don't have any heat. I'm trying to dance to make it go away, holding on to Mum's hand, but I can't dance; my legs won't move. The monster is coming closer to me, and it's showing me its teeth, rows and rows of them, sharp as scissors, and it's going to tear me up into little shreds and I sign to Mum, "Help me!" and she puts on the engine. Straight away.

The heater's been on for three minutes and Mum has put on the proper light and my laptop is charging up. The window has to be open, but just a little crack. The ice on the windscreen is still thick and swirly and you can see your breath, but the air doesn't sting so much when you breathe it in and the monster has slithered a little way away, but he's watching us, right there in the dark. Mum opens up my blog page and I wish she'd close it.

"How much longer do we have?" I ask Mum.

"Two minutes."

I try not to be afraid of turning the heater off again.

"It's a great blog, Ruby. I read it while you were asleep."

I shake my head and I'm angry; I was so stupid to think those emails were from Dad.

"I wrote something for you. Not a blog. Just something interesting."

I look at the laptop and go on my blog and see she's typed . And it takes up a whole page on its own.

"What's that?"

"I'll tell you in a minute. I'm saving it for my interesting thing for you."

One minute left and the monster is prowling around us, his claws scratching at the windscreen, waiting to break through it, and Mum must know that because she takes hold of my hand in hers and squeezes it. And then she takes her hand away so she can sign to me and she says, "This storm will end. And we will be all right." And I try and be like her and be brave.

"I have to turn the engine off again now. I'm sorry."


The cab had warmed up to twenty-eight with the engine running; it hadn't even got to freezing and it would plummet again now. Yasmin was afraid that the temperature would drop much lower this time.

"OK, you park an aeroplane and I'll tell you an interesting fact."

"About the full stop?" Ruby's signing was slow.

"Yes."

Ruby stood up, and Yasmin saw that it was hard for her to balance. She hadn't warmed up enough. Yasmin would have to turn the engine on again soon, but she'd leave it as long as she possibly could.


"If you printed out that page from your laptop," Mum says, "the white paper would be space, and the full stop is the size of the Earth."

I look at the . and think of Mum and me and Dad living in a . and how we would fit.

"It's not very accurate," Mum says. "The full stop should be in a whole book of blank pages. And not just one book but hundreds of thousands of books in thousands of libraries."

I look at that . We're so teeny-weeny-incy small. Like we don't matter at all.

Mum is smiling. "And you know what's amazing?" she asks, and

I shake my head. "That there is a full stop! That there's this amazing planet called Earth, with water and an atmosphere that can support life. And we are here. What are the chances of that, Ruby?"

I try to smile back at Mum, but it's tiring to move my lips into a smile.

"Keep waving your arms," Mum says, but I can't wave my arms. My jumbo airbus will crash into the plane next to it.

"Tell me about your visit to the school for the deaf," she says.

She knows that's something that would wake me up. But I'd like her to tell me more about our full-stop planet. And it's her turn to tell me interesting things.

"I'd really like to hear about it," she says.


Yasmin remembered Ruby and Matt coming home. Ruby had said, "It was just school, Mum," and she'd been relieved that Ruby hadn't pleaded to go there.

But just-school-Mum was huge. Her mainstream school was lonely, exhausting, often cruel. Never just school.

Ruby was signing, but her movements were slurred and Yasmin couldn't understand her.


I want to tell Mum that I wasn't the-deaf-girl, I was Ruby. But when I try to sign the words my fingers won't work properly. I want to tell her that at the school for the deaf you could be good at silly faces or rubbish at maths, but think of brilliant games at break time and tell ginormous lies, which are funny so no one minds and everyone gets your jokes the first time and understands you and gets to know you. And even if they don't right away, they will. And the best part is that if people get it wrong about you, you can change that. The girls there probably like ponies and kittens more than river otters too, but I can tell them why river otters are super-coolio.

My thoughts are like that pretend little rabbit whizzing round the racetrack and my fingers are the greyhounds trying to catch the thoughts and turn them into words, but my fingers are too slow and I can't sign to Mum.

I can feel that little rabbit getting slower and slower, then lying down. I'm being mugged by sleep and I know that I should STAY ALERT, RUBY, but sleep will be warm. My head feels heavy, like I'm a bobblehead; like all of me is now just my head and the rest of me is made of rubber.

Mum is tapping me, and signing, and she's saying, "RUBY, YOU MUST STAY AWAKE!"

He is right behind me. My legs are too heavy to move. I can't run away. The monster clamps his jaws all the way around my face and my arms and legs and his scissor teeth are biting into every bit of me.

Ruby was losing consciousness. Yasmin fumbled with the ignition and turned on the engine. Carbon monoxide poisoning was a risk, but she would die of hypothermia if Yasmin couldn't get her warm. The temperature in the cab had dropped to minus four. Outside it was minus fifty-five. Ruby was unconscious.

They'd had the heater on for ten minutes now. It was minus three in the cab. Yasmin took off Ruby's face mask and saw how pale she was. She put her mouth against Ruby's face and breathed warmed air from her body onto Ruby's cold skin. She wished that she could shout and wake her up with sound waves beating against the drums in her ears so close to her unconscious brain. But she could only use touch. And she couldn't wake her up.

How could she have done this to Ruby? She could no longer remember the steps and decisions that had led to Ruby being un-conscious next to her. Could no longer remember her reasons and justifications. But she couldn't use energy on self-hate, not yet; she had to stop Ruby from dying.

She knew what she had to do, but wasn't sure how she knew, wasn't convinced she'd remembered correctly. It was counterintuitive, but she undressed, her fingers fumbling and painful. The warm air from the heater stripped the layer of numbness off her body and the cold was skinning her alive. She undressed Ruby too, trying to keep her in the sleeping bag, and keeping on her face mask and hat. Then she squeezed into the sleeping bag with Ruby. Ruby seemed smaller and slighter, as if getting this cold had taken away her weight.

Ruby was shivering violently as Yasmin held her. She felt her own body getting colder and hoped that her warmth was going into Ruby's body.

She'd seen cold as a predator, made of the dark, as if it were alive. But she felt it now as vastly cruelly impersonal, a frozen darkness absorbing you into itself. She felt it filling her hollow spaces, embedding itself as icy marrow in her bones, and then consciousness seeped away from her into the Arctic blackness.

## 18

Ruby wasn't shivering anymore. Yasmin felt raw dread. Then she heard Ruby's breathing, even and steady, and felt the warmth of Ruby's skin. The thermometer showed that the temperature of the cab had risen to fifty-three; outside it was minus fifteen.

Yasmin had been asleep for almost two hours, with the engine running and heater on. It was only luck that there hadn't been a fault in the exhaust system under the cab and no carbon monoxide leak. But surely they were due a dollop of luck. The ice on the inside of the windscreen had thawed into puddles.

Mum wakes me up, smiling at me, and I feel happy but I don't know why.

The storm is over! It's NOT COLD ANYMORE! The ice monster is melted all over the dashboard and I am pouring Mum bubbly champagne and pulling party poppers and I feel tingly alive, like every single cell of me is alive and cheering and throwing firecrackers out of the windows and into the snow.

The cab isn't rocking at all anymore, not even a teeny bit. And things smell again; my hair smells of toothpaste! Mum signs to me that the police will be here soon. I say, "And you'll make them get Dad in their goddaM helicopter?" Mum says "Absolutely!" and not to swear and to put some clothes on. It ought to feel weird that I'm not wearing anything but it isn't.

She says I am her brave girl.

When they'd arrived at this place in the storm, Yasmin had only been able to see a few meters ahead; now the headlights revealed a snow-covered expanse, stretching as far as the headlights shone and then on into the darkness to the Arctic Ocean. She knew now that there were animals and birds out there surviving the cold and dark, and knowledge of them softened the barren harshness of the landscape and gave it a beating warmth.

"What if it's really hard to hijack the police's helicopter to go to Daddy?" Ruby asked.

"I don't think a hijack will be needed. I think we'll have earned their respect by crossing over a mountain range, beating an avalanche, and surviving a polar storm in the middle of the tundra. They'll listen to us now."

Ruby laughed. "Yes."

The police would also believe her now about the tanker chasing them, because surely no one would drive over the Atigun Pass in an Arctic storm because of a phantom.

"But what if they think we went over the edge of the mountain?" Ruby said. "When we threw Mr. Azizi's clothes out of the window and made the tracks?"

"The snow will have covered our tracks and the clothes before the storm finished even. The police will find us soon."

We don't say anything for a little bit, just feeling happy and warm, and then Mum signs to me, "Why don't you like using your mouth to speak?" I'm worried she's telling me off; that I've failed, like I always do. But she's not. I can see she's not. She just really wants to know.

"When I sign or type I see the same words as the person I'm talking to," I tell Mum. "Like now. I see my hands and you see my hands and we see the words together. But if I speak with my mouth, then only the hearing person hears my words. I don't."

I stop talking, because I'm a fail, but I'll tell her, "I'm frightened when I talk with my mouth-voice."

Mum doesn't hug me, which is good, because I don't want her to hug me. She looks at me really seriously like she wants to know more.

"It's like I'm not there anymore," I say. "When I talk with my mouth-voice I disappear."

Mum nods. I can see she understands.


Yasmin remembered shouting for Matt in the storm. But although her mouth and tongue had made the right shapes for his name and her lungs had forced out her breath as loudly as she could, his yelled name had been obliterated by the hurricane-force wind and she hadn't known if she'd made any sound at all. It had made her feel disorientated and exposed, as if she'd created a void around herself.

However much breath Ruby forced from her lungs, however perfect her movements and coordination of tongue and lips and palate, her voice would remain unheard by her, and the world would be silent around her. Since she'd been three years old Ruby had wanted a mirror in every room. Yasmin understood now her need to verify her physical presence in a place.

They put on their Arctic clothes before getting out of the cab. The temperature was no longer the killing cold of the storm, but was minus thirteen Fahrenheit and it was still dark.


We've got out of the cab and we're super-stiff, like we're dolls that have been packed into a too-small box. I bet Dad's doing what we're doing, because an aputiak isn't very big either, so he'll be stretching and doing jumbo steps too. I'm looking out for animals, but I can't see much in the dark. And I don't want to look too hard because I'm scared that I might see the man who's killing the animals, though he hasn't emailed us for ages and Mum says she thinks he's given up now. And anyway the police will be here soon.

Mum taps me lightly on the shoulder. Her hands in the light from the cab tell me to look up.

It's SUPER-COOLIO-AWESOME-SAUCE-BEAUTIFUL!!! There's gazillions of stars above us and everywhere you look, the roof and walls of the sky glittering and shining. And it's not like home when you see stars because the thing is, it's so so dark here. Just dark everywhere you look. Black black black. But in the ginormous sky there's diamonds and laser-bright dots and thousands of bits of sunlight caught and held up in the sky. Like glitter on velvet and light breaking on glass and they are magic and they are real!

Mum's staring up, her head tilted right back, and I can see that she's thinking

SUPER-COOLIO-AWESOME-SAUCE-BEAUTIFUL!!!


Yasmin had never seen a night sky as beautiful or as clear and perfect as this one; no man-made light pollution at all, with the air washed clean. During the storm, she'd clung to her belief that Matt was safe. Looking at this extraordinary night sky strengthened her belief. He had survived and the police would find him and they would all be together.

She searched the sky for Polaris. Since the age of thirteen she'd scanned the night sky, first with binoculars, then later with a telescope and trips to an observatory, and each and every time, in order to orientate herself in relation to the stars, she would first locate Polaris, the constant Pole Star, marker of due north. And she'd feel kinship with the sailors and explorers centuries before who had navigated using this star.

She found Polaris and it was high in the sky above her. She was standing at the top of the planet.

We're looking at the sky for a police helicopter and while we do that Mum shows me the Big Dipper and from the Big Dipper how to find a star called Polaris, which shows due north.

"Is that the same as the North Star?" I ask.

"Yes. We're at the very top of the Earth, Ruby," she says. "The world is revolving around us."

I laugh, but she says, "It's true! Imagine an invisible string going from space—down through where our feet are right now—all the way through the Earth and out again at the bottom, which is the South Pole. The Earth spins on that string, so it really is spinning around us."

I love that.

She's still staring up at the sky, but her face has got really serious-looking.

"I need to use your laptop, OK?"

She goes inside and I go after her because I want to tell her something she might not know. Dad told me that when birds migrate they use the North Star. It's how they find their way home in the dark. Baby birds study the stars in the night sky so they can learn about them. Cross-my-heart true! I think she and Dad should compare notes on the super-coolio North Star.

She's opened my laptop and is looking at the photo of the poor musk ox all torn apart and now she's scrolling down to the numbers at the bottom: 68950119 149994621.

"I thought these numbers were linked to the subject numbers, the DSC ones, but they're not," she says. "I'd guess that the DSC ones are something to do with a camera file, but these longer numbers are different."

She must see that I'm confused because she signs really carefully.

"We divide the Earth up into segments like a peeled satsuma," she says. "And the lines between the segments are called lines of longitude. They all meet at the North Pole, very near to where we are now, and at the South Pole, where the piece of invisible string comes out the other side."

She opens the photo of the poor wolves. I can see she really wants to hurry with something, but she's taking time to talk to me with her hands.

"And there are invisible circles going the other way; like hula hoops around the Earth and they are lines of latitude. One of the really important hula hoops is the Arctic Circle. Its latitude is sixty-six point five six then some smaller numbers, two five, if I remember properly. The Antarctic Circle is exactly the same but with an S for south."

She points at the numbers under the wolves photograph: 68945304 149992659.

"A decimal point in the first set of numbers makes it a latitude reading—a little way north of the Arctic Circle."

I don't understand, but it doesn't really matter because it's like she's talking to herself in sign. Dad does that sometimes too, but I've never seen Mum do it.

She writes 68.945304.

"Then we do the same with the second set of numbers, with a minus sign as I'm pretty sure it's a longitude reading west of the prime meridian."

She writes "–149.992659" and I have no clue what she means. Then she opens each email and writes all the numbers on the back of Mr. Azizi's map; she says that my job is to keep a lookout for the police helicopter.

———

Yasmin had once thought that latitude and longitude, as well as being an inventive practical tool, was a way of mankind claiming ownership of the planet. She'd liked these global invisible markings far more than the arbitrary and bloody lines drawn for countries. The encompassing nature of the bisecting lines, their impartial mathematical logic and scientific precision, had made the world feel more secure to her. She'd liked it too that a historic way of mapping the planet was used every day in humdrum modern life as people drove their cars using GPS, not realizing that they were being safely guided by longitude and latitude coordinates, obtained through the triangulation of satellite signals in space.

Perhaps it was because she'd long associated longitude and latitude with security and order that she hadn't realized what the numbers were. Their juxtaposition with the grotesque photographs had camouflaged them, allowing them to get past her usually scientific brain unidentified. Or perhaps it was simply that those terrible images had demanded all her attention; afraid and tired, she hadn't had the calm or the clarity to recognize them.

Trying to still her anxiety, she opened up Google Earth on Ruby's computer. The numbers would pinpoint this man's location to within a few feet. He would soon have a physical presence in a specific place out there in the darkness.

In the search box, she typed in the numbers that were under the photo of the mutilated musk ox, adding decimal points and a minus sign: 68.950119, –149.994621.

The screen showed a globe, then it spun to show the north of the planet—Russia, Canada, and Alaska—then it homed in to show just Alaska, moving across Alaska before it stopped.

This must be the place where he'd killed and photographed the musk ox.

She dropped a pin icon to mark the location of the musk ox and moved the cursor in for more detail.

She saw Anaktue marked on the map.

Using the ruler tool, she measured the distance between the butchered musk ox and Anaktue. It was eight miles.

Why did he send her a location? It must have been unintentional. She thought his satellite terminal must have a built-in GPS and had tagged the photo automatically and he hadn't realized.

She put the numbers that had come with the raven photo into the search box: 69.051605, −150.116989.

The raven's location was exactly at Anaktue. Had Matt seen this man?

She wasn't sure that the time frame of when the emails were sent matched the distances traveled, but there must be glitches in sending emails in a place this remote.

She typed in the numbers that were under the photo of the wolves: 68.945304, −149.992659.

Again, she dropped a pin and measured. The location of the wolves was barely half a mile from the musk ox.

She put in the numbers in the last email she'd received, the Arctic fox cub: 68.733615, −149.695998.

He'd moved eighteen miles away from the wolves, heading away from Anaktue.

She opened her email account. A new email had arrived an hour ago, while they were still asleep.


This is the worst photo. A family of river otters. A mother and father and three babies. River otters are really shy, but when no one's watching they play games, the grown-ups too: hide-and-seek and catch, all sorts of games. And they're graceful swimmers, and they build these super-coolio dens, with just a teeny opening to go in and out so that they'll be safe. But they weren't safe.

Mum's asking me to put the coordinates into Google Earth. I think she wants to take my mind off the poor otters, but even if I'm not looking at the photo I can still see them really clearly.

---

Yasmin left the cab. Standing on the top step, she scanned the sky for a helicopter but couldn't see any lights apart from the stars. She listened, but there was nothing, not even the wind; an immense silence and stillness.

She thought she heard breathing and a footstep. Surely she was conjuring up the sounds in her own imagination, spooking herself.

Ruby was banging on the cab window.

There was another email.

A photo of stars filled the backlit screen, their light puncturing the darkness; the same sky that was above them now. Yasmin felt abruptly shockingly vulnerable, as if she were standing naked in front of him. How did he know to send her this? It was as if he knew the hiding places of her mind.

Ruby had put the coordinates of the otters email into Google Earth. He'd moved nine and a half miles away from the fox cub email, and he was still moving away from Anaktue.

She entered the coordinates of the stars photo: 69.602132, −147 .680371.

The picture of stars was taken six and a half miles from the otters. Again he was moving farther away from Anaktue.

He must be running away.

She thought the stars photograph was a final act of intimidation, but instead of threatening her he had given her his location. She could tell the police exactly where he was.

She pulled down the CB.

There was no connection.

She tried again and again to get a connection, but there was nothing. She felt dread slipping inside her.

"Here's what we're going to do," she said to Ruby. "I want you to try to get hold of the police by email and tell them we need them to get to us as quickly as possible. Tell them that we don't have the CB radio anymore. Can you try to do that?"

Ruby nodded.

"Good girl. I am going to chip the ice out of the wheels. I don't want Mr. Azizi's truck to be left here. I'd like to get it ready for a policeman to drive it back for him."

She hoped Ruby didn't know she was lying and that she had to get them away as fast as possible. She fastened her gloves, took the ice pick out of Adeeb's toolbox, and went outside.

On the top step, she listened again for footsteps and breathing but could hear nothing. The hurricane-force wind had blown the snow wheeling over the road and across the tundra; it hadn't settled around the truck as she'd feared.

She crawled under the truck with Adeeb's torch. She positioned the torch and got out the ice pick. Her ice-scalded left hand was sharply painful as it supported her while her right hand chipped at the ice.


Mum and Dad don't let me Google things on my own, and teachers always give us a website to go to if we need the Internet for homework so I haven't done anything like this before. I've put "Alaska police" into the box and there are lots and lots of things, but I don't know which one is right. I thought I'd found a website that would help us but it's just for jobs. I'm typing "police in Fairbanks" because that's the only town I know, apart from Deadhorse, and I don't know if Deadhorse even has any police. A website! It's got phone numbers but we don't have a phone. I look and look because there must be an email address, but there isn't and I don't know what to do.

My bracelet vibrates and the Internet connection stops at the exact same time.

Mum is running towards me and she's hurrying up the steps and getting in. She sees me and her whole face seems to smile, though she still looks really worried. She tells me to put on my seat belt, but before I have she's already driving. My bracelet only vibrates if there's a loud noise.

Mum's breathing is super-fast; I can see it even through all her layers of clothes. She must have got the ice out because the truck isn't juddering.

I put on Voice Magic because I know she can't sign when she's driving. Voice Magic doesn't need the Internet.

"Did you tell the police?" she asks me.

"I'm sorry," I say.

She's just looking straight ahead and driving. And after a little bit, she must see how bad I feel, because her face looks all soft and she says, "It's OK, really. The police will already be on their way."


Yasmin had just finished chipping the worst of the ice out when she'd heard a shot splintering through the frozen silence and the crack as it hit something on the truck. She'd seen the satellite receiver crash down. She'd run towards Ruby and seen a torch heading away from her along the road; briefly its light had glinted off metal on the tanker. All this time he hadn't been on the other side of the avalanche but waiting the storm out. And then he'd crept up on them in the dark, snapping off the antenna of the CB, shooting down the satellite receiver.

He'd probably intended to do worse and had first wanted to make sure they couldn't call for help by CB or satellite.

She was driving fast now, swerving twice to avoid snowdrifts that had gathered on the road.

"What was the loud noise?" Ruby asked.

She didn't know what to tell her.

"Mum?"

"Someone broke the satellite dish," she said. "I think whoever it is doesn't want us talking to anyone. But the police won't be much longer."

The police would spot them easily. There were no trees or even bushes, added to which they had a bloody huge prefab on their truck. How hard could it be to see them?

They had no CB. No satellite connection. The nearest house was over a hundred miles away.

I should have emailed someone at school; Jimmy, because I know his email by heart. I did think of that, but I thought it was night in England and he wouldn't get my email till morning and that was too long. But I don't know if it is night at home. I don't even know if it's night here. It feels like it's night everywhere; like night has swallowed up the days.

I'm looking out of my window, because I'm hoping to see ptarmigan wing prints again, but there's only snow and darkness.

I suddenly know what I should have done, and it makes me feel sick.

"I should have tweeted," I say to Mum.

"There was nothing you could have done. Really."

She probably thinks it's a stupid idea. But it isn't. And now it's too late.

Before Dad went to Alaska he said he wanted to make sure no trolls had sneaked their way into my Twitter followers, like in "Three Billy Goats Gruff," with me as a billy goat.

He said, "Your followers are retweeting you like crazy. It's like you've got six hundred baby three-wattled bellbirds."

He said that because only baby birds make a tweeting sound, and the three-wattled bellbirds are really really loud, so their babies tweeting would be really noisy too.

"Although," Dad said, "some people say the superb lyrebird is louder."

I laughed, because I think it's super-coolio to have "superb" as a part of your name.

Then he said, "How about I call you the Superb Ruby?"

That would just be embarrassing.

And then he said, "Have you seen this? You have followers all over the place. America, Australia, Japan, Canada, all over Europe, everywhere."

So somewhere it must be daytime and somebody would have been up and seen my tweet asking for help, and they'd be a grown-up and know what to do.

Now it's too late.

Mum gives my hand a quick squeeze. "It's OK," she says. "Really."

I don't think it is OK.

"He's turned around," Mum says. "There's no lights behind us. There hasn't been for ages."

I twist around and check and she's right. It's just black behind us.

"He knows there's a police helicopter looking for us and doesn't want them to find him too," Mum says. "He's running away. And so is the man who sent us the emails."

I do a hoorah sign, which makes Mum laugh.

We drive on and on, for ages, and I keep checking and there's still nobody there.


Yasmin felt Ruby tapping her arm. Ruby pointed out of her passenger window. On the side of the road there was a post sticking up out of the snow, splintered wood at the top where the sign had been ripped away. Next to the broken signpost was a turning.

If Ruby hadn't been looking out of the passenger window and alerted her, Yasmin would never have seen it. She remembered checking Adeeb's map, hoping there was a river road they could drive on to Anaktue. She'd seen the River Alatnak looping close to the highway. They'd now reached that point. Adeeb had said it would only be possible to drive on the river road if a link road had been built to it. This must be the link road. She guessed that Soagil Energy had already started building their infrastructure.

Anaktue was thirty-five miles away. If the river road was safe, she could drive to Matt and be with him in less than two hours. The police helicopter would still spot them; they'd be close to the Dalton and their truck was huge. She could lead the police to him.

She turned off the Dalton and onto the rudimentary link road.

## 19

The link road stopped as it met the river road in a T junction. To the north was Anaktue. The ice on the river in that direction had no markers or any sign that a vehicle had driven on it. It curved sharply thirty or so yards away, and Yasmin couldn't see what lay beyond. In the other direction the river road had delineators on the ice and had clearly been used as a road. Yasmin guessed that the man killing the animals and sending her emails might have used this road as he ran away from Anaktue.

It would be far too dangerous to drive to Matt on the unmarked and untested river ice. She had to turn around. She started the maneuver, but the truck was huge and cumbersome and her turning circle too wide to get it turned around.

She'd just have to do a three-point turn. She would turn right onto the road with delineators then reverse onto the iced-over river towards Anaktue, then turn the truck back onto the link road.

She turned right onto the road with delineators with no problem, then started reversing. As the back wheels hit the iced-over river towards Anaktue, the rig juddered and she feared the ice was thin and unstable. She moved forward again so that the whole truck was on the river road with delineators. She couldn't reverse onto the link road because it was too tight to turn. They would just have to wait here.

She opened her window, cutting the engine, and strained to hear the sound of a helicopter. Instead, she heard the ice creaking. Despite being within the delineators, they were too heavy for the ice. The road couldn't have been driven on by a truck as heavy as theirs. She didn't know how to uncouple the load and make themselves lighter. She was afraid of even trying because her experience with the snow chains meant that even if she knew what she was doing, which she didn't, she had little confidence in getting things done quickly in subzero temperatures. She would just keep moving slowly to shift the truck onto the next section of ice.

It would still be easy for the police helicopter to see them; they weren't far from the Dalton and the river road was exposed.

Imagine a huge river. Then imagine it covered with ice in the dark. And we're driving on it! Mum says the ice is so thick we won't go through and that other people have driven here before us because of the delineators, which is what the posts are called. It's funny to think that underneath us there'll be frogs, right at the bottom of the river because that's the warmest place. There'll be loads of sorts of fish too, but I don't know much about fish.

"Shall we tell each other more interesting facts?" Mum says. Perhaps she's a bit frightened too.

"Yes."

"Would you like to start?" she says.

"OK. You know you asked me about the school for the deaf?"

Mum nods. In the storm I was too cold to tell her, but now I can.

"A girl there told me that sometimes the deaf community give you a sign name."

*Deaf community* sounds kind of strict but Anna, that's the nice girl, said it's cool. I said, *Super-coolio?* And she said, straight back, *Yes, super-coolio!*

"What kind of name?" Mum asks.

"Anna laughs a lot so her sign name is Giggle. And Anna's dad laughed at a friend's joke in the pub—Anna says all her family laugh a lot—but when her dad laughed his beer went down his front and now he's called Dribble."

"Dribble? Really?"

"Yes. But lots of people have names that aren't funny."

"What name would you be?"

"I can't choose it. It's chosen for me."

I think Mum looks a bit sad.

"I'll still be Ruby," I tell her. "But I'd be another name as well. I can be me but more than me too."

Mum doesn't say anything for a little bit and I'm worried she thinks it's awful, because she and Dad chose the name Ruby for me.

"I think that's great," Mum says.

I think so too, as long as it's not Dribble.

"What kind of interesting fact would you like?" she asks.

"Something about space."

"OK. Did you know that in space it's totally quiet? Even when stars explode, they don't make any sound at all."

"So in space everyone hears like me."

"Yes. I like thinking how quiet it is up there. Billions and billions of light-years of quietness."

I like that too.


Yasmin thought about the silence in space. The philosophy course she had knitted through had addressed issues such as "If the tree fell and no one saw it, did it really happen?" put into slightly more, but not much more, grown-up language of bundle theory and subjective idealism. For Yasmin, after Ruby was diagnosed as deaf, it became "If the tree fell and only Ruby was there, did the tree make any noise?" She thought that if the sound waves didn't ping against an eardrum and get turned into nerve impulses to a brain, then they existed as a vibration in the woodland air, a soft tremor over mossy ground, a nearby tree swaying, a leaf brushing in a minute stroke against her daughter's face.

"Your turn again," she said to Ruby.

"OK. Did you know that Inupiat people have sign language as part of their regular language? Like it's just a normal kind of thing."

"No, I didn't. That's great."

"Dad told everyone in the village about me and there's an old lady who's going to teach me some of their signs."

She hadn't yet told Ruby that everyone in the village had died in the fire; she didn't know how.

"Dad says if it's freezing cold and the wind is blowing, you have a scarf over your face and it's difficult to answer questions with your mouth-voice, so if you raise your eyebrows it means 'yes' and if you squint your eyes quickly it means 'I don't know.' But they have signs for complicated things too."

She would have to tell her soon.

"And they've got these really great words for things. There's a word that means 'guest expecting food.' Dad said that's a really useful word. And—Stop! We have to stop!"


Mum's stopped the truck and I'm jumping down out of the cab onto the ice. It's the family of otters.

The babies and parents are huddled up together on the ice. It's not like the photo. I can see their damp fur and their open eyes and their whiskers. I touch one of the otters, kind of stroking him, and then I see that he doesn't have a leg.

Suddenly, there's all these colors on the ice, pinks and greens and blues and I look up and there's dancing sheets of lights in the sky and I hate them. It's like a cheesy Disney film. But if it was a cheesy film, the family of otters wouldn't be dead. There's a husky dog. He's dead too. He must belong to the man because huskies aren't wild. And the lights are still dancing as if everything is pretty, like it's the ball at the end of *Sleeping Beauty* with the fairies turning her ball dress blue/pink/blue/pink and I want them to STOP and for it to be just dark again.

Tears were streaming down Ruby's unprotected face. It was the first time in all of this that Yasmin had seen Ruby properly cry.

"How could someone do this?" Ruby shouted with her hands. "Why?"

Yasmin put her arm around her, because her own hands could form no answer. She saw that Ruby's tears were freezing to her cheeks. Above them the sky was luminous green and pink, billowing lights across the whole of the sky. She heard the ice creaking more loudly than before.

She hurried Ruby back towards the cab and just to the side of their truck saw a deep gash in the ice. They'd missed it by a foot or so. On the other side of the truck was a perfectly round small hole with small cracks in the ice emanating from it. It looked as if it had been made by a bullet or a drill. She wondered if the person who had ripped down the sign had also tried to destabilize the ice and destroy the route. She had driven between the two holes.

They got back in the cab.

The photo of the otters was only six and a half miles from his last location.

She started driving, inching along, just enough to move the weight of the truck onto the next section of ice. If she drove slowly enough the police would easily reach them before they got near to him.

Around them the aurora blazed and the lights were radiantly stunning.

"It's very beautiful, isn't it?"

But Ruby didn't respond.

If you think something is horrible for being beautiful, then it isn't beautiful anymore, is it?

"Alaska is really famous for the aurora borealis," Mum says. "People come from all over the world just to see it."

I don't want her to tell me about the aurora borealis because it's probably a trick. She'll tell me that they're not really there and it's made by something else, like the paraselenae.

"Up above planet Earth," Mum says, "it's like a war."

Ruby turned to look at her. Yasmin understood that Ruby needed a cosmic counterpart to the dead creatures on the ice, that it was good and evil now for Ruby; the childish world of the small scale had gone for her.

"The sun hurls solar wind at us. It travels at millions of miles an hour towards us. Sometimes it throws a coronal mass ejection towards us. And it's about ten billion tons of plasma, which is the same as a hundred thousand battleships and it can be as wide as thirty million miles. And these ejections mean solar wind comes at us at supersonic speed."

Ruby nodded. Yasmin saw that she was watching the lights now.

"The Earth has a magnetic shield all the way around it. An invisible bubble. It's called the magnetosphere. The solar wind hits the shield. And that's what we're watching now. Those lights are the shield protecting our planet."

As Ruby looked at the sky, Yasmin thought about the metal at the core of the Earth creating a magnetic field as the Earth turned that traveled for thousands of miles into space and protected them.

For the first time the darkness around them was alive with colors.

The emailed photos of animals and birds, despite their menace, had allowed Yasmin to trust Matt, and Ruby's blog had given her some understanding of why he'd want to be in Alaska, but when she had seen the unparalleled beauty of the night sky here, when she'd seen Polaris and known that she was on the axis of the Earth, when she saw the aurora borealis playing out a cosmic battle in the heavens above her, she shared Matt's passion for this place. She'd come to the other side of the world for this, in winter too, and her trust in him went deeper.

Then the lights stopped and they were back in darkness.

She saw two small blue moons in her mirror. She thought it was an optical trick, because surely this couldn't be true. He couldn't be coming after them.

The blue headlights were vividly clear behind them.

Why would he risk being found so close to them? Surely he'd listened to the CB, heard the police say they would get her and Ruby after the storm. For crying out loud, the man had gone on the CB earlier and talked to the police himself. She remembered his lies, the stranger's voice that was familiar, saying that he was going south, not north; that he'd passed her twenty miles back and there was no one behind her. He'd even given a precise sham location, MP 181. At the time she hadn't thought about how specific he'd been. But now it felt wrong. She was afraid that scrutiny would bring forth something frightening, but had no choice but to think this through.

So he'd given his location, MP 181. That hadn't seemed particularly important; just a false detail in a larger lie. And then he said he'd passed her twenty miles back. Doing the maths—which surely the police would have done—her position at twenty miles further north of him would put her at MP 201.

She paused for no more than ten seconds, to look at Adeeb's map. MP 201 was about thirty miles south of where they had actually been. He hadn't just been falsifying his own location, he'd been falsifying theirs.

But surely to God she'd told the police where they were. Surely they'd asked for her location. No, because they thought they already knew it from the helpful tanker driver. And she'd been too preoccupied and frightened to think clearly.

She remembered the truck tilting in the violent wind, the squalling snow hitting against the windscreen as he'd lied to the police; an hour later the Arctic storm had hit at full force. The police would assume that she'd driven ten miles at the very most in those conditions. They'd never think that they'd crossed the Atigun Pass.

The police were looking for her and Ruby south of the Brooks Mountains. No one was looking for them out here on the northern tundra.

The tanker man is behind us again. But the police will get to us soon and they will find him and put him in jail, but first Mum'll make them take us to get Dad.

It feels even darker because the aurora borealis was in the sky and now it's gone it's left a shadow of itself, like another layer of dark.

The river road is getting narrower and narrower and I think this is a little bit what growing up is like. You can't turn around and go back, even if you're frightened and really want to. You can never be a little Reception child again.

It's getting colder outside. Mr. Azizi's thermometer says it's nearly minus eighteen.

Yasmin had to keep Ruby away from the tanker driver. But the faster she drove away from him, the nearer they came to the man who'd sent the emails.

She and Ruby weren't wearing seat belts. If the truck did go through the ice, she didn't know how long they would have to get out. She did know, from Adeeb, that once you went in the water you died of hypothermia long before you had time to drown.

Under threat from behind and in front and underneath, she looked up at the stars, but they could no longer comfort her or make her brave. Instead, she felt her cowardice. It was her lack of courage that meant Ruby was in such danger.

Ever since the policeman in Fairbanks told her that Matt was dead, she hadn't dared to stop moving, but had gone forward, ignoring everyone, risking Ruby's safety, going forward to find him because she was too afraid to stand still and look at their facts. It wasn't just that Matt needed her to rescue him, but that she desperately needed him and wasn't brave enough to face a life without him.

In the storm, she'd believed that Matt was safe in an aputiak. But where was the proof? All she'd had, all she'd ever had, was faith, which by its very nature meant no evidence to support it. Faith was made up of love and hope and trust, nothing else.

When she'd received those horrifying photos, she'd chosen to believe it was because Matt was alive and this man didn't want her to find him. But now she wondered where the logic had been in that.

Mum's made me put on all my Arctic clothes. She's driving while she puts on her outdoor things so I'm helping her. I put on my face mask and goggles, but Mum doesn't put hers on yet because she won't be able to see clearly to drive.

The truck abruptly stopped. Yasmin pushed her foot hard down on the accelerator pedal but nothing happened. She felt something dragging them backward. She looked out of her window. She heard groaning and the cab was tilting. Their load had broken through the ice and was sinking.

I'm taking the torch like Mum said I should, but I've also got my laptop. I tuck it inside my parka, and then I jump down onto the ice. Mum is throwing our food in a bag down onto the ice and she's clambering down too and she's holding the flare and Mr. Azizi's sleeping bag.

The house is tipping down and making a big hole in the ice; our bag of food goes through and now our house is going through too, a bit at a time, like it's in slow motion. My bracelet is vibrating, so our truck must be making a loud noise as it sinks. The headlights tilt upward into the sky, like they're search beams. And then they go into the water too.

Mum and me are running because the ice is cracking all around us and we jump over the cracks. Now everything is blue.

I look behind us and see it's the tanker's headlights that are making everything blue. The river must be really deep because you can't even see our house or our cab anymore.

The blue light is fading because the tanker's headlights are shrinking. He must be reversing. I think he's afraid that the ice will crack more and he'll go through and then it will be one jumbo hole, with him in it as well.

Mum's holding my hand and we're running away from the tanker and over the ice. I've got a stitch and Mum must know because we just walk for a bit, still holding hands, and then we run again and then walk again.


When they'd jumped out of the sinking cab, Yasmin had heard a shot, but Ruby didn't know the tanker driver had fired at them. She hurried Ruby away over the creaking cracking ice. When she thought they'd gone about half a mile, she stopped. They were surely out of range of his bullets now, and the ice around them was stable.

She knelt down on the ice and tried to unwrap Adeeb's emergency flare, Ruby shining the torch so she could see. But her gloved fingers couldn't tear off the flimsy wrapping, so she took off the gloves and worked wearing liners. She panicked that she didn't have matches but found that the lid of the container could be used to strike the end of the flare. It took six strikes before it caught. The flare went into the sky, crimson red, a trail of light behind it. She hurriedly replaced her gloves.

She and Ruby watched the red flare as it stayed in the night sky, as if it had joined the stars. Maybe the police had widened their search and would spot it, or perhaps other planes were flying again and one of them would see it. The flare fizzled out and it was just stars above them again.

She guessed that the man who'd sent the emails was only about half a mile away and he would have seen the flare. But she'd had to try to get help. With no shelter or way of keeping warm, Ruby wouldn't survive for long. They had Ruby's laptop, but without a satellite terminal it was useless to them.

Crouched on the ice, Ruby took off her gloves and opened her laptop. Wearing her silk glove liners, she typed:

> Shall I tell you the story about the raven? The one
> Inupiat people believe in?

> I'd love to hear the story. Why don't you try typing with
> the special gloves Dad got us?

> I can't type in gloves. Liners will be fine for a bit, Mum.
> When my fingers get cold I'll put on my gloves.

At the beginning of time, Raven made the world with the beating of his wings. There's a long bit about a sparrow but I'll skip that bit because it isn't the best bit.

Ok

Raven loved all the people and animals he'd made and wanted to know more about them. One day when Raven was out paddling in his kayak he saw a whale and when the whale yawned he paddled inside.

The whale closed his mouth and it was very dark. Raven kept on paddling till he came to the white ribs of the whale rising up all around him. Dad said the white ribs were like ivory columns. And in the middle there was a beautiful girl who was dancing.

I need to put on my gloves now.

Ruby put on her gloves and they walked in large circles, swinging their arms. Yasmin flashed on Adeeb's torch to see where they were going, then hurriedly turned it off. They needed to conserve the torch battery. She should have thought of bringing something to start a fire, for light as much as warmth. She put her hand on Ruby to slow her down. They had to keep their circulation going but not sweat, because sweat would evaporate off their skin, draining their bodies of heat, hastening hypothermia. She'd feared sweating when she and Ruby had run away from the tanker driver and the cracking ice, and so had made them walk as well as run.

She kept looking at the sky, hoping to see small moving lights of a plane or a helicopter that had spotted their flare, but there was nothing.

Ruby was crouching on the ice again, typing on the laptop in her glove liners.

Why aren't the police here?

I'm sure they will be soon. Someone will have seen our flare. It's a lovely story. Can you tell me the rest of it in sign?

But we'd have to use the torch for you to see my hands and we'd be using up the battery.

Raven saw that there were strings attached to the dancing girl's feet and hands. The strings were also attached to the whale's heart.

Raven fell in love with the girl and he took off his beak and showed her his human face.

Raven wanted to take the beautiful coolio girl out of the whale and marry her. But the girl said she couldn't leave the whale because she was the whale's heart and soul.

My fingers are too cold.

Ruby stopped typing and put on her gloves over her liners. She closed the laptop so there was no light.

Yasmin heard Ruby's voice in the darkness.

"The beautiful girl danced inside the whale. Raven saw that when she danced fast the whale swam fast and when she danced slowly the whale swam slowly."

Ruby's oral voice was quiet but clear and beautiful to Yasmin. She heard Ruby's courage as she spoke.

"Raven forgot the girl couldn't leave the whale and he picked her up and flew her outside."


I don't like doing this at all: making my mouth into shapes and doing special teeny movements with my tongue and teeth and lips and hoping the right noises are coming out as words. But it's the only way of talking in the dark. Mum is holding my hand tightly and that's one good thing about mouth-talking, we can hold hands at the same time. But I can't hear anything Mum says back to me; maybe that's why she's holding my hand.

I've been practicing with Voice Magic and Dragon Dictate. I say something and I look at what gets typed and then I keep on trying. I use a mirror too, like my speech therapist tells me to, and put my hand on my throat to feel the vibrations and in front of my mouth to feel the little puffs of air. Some days my typed words stay gobbledygook. But some days it gets better. It was nice and private and I could do it when I wanted to and no one else was there to hear me make mistakes. Or to hear me do well. I want my mouth-voice to just be something I choose to do. I hope Mum can understand the story.

"As Raven flew with the beautiful girl into the sky all the strings snapped," I say with my mouth-voice. "In the sea the whale got stiller and stiller."

———

Yasmin had thought that she'd been waiting for this moment for years, but Ruby had been using her voice since she first learned to sign, only Yasmin hadn't been listening.

"The whale died and the girl in Raven's arms got smaller and smaller until she disappeared," Ruby said. "And then Raven knew that everything that is alive has a heart and a soul."

Ruby finished speaking and the silence sounded so loud to Yasmin that it jolted her.

She strained to listen, but the snow absorbed any sounds into itself. She looked out into the darkness and it had absorbed all light and color. They couldn't go further forward because the man who'd sent the emails was in front of them. They couldn't turn and walk away because they risked coming within range of the tanker driver's bullets. She and Ruby were trapped within these fearful boundaries, and beyond them were the impassable confines of the Brooks Mountains and the Arctic Ocean: box within box.

As long as she was on her way to find him, she could believe Matt was alive; she could outrun the facts. But now they confronted her, as if they'd pursued her from Lieutenant Reeve's office in Fairbanks, and here in the icy wilderness surrounded her.

Matt had told her the truth about his wedding ring and the animals, yes, and therefore about Corazon too, but that didn't mean he was alive.

Her loving him didn't mean he was alive.

She could no longer move any closer towards him, and neither could she run from her fear.

She felt her stasis shadowed by the frozen immobility of the treeless tundra, a forced stillness within a vaster stillness.

Above her the stars were unreachable light-years away.

In the darkness and silence, she finally had to face the truth.

He was dead.

He had died on Monday afternoon while she and Ruby were still in London.

She screamed her grief, fracturing the silence, and surely Ruby could feel it against her skin, this monstrous sound.

She heard her name coming back towards her in the darkness.

She knew it couldn't be true.

Matt called her name again.

## 20

Mum's running and she's holding my hand and I'm having to run super-fast to keep up with her, but it's icy and slippery so she's kind of holding me up too. In her other hand she's holding Mr. Azizi's torch and its light jiggles as we run.

There's a light shining towards us. I'm frightened it's the man who killed the animals. It's getting bigger quickly; he must be running too and he's getting closer.

Someone is shining a torch into my face and I can't see anything. He's pulling me towards him and he puts his arms around me and I feel a warm cushion of air inside his furry hood and I see his face. I hurl myself against him, like I can disappear myself inside him.

Daddy's holding me tightly and he's looking at Mum.

"How are you here?" he says to her. "How is it possible that you are here?"

Yasmin needed to touch him to believe him alive. He went towards her, holding Ruby's hand; she pulled down her face mask, wanting his skin against hers. She put her face to his and kissed him and felt his warmth, tasted his breath and his lips and smelled his body and wanted the taste and smell to be strong, so that every sense in her could believe that she had found him.

She thought this land of darkness and ice had been her Hades, fraught with danger, and it had been like a pact—if she overcame her terror, risked everything she had, then she would be able to bring him back from the dead. She put her arms around him as he kissed her, holding on to him as if he might be taken from her.

Matt looked at her face and saw the cost of her reaching him—her skin raw and bleeding, exhaustion in the shadows under her eyes; so glorious and impossibly brave. He took off his glove and as he traced her cheek he allowed himself to believe that she was here with him and that he could hold her again.

He felt Ruby move closer to the two of them. He needed to get them to warmth.

Mum and Dad are looking at each other like the other one is a magic trick, but a lot better; like each other's face is a beautiful awesome-sauce miracle.

Happiness is like a huge balloon inside me. If I went outside everything would jump into bright colors; there's no way it could stay dark and cold. But I don't want to go outside, I want to stay right here with Dad and Mum.

Dad's aputiak is the coziest place you can ever imagine. Mum and Dad and me are all inside and there's a qulliq, which makes it light and warm. There's quite a long tunnel as the entrance, with a caribou skin as a flap-door and a little hole in the roof for the smoke from the qulliq.

Mum wants me to get into my sleeping bag, which she took from Mr. Azizi's cab. I feel warm already, but she says "just in case." There's loads of room to stretch out. Daddy said he built it for the huskies too, so he could keep an eye on them, but I think they must be outside cooling off. Huskies get too hot even when it's freezing cold. Dad says his supplies ran out yesterday and the qulliq will only burn for a few more hours, which I think is Mum's *just in case*. There's a bonfire outside, near our aputiak, but Dad says it will be out in an hour or so. He looks really worried when he says that, but I'm not worried at all. Not anymore.

Dad's got a beard, all frozen up, and the ice on it is melting because of the qulliq. He said he saw our red flare and ran to find who it was; he never thought it was us, and then he heard Mum.

Dad doesn't understand how we got here and Mum's all shaky and teary, so I tell him how we got a lift in a truck and then about Mr. Azizi getting ill, so Mum drove it herself. "Across northern Alaska?" Dad asks, like he can't believe it. And I say yes, and I can see how proud he is of her—the Superb Mum!

"You were out in the big storm?" he asks me, and I nod.

"You must have been frightened," he says.

"I was cold."

"I bet you were."

"Mum and I danced to keep warm."

I tell him about the tanker man too, but I say we don't need to worry about him anymore because he stopped chasing us when our lorry went through the ice.

As I talk to him, he takes Mum's hand and I think it's to make sure she's really OK and she's really here.

"You sent us the emails, didn't you?" I say to Dad.

"Yes. But I never thought . . ." His fingers stop moving, like he doesn't know what to say. "I thought you were safe in Fairbanks or were back in London. I never dreamed . . ."

His fingers don't have the words again, and he looks so tired and hurt. I didn't see that before. The balloon was too big. But his lips are all cracked and bleeding.

"Did everybody die?" Mum asks him.

"Yes."

He means the whole village; all his friends; the old lady who was going to teach me Inupiaq signs. Everyone. But Daddy didn't die.

"Corazon?" Mum asks, and she looks so sad.

He nods, and they speak with their eyes to each other and I think it's a language that no one else could ever understand.

His hands move, slowly, like the words sting.

"And Kaiyuk, her twin; everyone. I should have been there."

He starts to say something, but then he stops and my bracelet is vibrating. There's a light shining from outside and the snow walls of our aputiak turn pale icy gold. Mum and Dad are putting on their goggles and hurrying out and I wriggle out of the sleeping bag and go after them.

I'm blown right over, like there's a whirlwind sucking the air out from underneath me, and there's a glare so bright it's like looking at the sun and a noise is rattling my teeth.

The bright light snaps off and the jangling stops. I blink a few times because I'm still blinded and then the darkness comes back. Mum is shining a torch and I can see there's a helicopter on the snow; it looks like a giant black dragonfly with its wings getting slower until they are still. There's writing on the side: "Alaska State Troopers." A man is getting out; his face is covered in a black rubber mask and goggles and he looks like an insect too. He's got a badge on his sleeve with "State Trooper Alaska." He turns to close the door behind him, and he must whack it shut because my bracelet vibrates again. Now he's coming towards us.


Captain Grayling saw the group on the snow, the parents and the little girl, a family out here in the middle of the twenty-below wilderness; relief punched him almost over.

"Oh thank God, thank God. You're all right? Your little girl, she's all right too?"

"Yes," Yasmin Alfredson said.

He bent down on the snow to be at the little girl's height, and she backed away from him. He pulled down his face mask. "I'm sorry, scary mask."

But she still didn't go near him and he felt his culpability. He was the reason that she and her mother had ventured into the Arctic wilderness. He hadn't protected them. No wonder the little girl wanted nothing to do with him, and he admired her spirit.

He took hold of Matthew Alfredson's arm, more of an embrace than a handshake.

"How do you apologize to a man for thinking he's dead?"

Captain Grayling was older than Yasmin had imagined, his face finer and more careworn. He came with them into the aputiak, crawling through the tunnel entrance.

"Did you see the tanker?" she asked.

"Yes. The driver's in the chopper. Turns out he's not so great at reversing."

"Do you know who he is?"

"He's not saying anything at the moment, but I'll get the truth out of him."

He paused a moment, and Yasmin saw guilt in his face.

"I started searching for you the moment I knew you were on the Dalton," he said. "But the storm hit and I couldn't control the chopper. I started looking again as soon as the winds dropped enough to fly. I scoured every mile of the Dalton south of the Atigun Pass and there was nothing. So I headed north."

She guessed he'd believed the tanker driver's location, and looking for them on the tundra had been a last-ditch effort motivated more by hope than a realistic expectation.

"The storm had eased; visibility was much better," he continued. "Then I saw your flare so I followed it. I found the tanker. Then came on to find you. The wind during the storm and the ice have damaged a blade. Made it here, but it's not safe to fly out again. I've radioed for help to come and get us all."

"How long till they get here?" Matt asked.

"An hour, maybe a little more. It's a trek even by chopper."

Captain Grayling saw Yasmin Alfredson signing to the little girl and only then realized that she was deaf. The child's utter vulnerability shocked him.

"You're angry with me, right?" he said to the child. "I'm angry with me too."

Yasmin translated his words into sign, but she didn't soften.

"I should have believed your mother," he said to her. "It's my fault you went on such a frightening journey. I should have looked for your dad myself."

Yasmin translated and this time the little girl nodded, her body no longer so pointedly removed from him. She said something to her mother.

"Do you know if Adeeb Azizi is all right?" Yasmin asked.

He nodded, smiling, and made the sign for "OK," the only sign he knew.

"I did search for you," he said to Matt. "Flew over the whole area around Anaktue, God knows how many times, checking and rechecking."

"When was that?" Matt asked.

"Monday afternoon and into the night."

"I was over thirty miles away by then," Matt said.

Dad's talking with his mouth-voice for the state trooper and sign-voice for me. He does that when he's with me and someone who can't sign; it's a really hard thing to do because in sign language the grammar's different and you need to use your face too. And Daddy looks so tired.

"I left Anaktue twice," he says. "The first time was last Wednesday. That's at least a week ago, isn't it?"

Captain Grayling nods, but I don't know what day it is today; it feels like we've been driving for one long night, because of night swallowing up the days.

Yasmin had so many questions for Matt but knew she needed to listen to his story of the last few days, the details and facets of it, as he would need to listen to hers, because they were days that broke you down and made you again, different from how you were before.

"You said you left Anaktue last Wednesday?" Captain Grayling said.

## 21

Matt had woken early that morning, a sleepless night spent on a camp bed, a journey ahead of him. Corazon was in her bedroom asleep, but her twin, Kaiyuk, was already up tending to his huskies. Matt heard their barks across the stillness of the early morning and Kaiyuk's voice as he fed them. He and Kaiyuk had talked long into the night, and Matt guessed he'd decided not to go to bed at all.

Pulling on his atikluk over his atigi parka, he went outside and was disorientated as he was every morning by the stars and moon still being in the sky, as if they hadn't got the hint. The blast of cold air wiped sleep away from him.

He walked past the cluster of wooden houses and cabins, the buzzing from the generator building, towards the kennels. From here you could see that two of the wooden houses were tilted, their foundations built into the permafrost, which in the last few years had started to thaw.

Kaiyuk already had the dogs harnessed up for him in a gangline, each dog attached by a separate tug line. This would only be Matt's second time out alone with a husky team and for longer than before. Kaiyuk gave him some last-minute advice about the musher being the leader of the pack, and to make sure the dogs always knew that. Then he'd given Matt a crescent-shaped lamp carved from stone; his own qulliq. "If you're going native . . ." he said to Matt, grinning at him.

Then the two men had embraced and Matt felt the solidity of their friendship. He hadn't woken up anyone else to say good-bye before his trip; it hadn't seemed necessary.

He looked at Yasmin and Ruby, close to him in the aputiak, and then at Captain Grayling. He wasn't sure how long he'd been silent but thought it was only a few moments and that memories like dreams stretch out as you experience them but objectively last hardly any time at all.

"I left the village early, about six," he said. "Almost everyone was still asleep. We'd had a party the night before for Akiak, a welcome-home bash."

"Akiak Iqua?" Grayling asked.

"Yes."

"Our records had him working at a well at Prudhoe," Captain Grayling said.

"He didn't tell anyone official he was leaving."

Akiak had wanted to leave before Soagil Energy fired him; didn't want to give the bastards the satisfaction.

"Akiak found out my laptop had broken and gave me his at the party. Said it had been a gift from Soagil Energy in their bribery stage, but now that they'd reached threats he didn't want anything to do with them or their gifts."

Matt had taken the MacBook Air, but as it didn't come with a protective cover he'd feared that it might not work outside in the sub-zero cold. Hoping for the best, he'd wrapped it in his old cover, which didn't fit properly, before putting it in a knapsack for his trip.

"Did you use a snowmobile?" Captain Grayling asked, and Yasmin surmised that he was unsure of any of his facts now.

"No, a sled and huskies."

Kaiyuk used his dogs for racing and, like everyone else in the village, thought Matt a little nuts not to use a snowmobile for his expedition but had offered him the use of the team anyway. Matt had made up some excuse about not wanting to frighten away the snowy owl he hoped to find, and everyone was generous enough not to point out that eight huskies were as likely to frighten off a snowy owl as a snowmobile.

As he'd left the village, he saw Kaiyuk with Akiak, still looking drunkenly cheerful from his party, and both men waved to him. He heard children's voices as they played in the snow over the sound of the old grumbling generator.

For four hours, Matt concentrated entirely on guiding the dogs and making sure he stayed steady on the sled. He thought that one of the two leader dogs, an intelligent female called Puqik, was simply indulging him in his role as leader of her pack.

When he'd arrived at Anaktue, his outdoor clothes had come from a specialist Internet shop; now he was wearing an atikluk and atigi, with caribou fur on the inside and mukluks instead of snow boots. Nobody had teased him for going native about that.

The stars and moon were still above him, as they had been when he'd gone to bed the previous night, and it sometimes felt to him that out here he was living in an endless moment, that in the far north time stretched and grew vast. He thought of the translucent Arctic moth, spending up to fourteen winters as a larval caterpillar to emerge fully fledged for just a few days; to the Arctic moth each hour in those summer days must last years.

His head torch picked out only the white of the snow in front of him and the fur of the dogs' backs; the only sounds were the sled moving and the dogs breathing, intent on pulling. He could have been traveling a thousand years before and he'd have seen the same landscape, worn the same clothes, traveled the same way, and this thought put things in perspective, especially himself, which was necessary because he knew that for too long he'd made himself the star player in his life, and that was not only weak and egocentric but also out of kilter with the world. In the Arctic tundra, it was impossible to feel important but simple to feel connected to something uncircumscribed by time and distance.

He reached a natural rhythm with the dogs and sled, felt rather than conscious, and could think unhindered about Corazon. He saw that the closeness he had with her was shored up with the intimacy and love he also had with Kaiyuk, her twin; and that it wasn't romantic feelings, but a deep friendship that bound him to both of them; and perhaps he'd wanted a part of the love they had for each other, but it was exclusive and privileged between them. Corazon had kissed him back, out of friendship he thought, as if she'd felt his need and had attempted to temporarily meet it. She hadn't wanted anything more and he hoped that if she had, he would have stopped it from going any further. A kiss was betrayal enough.

And that was surely why he was out here on his own, the true reason for this trip—to man up to himself, to acknowledge properly that he had betrayed his wife.

He looked out at the huge tundra, ablated by cold, and felt the frozen calmness and thought it was easier to face your own big things calmly here. Above him the sky was immense, flooded with stars.

It had been four days since he'd kissed Corazon; two days since he'd spoken to Yasmin. But it wasn't the phone call that was vivid in the winter quiet around him; instead he remembered the sound of waves and shingles underfoot, his trainers sodden with pooled seawater. He'd looked through her telescope at the seaside night sky and she had shown him galaxies. But in truth he'd been looking at her rather than the stars—a beautiful girl who didn't trade on her looks, seemed irritated by them, but demanded attention for her intellect; a guerrilla knitter who gazed at the stars; gifted, passionate, funny, vulnerable; the astonishing impossibility of her.

And he had remained in love with her; loved her as much out on the Alaskan tundra as he had that night when she lay in his arms on the beach at Cley. But he thought he had stayed in love with a girl who was no longer there, like one of those dead stars she'd once told him about, whose light we still see not because we are living in the star's future but because we are looking at the star's past.

*"I kissed her because I missed you."*

He felt his cowardice in grabbing hold of intimacy with Corazon and knew that no one could fill the hollow in him that Yasmin had left.

But he had a duty to Yasmin as the woman she was now, and to Ruby, to make the best of their life together, not absent himself from it. However compelling and extraordinary he found Alaska, he needed to return to them. He'd spend three days on this trip, then he'd pack his things in Anaktue and go back home.

He'd originally planned to spend another eight weeks here filming the birds, as well as animals, that didn't migrate but stayed and endured the cold. He'd brought his camera, terminal, and Akiak's laptop so he could email photos to his production company, but he left them all in his knapsack; there was no point now.

He fed the huskies, then pitched his tent and lit the qulliq lamp, using Arctic cotton for a wick as Kaiyuk had shown him. The heat surprised him; afraid of burning down his tent, he'd put it out.

He looked out at a wilderness that appeared rugged and immense, but he knew that under the snow the tundra was composed of tiny plants, a fragile ecosystem easily spoiled and impossible to repair. There were still tire marks in the Russian Arctic tundra made by vehicles in World War Two.

From here, London was frenetic, its streets and houses frantic and shrill, crammed with objects that demanded attention; no one could stand out against such a canvas. In Alaska, people were more clearly defined. But recently the village itself had become louder and less settled, as people argued about how to prevent Soagil Energy's bid to frack their land. Corazon was coordinating the opposition to the company, unifying the villagers. She sometimes used his terminal to access the Internet; when he returned to England he'd leave it with her.

Without a lens separating him from the land, he saw it more clearly and felt its magnetic draw on him more strongly. Untainted by man, this land had its own identity, a soul and a being, and he understood the Inupiaq belief that all things have a spirit.

Early one morning, the snowy landscape had eyes, looking at him with bright intent. Only when the snow moved did he see that a part of the snow was the feathers of a white ptarmigan, nestling a foot away from him.

In summer he'd come here and seen fawn-feathered ptarmigans and brown-furred hares and tawny-gray foxes and brindled wolves; now their feathers and fur were white, as if they were made out of the snow itself. On his final evening, he saw a snowy owl in flight, its white wings spanning five feet across; it was as if the bird had been cut from the sky.

The land's purity and huge aloneness, its balance of details in a larger whole, made it feel to him more like a living poem than a place.

His last night, the sky was cloudless with a full moon lighting the snowy terrain in an opalescent blue light. He remembered Yasmin telling him that the moonlight that reaches Earth is mainly the reflected light from the sun with some starlight and Earthlight thrown in. She'd told him that the light wasn't really blue, it was because of the Purkinje effect, a flaw in the human eye, that made it so. And he'd thought that what we know is filtered by our flaws, and sometimes turned more beautiful by them.

He looked at Yasmin in the light of the qulliq and saw the girl he'd loved so much in the past returned to him and the exhausted, extraordinary woman she was now, so courageous in her love for him. He took her face in his hands.

———

Captain Grayling watched Matt sign to Yasmin. He'd been surprised by their clear and deep love for each other. He'd found Matt's wedding ring among the charred remains of Anaktue, and he'd thought the marriage it symbolized was over. He found their closeness moving and painful. He and his wife had separated, quietly and desperately, a year after their son died. He saw that the little girl had turned away from her father's hands, giving them privacy, but he needed to know the rest of Matt's story.

"What happened then?" he asked Matt.

Matt turned to him. "On Friday morning there was an ice storm. I waited for it to finish before heading back to Anaktue."

The rain had frozen onto everything it touched, covering the dogs' harnesses and lead lines and his tent with ice. He'd chipped it off, then set out, looking forward to seeing his friends, the chat and banter at dinner that night. He would tell them that he was going back to England but was pretty sure most of them were surprised he'd come out here for the winter months at all. He'd enjoy telling Kaiyuk about the husky team, being a little boastful about how well he'd managed them.

Before he'd left, Corazon and he had swiftly reverted back to their easy close friendship with little awkwardness. She'd given him a snow knife for his mad sledding trip, not an antique but a modern one, like her, she'd said. He'd have to admit that he didn't use it. And own up to using a tent and Arctic sleeping bag. He was no Inupiaq hunter with skill at surviving the wilderness. She'd laugh at him, he imagined.

———

"It was midday when I got back to Anaktue," Matt said.

As he'd neared the village, one of the huskies had tried to tug away and he'd had to make the dog continue on.

"There were no lights and no sound. I thought it was the middle of the night and my watch must have broken."

There were stars above him and it was dark, but that was the same day or night. Time here was like the snow-covered treeless tundra with no distinguishing marks with which to orientate yourself.

But surely it couldn't be midday because there would be lights on and voices and doors opening and cooking sounds coming from inside into the frozen air.

He strained to listen. But there was nothing. It was never silent here. Even in the middle of the night the diesel-fueled generator would make its mechanical buzzing and grumbling. If it went out, people realized quickly and someone would come and restart it. Temperatures dropped too fast in late November for no one to notice.

In the beam of his torch, Anaktue shone. The ice storm had hit Anaktue too, glazing the village in an unbroken sheet of ice, encasing each of the houses and cabins as if in glass. The snow on the ground was glazed over. But surely someone would have walked on the ice, opened a door or a window and cracked it. It was like a village under an enchantment or curse.

Breaking an ice-sealed door, he went into the first cabin, where his friend Hiti and his family lived. Despite the biting cold inside, the cabin smelled of diarrhea and faintly of garlic. He shone his torch around the cabin.

Hiti was lying on the floor of the kitchen, holding a blanket around his twelve-year-old son. Matt pulled the blanket back a little way, exposing the child's face. He saw that Hiti's hands were stained blue, as if he'd dipped them in ink. His wife was a few feet away, holding their younger child, also wrapped in a blanket, his face covered. Matt thought that their children had died first and the parents had wrapped them before they too had died. He heard a noise in the silence and turned, startled. A large bird was in the cabin. It must have followed him in, its frenzied movements making it a blur of black; then it flew past him and back outside.

He ran into cabin after cabin. The same smell. No one alive. Only Kaiyuk and Akiak unaccounted for. Both fit and young; he hoped they'd managed to escape whatever had happened here. He found them fifty or so yards away from the village. They must have been trying to go for help.

Corazon was in her elderly neighbor's cabin, and he thought she had gone to look after him. Like the others, her hands were colored blue, diarrhea staining the floor.

Adrenaline had coursed through him, making him run, his body taut, his mind racing with desperate urgency. Then his torch shone on a dead black bird on the white snow. A raven. He'd been abruptly stilled. The urgency to help them was before they'd died. There was nothing he could do for them; nothing he could ever do for them. His sense that time here expanded into an endless vast moment was horrifyingly true of death and remorse.

He returned to Hiti's cabin and carefully replaced the blanket over his son's face. He saw the boy's prized caribou hide hung on the wall of the cabin; it was his *anjungaun,* a young hunter's first game.

The boy had shot the caribou with Hiti in September and had confided in Matt that he'd cried when he'd killed it; that he'd felt like a monster. But then his father and he had cut the animal's windpipe to release its spirit. They'd butchered it together and his mother had frozen the meat into different cuts and pieces for stewing that they'd be eating through this long winter until springtime, and the fat would be used to light their qulliq and the hide would be used for bedding or clothes. But as it was his anjungaun, they had displayed it on the wall; in the summer he would be allowed to go on an overnight hunting trip and he'd take it with him and use it in an aputiak. His father said one day he would surely be an isiqsuruk, a strong and enduring hunter. The boy said that because they'd released the animal's spirit and not wasted a single part of its body, he was proud of his first hunt.

Matt took the caribou hide off the wall and held it as he wept.

## 22

In the quiet aputiak, Matt remembered the noise of the dogs, Kaiyuk's dogs, howling at the black sky, the stars shrouded in clouds; the dogs' sound a violent keening.

Yasmin was holding his hand tightly in hers, as if she'd been going into the cabins with him. He wasn't signing these details to Ruby; he didn't want her to have these images in her head, and didn't want her to know how he'd failed his friends.

"They had no way of getting help," he said. "I'd taken the satellite terminal with me. I didn't even use it."

"It wasn't your fault," Yasmin said. "Matt, listen to me, please. It wasn't your fault. You had no way of knowing."

Captain Grayling's face appeared slackened by the horror of what Matt was telling him.

"Do you think they died painfully?" he asked, and Matt was taken aback by the humanity of the state trooper's question.

"Yes. But I didn't know it then."

"You found them last Friday?" he asked.

"Yes."

"The police thought everyone died in a fire," Yasmin said to him.

"I don't understand."

"There was a terrible fire," Captain Grayling said. "Burned everything to the ground. There was no way of knowing that they died before."

"Someone set fire to the village?" Matt asked, appalled.

"It could have been an accident," Grayling said, as if he wanted to believe it. "Maybe a heater was left on when they died, or a cooker, that could have caused the initial fire that spread."

Yasmin remembered that Captain Grayling had led the search party at Anaktue; it must have been a brutal scene. She understood why he didn't want the fire to be deliberate: because it would be as if someone had killed them twice over.

"I thought the police would find them," Matt said. "Not for a few days, maybe, but I was sure they'd be found."

The villagers had friends and relatives outside Anaktue. It was remote but not totally cut off. People visited by taxi plane, and the villagers left the same way. He'd assumed that someone was bound to find them and tell the police.

Yasmin turned to Captain Grayling. "If you'd found them before the fire you'd have known Matt was alive. You would have seen there wasn't a Westerner's body among the dead."

Captain Grayling nodded. He took a few moments as if to collect himself.

"We will find out about the fire," he said to Matt. "But I'd like to know what really happened at Anaktue, before the fire. And I think you can help me."

Dad's taken off his special boots, and his feet are bleeding and some of his toes are black, like someone has put shoe polish on.

I tell Dad that I want to know what happened too, so I'll lip-read what he says. I don't want him to sign too because he looks so tired. I say that I'll look away if something's too horrible. I put my sleeping bag over his poor feet to try to warm them up, and when I do that, he smiles at me, just like old Dad again.

"Outside one of the houses, I saw the dead raven again," Dad says with his mouth-voice and in sign as well, even though I said he didn't need to.

Had he told them about the raven? Or just remembered it so vividly himself that he thought he must have done.

It had started snowing, the white flakes landing on the black bird.

"I photographed it."

It hadn't been about evidence or a trail then, but because the dead raven felt like an epitaph for the Inupiat villagers, expressing something that he would never be able to.

"And then I left the village for the second time."


His plan had been to go to the airstrip because surely a plane would fly over in the next few days. He'd still got his tent and provisions for himself and the huskies in the sled from his first trip. Kaiyuk had made him take double what he needed in case a storm had blown in. He could wait as long as it took for the plane.

The dogs hadn't wanted to leave. He'd had to use all his authority and strength to get them to budge. One of the leader dogs, Puqik, had seemed to understand that they needed to get away, and the others had eventually followed her.

As he left Anaktue, the snow became heavier. Behind him the village was lost in snow and darkness and he felt that he was abandoning them. The dogs pulled on, the snow getting denser, until he could no longer differentiate what was in front of him or beneath or above him, a one-dimensional whiteness in which he could have been traveling across the sky as much as across the land.

Eight miles from Anaktue the snow thinned and the different planes of a three-dimensional world established themselves again. His head torch showed black shapes lying on the snow.

As he got closer, the smell hit him, the same as in the village cabins, putrid even in the icy air. There was a herd of dead musk oxen, the smaller ones almost buried in the recent white-out. A large bull had been partially eaten, after it was dead because there was no blood on the snow.

Something glinted in his torch beam. A short distance away, there was a hole in the snow and he saw moving water beneath reflecting his torchlight. The river was frozen over here, then covered with snow. Musk oxen must have made the hole with their hooves in the thinnest part of the ice to get to water.

He looked into the hole. The river flowed fast under the ice. A lingcod, eighteen inches long, was trapped by a shard of ice just underneath; its gills were half dissolved.

He hadn't wanted to believe the evidence in front of him; hadn't wanted to think that this fragile and pure land, the white poem he'd lived in yesterday, was rank with poison.

Nor did he want to acknowledge that the smell of the musk oxen linked them to the villagers. It was too grotesque a detail, demeaning, had no relationship to the beauty of the people or the animals.

Half a mile away he found a pack of dead wolves, most of them buried by drifting snow. He thought that they must have fed on the musk oxen, or perhaps drunk from the river too.

The villagers would take water from the river to last two days at a stretch, keeping it in storage tanks; the task of hauling it falling to the fittest men and women. Akiak and Kaiyuk had been going to get water from the river when Matt left for his first trip. Akiak wouldn't have been on any roster, not when he'd unexpectedly returned, so it had been generous of him to help his friend.

But the villagers always boiled the water before drinking it.

It was still snowing, softly smothering the animals.

In the aputiak Matt told them how he'd taken photos of the musk ox and the wolves, using his satellite terminal to get a precise location. The terminal hadn't connected for long enough to attempt linking it to his laptop, but did give him latitude and longitude. He'd written the numbers on a notepad with a pencil. His biro had frozen.

"You used decimal coordinates," Yasmin said.

"It was faster to write. I thought it would be easy to fill in the decimal points later."

Yasmin imagined the physical and mental stamina of standing in minus twenty Fahrenheit, using a camera, then a terminal, then a pencil. And she understood why he wrote the minimum. He'd have had to write wearing just glove liners; he wouldn't risk frostbite in his fingers in case he couldn't talk to Ruby.

"Instead of heading east towards the airstrip, I went southwest, following the river and the dead animals and birds on its banks. I was going against the current, towards the source."

Yasmin understood that Matt had felt he owed it to the villagers to record what had happened and to find out the truth, but surely he could have gone to the airstrip and waited for a taxi plane, and then someone else, the police, could have done it. He must have sensed her question without her asking it.

"The snow was covering everything; the blizzard had almost buried the musk oxen and wolves. Another heavy snowfall and the animals would have been hidden and there'd have been nothing left to see, nothing left to follow."

She nodded and thought he must have hoped that the police would discover the villagers and then come searching for him. He didn't know about the fire and that because of the fire they'd thought him dead. He wouldn't have imagined being so totally alone for so long.

Kaiyuk's huskies were the only living connection he had to Anaktue. He'd called to each one above the sound of the wind, using their names, which Kaiyuk had taught him. At the front was Puqik, which meant Smart; next to her Umialik, meaning King; then Qaukliq, meaning Chief and Nuturuk, Firm Snow; then Siku, Ice with Koko, Chocolate; at the back was Qannik, Snowflake with Pamiuqilavuq, which Kaiyuk had said meant Wags-his-Tail, but Matt hadn't known if Kaiyuk had been teasing him about that.

"Puqik, one of the leader dogs, found some carrion by the river and ate it before I could stop her."

He'd stayed with Puqik until she died, for the first time in his career wishing that he had a gun. It had hurt his friends to die.

Without Puqik, the other dogs were difficult to manage, and he struggled to keep authority over them. The only light he had was a wind-up torch, and he'd let it get almost out before winding it again because he had to do that in just glove liners.

Sometimes he thought he'd lost the river, and then he'd spot a dark shape near its edge and know he'd found a poisoned animal or bird. He'd photograph it and get the coordinates and write them down; then he'd continue through the dark scarred land monitoring the poison.

"Is that what happened to your friends too, Dad?" Ruby asked. "Were they poisoned too? Was it poison, not a fire?"

Matt nodded, wishing that Ruby didn't need to know this story, but he was signing it to her because she'd asked to know what happened. He and Yasmin had agreed that they'd never use her deafness for some kind of advantage, even when it was to protect her.

"The second night my primus ran out of fuel," he said. "It was too windy to light the qulliq. I had food for the huskies, but no way of melting snow to get water for them."

Over the next two days, whenever the wind dropped enough he'd light the qulliq and melt snow for the dogs and himself.

"By Sunday night, I had traveled twenty-five miles. I pegged the huskies on their lines outside the tent. They were hungry. I'd been giving them half rations, trying to make the supplies last. The next morning two of the dogs were missing."

"Which dogs?" Ruby asked.

He'd told her all their names, after his first sledding trip with Kaiyuk.

"Pamiuqilavuq and Nuturuk. I found Nuturuk with a poisoned Arctic hare and he was ill too."

It had looked as if the dog was on solid ground, but as Matt went to get him the ground had given way.

"Dad? What happened?"

"He was on thin ice over the river and he went through. He died because the water was so cold."

"But he's got special thick fur, Daddy. You told me that. You said huskies got too hot even when it was freezing cold."

"He was ill, so he got too cold very fast."

The part of the river where he and the dog went through was relatively shallow, but it was fast-flowing. Matt hadn't tried to rescue the dog, but had let him be borne away swiftly; drowning or hypothermia was a less brutal way to die.

"What about Pamiuqilavuq?" Ruby asked, making the sign of a "P" and a fast-wagging tail.

"I couldn't find him. I think that he must have fallen into the water too. It would have been very quick, Puggle."

"Yes."

"We went another four miles."


His feet and his outer trousers were wet from going through the ice in the river. He was wearing three layers, as Inupiaq hunters did, but the cold penetrated through. He felt frostbite as electric shocks in his feet and shins. His legs became weaker and his feet numb and he found it hard to balance in the sled. He kept on calling the dogs' names over the sound of the wind, but gradually he could no longer remember what they were called. He knew that he was suffering from exposure, that he would die if he didn't get warm soon.

He stopped the huskies. His wet clothes were leaching the remaining warmth away from his body and he had no way of drying them.

There was nothing with which to build a fire, not a tree or a twig. The wind was slicing like machetes with nothing to stand in its way. In this wind he wouldn't get the qulliq lit, let alone keep it alight. He had no source of warmth.

Dad says he knew a storm was coming because it was getting so windy and cold. He tried to put up his tent, but the ground was too hard to get the stakes in properly. And then this gust of wind came along and Dad says it just blew the tent away like it was a lacy handkerchief held down by drawing pins. He tried to chase after it but it disappeared.

He says he tried to tether the huskies, so they wouldn't escape and get poisoned, but it was hard to hammer the stakes in. And it's awful to think of Dad all cold and alone with the hard hard ground.

"Why didn't you email us?" I say. "And tell us it was you and ask us for help?"

"I wanted to, Puggle, but Akiak's laptop had frozen." He smiles. "Literally."

I do a carrier bag smile but I feel sad inside.

"It wouldn't even switch on," Dad says. "My cover hadn't protected it properly and I think it had got too cold to work. The screen had little cracks in it too."

He looks at Mum with that new look he has for her, and I can tell he's about to say something to her, probably in sign because that's more private, but the state trooper interrupts. Mum translates his words into sign for me.

"That must have been on Monday," the state trooper says. "When we were searching for you in the storm. But you built this."

"Not this. A first effort," Dad says, and gives me a proper smile. "I was pretty hopeless, Puggle. I'd never done it before, just watched Kaiyuk and Corazon. They could build an aputiak in twenty minutes. It took me hours. Even then it was a scrappy kind of thing."

He'd been thinking too much as a Londoner and not as an Inupiaq; if he was to survive he'd have to think what they would do. He took Corazon's snow knife and cut blocks of snow from a snowbank, his fingers struggling to coordinate. Some of the blocks crumbled and were useless and he had to start over. When he thought he had enough blocks, he started to build the aputiak.

All the time he was building it, his body wild with shivering, his feet stabbed with frostbite, he thought of Yasmin and Ruby, saw their faces in the dark as if at the end of a tunnel and if he built the aputiak he'd reach them. He remembered Kaiyuk's voice above the howling wind explaining to him patiently, "*Not row upon row, but a spiral; then we pack the joints with snow*"; but his voice was more vivid than a memory, as if he were with Matt on the snow, and he feared exposure was making him hallucinate, but the sound of Kaiyuk's voice comforted him nonetheless.

When it was done, he crawled inside, unutterably cold. It took him ten attempts to light the qulliq. The warmth startled him. He closed the opening with snow, then took off his damp clothes to dry. He took the battery out of Akiak's laptop, then put the battery and the laptop near the qulliq, hoping the warmth would get it to work again. He fell asleep, slipping in and out of consciousness, light from the qulliq shining on the snow walls.

He woke choking, the smoke from the qulliq filling the aputiak, and he had to get the knife and gouge a hole to let the smoke out. But he was no longer violently shivering.

The next morning, his frostbitten feet had turned red and blistered. Two of the huskies, Umialik and Qannik, had broken their lines and gone. He'd given them the last of the meager rations the night before and they must have gone off in search of food. He only had Koko, Qaukliq, and Siku left. It sickened him that before feeling the loss of the dogs, he'd felt relief he could remember their names. The next aputiak he built would be big enough for the dogs too.

He replaced Akiak's laptop battery and the laptop turned on for five seconds or so, but then the keyboard jammed and he saw that warming it had caused condensation inside the screen. He wrapped the laptop in a lightweight camping towel, hoping to draw the condensation away, then packed it in his knapsack.

He left his poorly built aputiak and walked for three miles along the river, his feet bloody and blackened with frostbite, the three remaining dogs pulling the sled without his weight. He had only a torch beam to see by, tiny in the immense black landscape, and he felt as if he were the only person alive on a planet of darkness and ice.

His torch beam shone on a delineator. It was the first evidence of humans he'd had for almost four days, and he knew he was reaching the source of the poison. He saw more delineators, marking the river as a road.

He'd walked, stumbling, a mile and a half along the river road, when he heard a faint crackling as the huskies pulled the sled over the ice.

He shone his torch, looking for the cause, and found a hole in the ice, cracks emanating around it from where the sled had gone over it. He widened the hole with his knife. Underneath, boulders sectioned off a part of the fast-flowing river. His torch beam shone on layers of dead fish and frogs, partially dissolved, a foot thick under the ice.

He walked a few paces and felt something soft and giving at his feet. He shone the torch and saw dead river otters on the ice.

He took a photo, but the camera was getting harder to operate and he feared that snow had got into the mechanism. He was desperate to get the photos onto the Net, where they wouldn't be subject to the freezing weather, but doubted he'd get Akiak's laptop to work. He remembered how in a strange way it had been easier to think about the problems he had with his camera and laptop than to focus on the family of river otters. Qannik had been next to them.

―――――

Dad says he saw the river otters too and he photographed them. He thought he was getting near the source of the poison.

I tell him that when I saw the family of otters I cried, and he nods, because he understands. It's like our stories are joining up now, Dad's with Mum's and mine, and we are all one story again.

When I saw the husky next to the otters, I thought the bad man had let him die, but now I know that Dad was trying to look after him. Qannik means Snowflake and although he looked soft and gentle, he was very strong and quite fierce.

Dad walked along the river road, like we did, and when he got to here he knew he'd found the poison. He says he checked further up the river and there were no dead fish and no dead animals. He says the poison started here.

Everyone is putting on their outdoor things and going out of the aputiak. Dad tells me to stay in the warm but there's no way I'm letting him out of my sight again, not for a minute.


The bonfire is super-bright, so I can see Mum's and Dad's hands. The flames look like genies trying to escape into the dark.

"It was burning when I got here," Dad says to the state trooper. "I'm not sure what they were trying to destroy. I kept it going hoping a plane would spot it."

The state trooper is saying something and Mum translates, "Regular planes don't fly over this way. We don't either unless we have a reason."

I know he means that he was looking for Mum and me, which is why he saw our flare, and a flare goes a lot higher than a bonfire. Our flare looked like a red star.

No one was even looking for Dad except Mum and me.

Dad puts a plank of something on the bonfire and it makes lots more flames and the darkness turns orange as the genies escape.

I can see a gigantic metal monster rising up into the marmalade sky.

"It's a fracking rig," Dad says.


He'd walked towards the glow of the bonfire and in its light had seen the towering rig, a hundred and thirty feet tall, like a medieval trebuchet made of metal attacking the land; and then he'd searched with his torch, its small beam shining on a huge compressor and storage tanks and well heads and frack pumps. There was a partially dismantled generator shed, floodlights lying on the ground. He'd found twenty-two wells within a mile of the rig. There were pits like moon craters, the size of lakes, which he thought must be the waste storage ponds. Even in the cold he smelled the chemical poisons, abrasive in his nose and throat. Despite the subzero temperature, the fluid in the pits wasn't covered in ice and instead of reflecting, his torch beam was absorbed by the murky viscous fluid.

For thousands of miles around this place the ancient tundra was white with snow, the delicate ecosystem beneath fragile and unspoiled. But here it was scarred with metal and craters, and underneath him the fracking pipes went two miles down into the earth, spreading out as veins and fracturing the land.

The villagers had feared that fracking would poison their land and water and destroy their way of life. They'd feared it could make them sick. He'd researched with Corazon the many ways that fracking was potentially dangerous. Horribly ironic, that it wasn't fracking wells right next to their village that had killed them, but wells owned by a different company over forty miles away.

––––––

"Do you know how the river was poisoned?" Captain Grayling asked.

"A casing in one of the fracking pipes could have cracked and leaked chemicals from the fracking fluid," Matt said. "Or when they fracked the rocks, they released poison naturally present. Or someone just dumped all the toxic waste. There's a whole load of ways. And any safeguards didn't work."

The state trooper has pulled off his mask and I can see from his face that he thinks this is a nasty place too. He might have taken off his mask because he knows I find it a bit scary, or because his face got too warm right next to the bonfire.

"And you built the really good aputiak?" I say to Dad, making our special sign for it.

"Yes."

"With a hole for the smoke and a door made of a hide," I say.

"Exactly. I'd learned a few lessons the hard way, Puggle."

When he'd finished building the aputiak, he lit the qulliq and put Akiak's laptop near it, wrapped in the camping towel. After four hours, the screen glowed and he felt he was no longer alone. He hadn't been there when the villagers were killed, when they had needed him, but now he was at least able to bear witness to what had happened. He attached his camera cable to Akiak's MacBook Air, which automatically went to iPhoto. He clicked "Import All" and his photos downloaded onto the laptop.

He opened the first photo and started typing the coordinates of where it was taken in the description box, but the screen flickered off and on and he was afraid he didn't have long before it packed up. He typed as fast as he could for each photo, just copying the numbers he'd written in pencil, no time for anything else.

He already knew the coordinates of Anaktue, and he put those with the photo of the raven.

He'd taken photos of the fracking wells and pits, shadowy in the light of the bonfire, and taken coordinates, but there was no proof in the photos of any poison; the proof was in his photos of animals and birds.

He needed to get the photos onto the Internet as a safe place for his record, away from the vagaries of ice and damp and extreme cold, but first he would email Yasmin, somehow translate his love for her into articulated thought and words.

He typed in her address, then the screen flickered again and failed. He wrapped the laptop up and put it by the qulliq. An hour later, the screen came on faintly. Only the trackpad worked. The keyboard didn't work at all. He pressed letter after letter, but none of them responded. He felt as if he'd been made mute. He thought about Ruby when people didn't understand that her signs were words and how brave she was.

Maybe he could still send the photos and coordinates. He had Yasmin's address and the trackpad worked. He left the aputiak.

"I emailed the photos from over there," Dad says. He points at a hill, like a huge black cutout against the orange light of the bonfire. "I had to get a clear line of sight to a satellite."

"It must have really hurt your feet," I say. Because inside the aputiak I saw his poor black toes.

"It hurt a bit, but not too much," he says. "Frostbite's not such a big deal in feet. Worst-case scenario is that I lose a toe or two, and you can get by missing the odd toe."

He says that just to me with his hand-voice.

I take his hands and look at all of his fingers, really carefully. He smiles and he signs that his fingers are all absolutely fine.

———

The climb had been hard, his feet numbed with frostbite, the ground uneven and treacherous with ice. He reached the top and tried to wedge his torch so he could see to plug in the connecting cable between the laptop and his terminal, but the torch kept falling over and getting covered in snow. If the laptop screen had been bright it would have been easier, but it was dim and cracked and gave no light for him to see by.

He took off his mittens and, wearing thin liners, felt along the connection holes with his fingertips to try to plug in the cable.

He got the terminal and laptop connected. The terminal searched for a satellite. Using the trackpad on the laptop, he opened iPhoto and then clicked on the photo of the musk ox. He clicked the "share" option and then "email." Using the trackpad, he checked the description box so the coordinates would be sent automatically with the photo. He'd typed in Yasmin's address before the keyboard had frozen, so he used the trackpad to copy and paste her address into the recipient box. The subject box automatically filled in with the number of the photo from his digital camera. Before he clicked the "send" icon he tried the keyboard, desperate for it to work, so he could write to Yasmin. The keyboard was still frozen.

The terminal got a satellite connection and he sent the musk ox photo, but when he tried to send the next photo, he lost the connection and had to start over. He knew he could only send a small sample of the photos he had taken. Every five minutes, he'd put his hands into his mittens until they were warm again. After half an hour the laptop screen went out. He had to return to the aputiak and wait till it flickered into life, then climb the icy slope again. His mind sluggish and his body clumsy, he lost all track of time. He kept on hoping that his keyboard would work, just enough, just for his initial even, to tell Yasmin it was him.

He'd felt the storm building all around him; the wind sharpening against him, the snow falling faster and thicker until it was blinding him. On his last trip down from the hill, he had to crawl, the glacial wind whipping around him, stripping him of warmth; the vicious cold felt vastly impersonal and intimately cruel.

He didn't know what day it was anymore and he thought out here there were no days, no turning of the Earth to reach the face of the sun, but a dark night of the soul in which only violent storms broke time into different pieces.

He reached the aputiak and, miraculous to him, the qulliq was still burning. As he sheltered, he thought of Kaiyuk and Corazon, sharing their skills with him.

Daddy hasn't said anything about Qaukliq, Koko, and Siku, but those are the only huskies he had left.

"Were Qaukliq, Koko, and Siku in the aputiak with you, in the megatron storm?" I ask him.

He looks sad and I know something horrible happened. He tells me they weren't there when he got back to the aputiak from sending his emails. He says they'd lost their proper musher and the lead dogs, and they were really hungry so they'd turned wild and half mad. They had gone out into the storm and he couldn't go and find them.

I want him not to be sad, not to think about the dogs.

"After the storm," I say, "did you see the stars?"

"Weren't they amazing?" he says.

We're signing to each other, so it's private.

"You sent Mum a photo," I say.

"I didn't know she was seeing them herself for real," he says, and he smiles at me. "Since when did you get so grown-up?" he asks. I think he knows I was trying to cheer him up.

"You kept your hands warm," I say.

"I had my toasty mittens and a qulliq."

"Did you think anyone was coming to rescue you?" I ask.

"Honestly?"

"Honestly."

"To start with, I thought maybe, but as time went on I wasn't very hopeful."

I think that means he was sure nobody would rescue him.

"Even with your coordinates?" I say. Because even though the co-ordinates were to show where the animals and birds were, they also showed where Dad was.

"I thought they were a bit cryptic," he says, and I know that "cryptic" means like a really hard crossword. "And no one knew it was me," he says.

"I did," I say. "For most of the time."

Dad takes my hand so for a little bit I can't talk.

"You didn't have any food left," I say.

"Not much."

"You said the qulliq only has a bit of time left and the bonfire's going to go out too."

"It was going to get very dark," he says.

It would be so frightening to be here on your own in the dark and cold.

"But Mum worked out the coordinates," I say.

"While driving all the way across Alaska," Dad says with a !! expression on his face.

"And you saw our flare," I say.

"And heard your mum making a big racket."

"And then you made a big racket back?"

"I did. And I saw you and Mum running towards me. You are both the most amazing people I have ever met in my entire life—"

My bracelet vibrates and Dad's hands aren't making words anymore.

———

A siren screeched across the darkness. Yasmin traced the sound to the helicopter, two hundred meters behind them.

"Isn't he handcuffed?" Matt said.

"No. Because he's not going anywhere," Captain Grayling said. "He isn't a threat now. You have my word. I'll go and stop that infernal racket."

While Yasmin had listened to Matt's story she'd been too preoccupied by the dangers of his journey to think about hers and so had been able to push the tanker driver aside.

When she'd looked out at the darkness, she'd looked towards the gently glowing aputiak in front of them, not to the helicopter. Now she felt him behind her again, oppressively close. She couldn't imagine him as a man with a face, but as blue lights stalking her, a siren as a voice.

The state trooper's gone to turn off the noise in the helicopter, so it's just Mum and Dad and me by the bonfire. They always sign everything in front of me or let me read their lips and I think they'd like to be private.

"I'll go to the aputiak," I say. "I'm a bit cold. And sleepy."

It's partly true. The aputiak is glowing all yellowy warm through its snow walls, a snug cave.

"I'll take you," Dad says.

"It's just over there, Dad. I'm grown-up enough to walk a little way on my own."

"You are," he says, and gives me his torch.

Yasmin pulled her mask over her face; the bonfire's warmth was ebbing.

"That photo of stars . . ." she said.

"It was a kind of good-bye," Matt said.

After the terrible storm, the sky turning bright with stars had been wondrous and he'd thought of Yasmin and taken the photo. He remembered how he'd concentrated on the practicality of it: taking the photo and plugging the lead from his camera into the laptop and using the trackpad to put the coordinates from the fracking well photos. The chance of her realizing the stars photo was from him, and of understanding the coordinates, was remote, and he'd known that wasn't the reason he was sending it.

"Good-bye was a bit pessimistic," she said, and even with a face mask on he could tell she was smiling.

"A bit," he admitted. "That wasn't the first time I thought I'd peg it."

"Peg it?"

"I'm trying to do understatement."

"You're doing it very well. That was in the first storm?"

"Yup. When my tent cartwheeled off across the tundra and my laptop was frozen and I hadn't thought about the aputiak. Couldn't think straight at all."

"You had exposure and frostbite and were exhausted. It's not surprising you couldn't think straight."

The sound of the siren snapped off. Captain Grayling must have reached the helicopter.

"But I did think of you," he said.

She kissed him.

"I need to see who's in the helicopter, don't I?" she said.

"You don't have to."

"That's why you let Ruby go off to the aputiak?"

"No. But I did know we'd need to talk about it."

She knew he felt violently protective and loved him for not making this about him; for not marching over to the helicopter saying he'd kill him; for not dominating her anxiety with his aggression.

"I'll have to see him at some point," she said.

"In a courtroom. When he's got big burly guards next to him."

"Yes."

But for so long he'd been at her back, stalking her. She had to turn round and face him.

I got near to Dad's aputiak when my torch shone on a little bit of brown fur on the snow. I knew it was Siku. He's the only husky with a stripe of brown down his back. I think he must have tried to get back to Dad to die.

I tried to pick him up but he's really heavy, so I'm dragging him over the snow. I'm not going to leave him. I know he can't really feel anything, but I still don't want him to be on his own in the snow.

I get him inside the aputiak. And then I cry a bit about everything Daddy's told me.

Fifty meters from the helicopter, Yasmin and Matt met Captain Grayling.

"Do you know who he is?" Yasmin said. "Have you found out?"

"His name is Jack Deering. He's owner and CEO of Am-Fuels. It's a hydraulic fracturing company."

"So these are his wells?" Matt asked.

"Yes."

Yasmin tried to remember where she had seen Am-Fuels' name. It was at the trucker stop when Adeeb was taken ill, in the parking area there'd been three Am-Fuels trucks with prefab houses. All of them had headed back to Fairbanks, clearing out. And at Fairbanks, before they'd even left, they'd had to wait to turn out of the trucker yard; Am-Fuels trucks had been coming in.

"I want to see him," Yasmin said.

She was pretty sure she knew who he was. She carried on walking towards the helicopter.

The light was on inside the passenger cabin. She went closer and through the window saw the side of his face; he hadn't yet seen her.

She remembered the airport and her desperation to get to Matt, the two merging so that her desperation had also felt frenetic and loud.

He had called himself Jack Williams, not Jack Deering. He'd told her the last flight for the day had left and offered to help. He'd seemed kind; he'd had his daughter with him. But Jack Deering and the girl in the queue hadn't interacted in any way; he'd needed an excuse to be there. He'd probably followed them from when they arrived off the flight from England.

She remembered that most of the men in the departure lounge had been wearing F.B.F. caps, but a few, including Jack, had been wearing Am-Fuels caps; Silesian Stennet had said F.B.F. had been taken over by Am-Fuels. No one had known who Jack was, because how often would the boss mingle with the workers? It was probably only their departure lounge that had the announcement about debris on the Deadhorse runway.

Jack's loathing of Silesian, the green activist, had been genuine, but not protective of them. And he'd come after them to make sure Silesian didn't say anything more. Because Silesian was on the right track. Only it wasn't poisonous fumes from Am-Fuels' wells traveling forty miles north to Anaktue that killed the villagers, but poison in the river.

It would have been easy for Jack to take a tanker; he probably owned a fleet of them.

Inside the helicopter, Jack turned. She met his look and held it. Just a man after all. He was the first to turn away.

"He'll be sent to prison," Matt said. "In America. So thousands of miles away from you and Ruby."

"Yes."

They walked back to the bonfire, from where they could see the warm glow of the aputiak, with Ruby safe inside. Grayling was in the cockpit, finding out how long the replacement chopper would be.

A few individual flakes of snow were falling to the ground, taking their time in the stillness.

I'm stroking Siku and I HATE the man who hurt him. I know it's the man in the helicopter. I want him to know what he's done to Siku and all the other animals. I want to tell him that I AM NOT AFRAID of him and he didn't stop us finding Dad. I want to be brave like Mum and Dad. I say good-bye to Siku and leave the aputiak. It's snowing a bit and the flakes sting like sparks and I have to pull up my face mask. I go around the edge of the bonfire so Mum and Dad don't see me. They're standing close, like two hands held together. Mum's face is inside his big parka hood and I'm sure they're kissing so it's good I left them on their own.

I'm getting closer to the helicopter; Mum and Dad and the bonfire are a long way behind me. Mum told me she used to be really really afraid of the dark, but one night she made herself pull up her bedroom blind and look at the dark and instead of just black she saw gazillions of stars.

I can see through the window of the helicopter. It's light inside. A man turns towards me and I quickly turn off my torch.

I thought it would be the man with the smelly hands, but it's the smiley smarmy one with the super-expensive watch that he just wears on any old day.

There's another man in there. It's the state trooper. I go a bit closer and I can see both their faces in the light and I don't think they can see me in the dark outside. The state trooper doesn't have his face mask on. The smiley smarmy man looks cross and he says, "Oh for God's sake, David . . ." Then something I can't see, then the smiley smarmy man says: "We found him . . ." and there's lots of other things, but I can't lip-read them clearly enough to be sure.

The state trooper is getting out of the helicopter. He looks angry, then he puts on his face mask.

I'm running to Mum and Dad by the bonfire. But I haven't put my torch on and I fall over. The state trooper walks right past me, not even seeing me.

He's with Mum and Dad by the bonfire. The flames show up his black rubber mask over his face.

I stand a little way behind him and sort of to the side, so that he can't see me, but I'm hoping Mum or Dad will. And them Mum sees me, and I put my fingers to my mouth—*shoosh*. Mum looks surprised, but she doesn't say anything to the state trooper. I sign to her, "The bad man called the state trooper David," I say, finger-spelling "state trooper" and "David." "And then he said, 'We found him.'"

Mum looks at the state trooper, like she's super-interested in what he's saying, so he won't see her hands by her waist finger-spelling to me: "Go to the aputiak as fast as you can." I don't want to leave Mum and Dad, but I will do what she says. She made Dad's and my sign for aputiak, so now it's her sign too.

Matt saw Yasmin signing to him. He thought she was going to say something intimate and wanted privacy in front of Captain Grayling, and Captain Grayling must have thought so too, because he smiled, a little paternally.

"Did you try to phone me?" she asked in sign. And then hurriedly, "Tell me in sign."

"Yes. In the first storm. When my tent blew away and I couldn't think straight. I needed to hear your voice."

His sat phone had been at the bottom of his knapsack, out of charge since the beginning of his first trip with the huskies and useless to him when he'd discovered the villagers dead. But in that first storm, suffering from exposure and frostbite and desperate, he'd remembered an idea he'd previously dismissed as apocryphal.

"I put the phone inside my clothes, against my skin," Matt signed. "I hoped body heat might warm up the battery, get some charge.

I ran. There was a hill and I climbed it, as fast as I could. And I called you."

As he did so, he'd thought it was futile. But in the darkness and howling wind he'd had a link to her for a few seconds that crossed continents and oceans.

"I lost the connection before I could speak to you."

Yasmin tried to disguise her emotions, signing to Matt, "He told me that he found your phone at the village."

She thought how close they'd come to this knowledge a little while earlier and wondered if it would have bought them any time or advantage. But she doubted it. They were in the middle of a wilderness with no means of escape or hiding or survival.

"Where's Ruby?" Matt signed.

"In the aputiak."

She was aware of Captain Grayling watching them, no longer paternally. She had backed a little away from him and maybe that was the moment he knew.

"It's not what you think," Captain Grayling said. "I've been trying to do the right thing."

Nearby was a huge waste pit, the smell of poison spiking through the frozen air.

"I never wanted you put in danger," he continued. "You must believe that. We just needed the chance to explain to you, so that you'd understand why this accident can't get out. If it does, then hydraulic fracturing might be permanently stopped in the rest of the U.S. We'd never break free of wars in the Middle East. I couldn't let that happen."

"How do you know Jack Deering?" Matt asked.

"We're cousins. He's prepared to offer you a huge amount of money."

"You think there's a price?" Matt asked.

"No, I don't," Grayling replied.

Yasmin felt visceral anger towards him. "You said you'd searched for Matt."

"I did," Grayling said. "I thought then that there'd just been a terrible fire and someone might have escaped it. I only gave up searching when we'd found twenty-four bodies, one more than the number of villagers. Visa records showed that a Matthew Alfredson was staying at Anaktue. I found a wedding ring with his initials."

Yasmin thought that he must have been decent once, and his voice still carried the remnant of that.

"It was only later that night that Jack called me," Grayling continued. "He told me there'd been a freak accident at a hydraulic fracturing well and he'd paid one of his men to set fire to the village to cover it up."

On the bonfire, a piece of painted wood caught, sending sparks skittering up into the black sky, the ash as it burned out landing on Yasmin's face mask.

"The people at Anaktue were dead," he continued. "It was an appalling accident. But there was nothing I could do to change it. I thought I was right to try to prevent a further disaster happening as a consequence."

He paused and the only sound was a hissing flame as flakes of snow landed on the bonfire.

"Jack told me it was a unique combination of circumstances that meant the fail-safes hadn't worked. I agreed with him that it would make this tragedy even worse if a chance-in-a-million accident meant fracking was stopped across the whole country, most probably forever. He was right to think about the wider implications."

Perhaps he believed this story, Yasmin thought. Perhaps he was able to cast himself in a decent light.

"You told me you'd found Matt's phone," she said, and thought he flinched from the anger in her voice.

"I was sure he was dead. I thought believing in this phone call as evidence he was alive would just prolong your agony."

"You lied out of kindness?"

"The phone was a distraction, a prop, something you needed to let go."

She thought she felt something ugly close to her in the dark.

"You'd taken part in a cover-up and so you lied to protect yourself," she said.

"No. I didn't know who'd phoned you but I knew it couldn't be him."

"Have you any idea what you did?" she said, wanting to crack the reasonableness in his voice, wanting him to sound like the man he was.

"I have to take some responsibility for that," Jack said.

He was coming towards them, his black Arctic clothes making him almost invisible in the darkness, only flames reflecting orange in his goggles marking his presence as he approached.

He stood close to Yasmin, his voice quiet.

"You frightened him when you arrived with your tale of your husband calling you. He phoned me straight away."

Jack's voice was different; he must have disguised his accent at the airport and on the CB.

"I told him the worker I'd paid to set the fire had seen a Caucasian man among the dead," Jack continued. "If I hadn't told him that, he'd have gotten all his trooper pals and PSOs out searching for your hubby, all the toys out of the cupboard with their sirens and lights with him at the center. He'd have taken his eye off the bigger picture."

She signed to Matt, telling him she thought Grayling might help them, maybe he wasn't all bad. Jack took hold of her hands in his, holding them tightly, gagging her.

"And then you came on the CB complaining about a tanker chasing you," he said. "Davey heard. Made the connection fairly fast. Phoned me on the sat phone and got me to admit I hadn't been totally straightforward with him. He wasn't pleased, were you, Davey?

Still thought we were kids and he could get on his high horse and tell me off."

Yasmin pulled her hands away from his, but there was barely enough light from the bonfire to see by now, so they wouldn't be able to sign.

"When I'd calmed him down enough so he'd listen," Jack continued, "I explained that I wasn't chasing you but following you. I pointed out that Matthew Alfredson probably knew about the accident. And he was probably going to call his wife again. You would lead us to him and that way we'd have the chance to talk to both of you, explain what was at stake without a whole load of troopers getting in the way."

Yasmin thought Jack was enjoying himself and it wasn't the enjoyment of power over them, but over Grayling.

"But if Matt had phoned me again," she said to Grayling, "then I'd have known you'd lied to me."

"Not Davey," Jack said. "The state troopers. The police. You wouldn't have known who to trust. I thought it would work to our advantage. And it's not that far from the truth. Fracking has supporters in very powerful places."

"Why the hell did you go along with this?" Matt asked Grayling. He'd felt the man's decency, in the way he'd behaved towards them up until this point, and found it hard to reconcile with the man now standing a foot away from him.

"I needed the opportunity to explain things to you," Grayling said. "I thought it was important to keep looking at the bigger picture. There was a greater good here and I had to keep hold of that."

"There was a storm," Yasmin said. "And we were out in it because he didn't let us turn around."

"I told him I'd take care of you out on the road," Jack said. "Make sure nothing happened."

Yasmin didn't think he was making excuses for Grayling but again flaunting his power over him.

"You believed him?" Yasmin asked Grayling.

Grayling was silent.

"Because it fitted with what you wanted. Because otherwise you were compromised?"

"I was looking for you," Grayling said. "Kept on searching until the chopper wouldn't fly. As soon as the storm allowed it, I searched for you again. No one was supposed to get hurt. I promise you. And no one is going to hurt you now."

"Is your helicopter broken?" Matt asked him.

Grayling waited before replying, "As I said, I just needed some time to talk to you, explain things—"

Matt interrupted, "Have you radioed anyone? Is anyone coming?"

Grayling didn't respond. The wind blew ash from the bonfire, spiraling up against the falling snowflakes.

"I am going to be with our daughter," Matt said, and walked away from Grayling and Jack towards the aputiak. Yasmin thought that they allowed him to leave because there was nowhere for them to run to or seek help.

"What location do the police have for us?" Yasmin asked Grayling.

He didn't reply.

"The one Jack gave, south of the Atigun Pass?" she asked.

Again he didn't reply, and Yasmin was sickened by him.

"I wasn't trying to catch you," Jack said to Yasmin, his voice soft in the darkness. "I just needed you to lead me to your husband."

But she'd already guessed why he hadn't let her turn around. Once she reached the river road that led to this place, he must have known where she was going. It was only then that he had fired at Ruby and her.

She turned away from the men and went after Matt.

As she walked towards the aputiak through the black icy landscape, she didn't think about Jack or Grayling or what was happening now, but of the photo of stars Matt had sent her, and of him running with exposure and frostbite, a phone next to his skin, so he could hear her voice.

Matt was coming out of the aputiak. She knew from the way he was standing, and then from his face, that something was terribly wrong.

I've got my laptop open and I'm using its light to see the way ahead because I left the torch behind for Mum and Dad; it makes the snow and ice look greeny and I look at the greeny snow, not at the dark. I've got Dad's backpack on with the terminal, so it's safe and dry and my laptop's got Dad's special cover on it and there's clear plastic over the screen. It's snowing, but only a bit. A fat flake landed splat in the middle of the screen, but I just wiped it off with my mitten.

I'm quite high because when I look down I can just see the bonfire, like it's an orange dot. And near it is the aputiak and it's a little yellow glow. If I keep the orange dot and the little yellow glow behind me, and I'm climbing up, not down, then I'm going the right way and I'll get to the top.

The vast darkness surrounded them, and somewhere out there was Ruby. Ten years old. Minus twenty. She had taken the laptop and terminal. If Jack and Grayling found out, God knows what they would do to her. They were mute with fear, bonded by something that was larger than love.

If they went after her, then Jack and Grayling would know that she'd gone, but how could they not look for her?

Yasmin retched, her terror physical. Ruby was in danger of frostbite and hypothermia. What if they couldn't find her? She would die alone.

They saw shapes in the dark coming towards them. Jack arrived, pulling down his face mask; he was holding a gun. Behind him was Grayling.

Matt thought of Siku in the aputiak. Only a child would do that, he thought; only a child would rescue a dead dog and bring it inside to look after it. And only a child would think to put a sleeping bag over it to make it look like she was there; as if that would work. Her innocence was terrible against these men.

"Where's your laptop with the photos on it?" Jack asked Yasmin.

"It was in the truck when it went through the ice."

"You're not a good liar," Jack said, and turned to Matt. "Your terminal? Is that in the igloo as well?"

"The cold stopped it from working," Matt said, "so I just left it."

Jack started moving closer to the aputiak, but Yasmin stood in front of him, barring his way.

"Our daughter needs to sleep," she said. "She's been terrified and she's exhausted."

Maybe she should tell them the truth, and then they could go and look for her. Because what threat was Ruby to them? She was ten, a slight little girl. Even if Ruby got the terminal and laptop working, and surely she couldn't, not in the dark in minus twenty, on her own. But even if she did, who would she email? Who could she ask for help? Did she even know anyone's email address?

"I want to hear what you've got to say," Matt said to Grayling. "You told us you wanted to explain things; well, I'd like to know."

He thought the only way they could ensure Ruby's survival was to stop these men going after her, to keep them talking, and Yasmin knew he was right. Even if Ruby wasn't a threat, they'd still see her as a potential risk and go after her.

"OK," Grayling said. "Let's talk by the bonfire, let the child sleep."

It was as if he was doing a small kindness to make up for larger brutality. He turned to Jack.

"That was always our plan," he said to Jack. "That we would explain."

They walked towards the bonfire; the last piece of debris was burning.

"So what exactly happened here?" Matt asked.

"A well casing had a hairline crack," Jack said. "Fracking the well forced it wide apart. The blowback got contaminated. Probably with arsenic. Traveled as a plume down the river." His tone was undramatic, almost nonchalant. "First I knew was my foreman getting hysterical. All these dead animals and fish. It's routine to have dead animals near a fracking site, but this was different. I knew there were Eskimos downriver, sent one of my workers to check it out. Told him what to do."

Matt thought he saw a shape in the darkness and his eye muscles tightened to focus, but the shape was a shadow of the last flames of the bonfire, nothing more.

"The people living in Anaktue boiled their water for drinking," Matt said.

"Boiling just concentrates the level of arsenic," Jack said, his tone still neutral.

"Are there any other people who—"

Jack interrupted, "Just one Eskimo village that no one's ever heard of."

"Weren't there any inspections or tests—"

"The well was inspected and signed off as safe."

"But the pipe had a fracture?"

"Hairline. A mile or more down. And he was a junior, wanted to hightail it home fast as he could. Freezing his bollocks off in a thin parka, dropping his little camera into a well, in the dark, with another fifteen wells to go."

"And after the arsenic leak you destroyed the evidence?"

"I just paid a man to light a fire. The snow did the rest."

"And here?"

"My foreman panicked, fucking idiot, started dismantling everything. Lit the bonfire."

"He needn't have bothered?" Matt said.

"There was nothing to show there'd ever been a problem. It's a fast-flowing river, five, perhaps ten miles an hour; the arsenic plume would've reached the Arctic Ocean and the river would have tested clean. But like I said, the guy panicked, made everyone pack up and leave, even destroyed the fucking road."

Yasmin was searching the darkness for Ruby and she knew it was an effort for Matt not to do the same, that he was forcing himself to look at Jack.

"All of the waste ponds are full," Matt said to Jack. "Were they full before the arsenic leak?"

"People aren't always as safety conscious as they should be."

"So you dumped the poisonous blowback in the river?" he asked.

"Like I just said, people aren't as safety conscious as they should be. Some of them are plain lazy. And Junior in his thin parka isn't going to come back and check."

"If the river flows at ten miles an hour," Matt said, "it would only have taken four hours for the arsenic plume to reach the village."

"No one realized in time to warn them," Grayling said, and Yasmin thought she heard genuine sadness in his voice. She tried to see his eyes, hoping to find some charity there, but the dying light from the bonfire reflected off his goggles and she couldn't see behind them.

"The problem we have," Jack said, "is that this isn't a leak that poisoned a well, like most fracking accidents. People who make decisions on energy policy aren't a load of hillbillies getting their water from a fucking well."

The bonfire was going out; the rig and the detritus of the fracking site were no longer visible in the darkness. Yasmin feared that soon there would be nothing to guide Ruby back to them. But it would be worse if these men went after her.

"You said there was a good reason for covering this up," Matt said to Grayling. "I still haven't heard it."

"A river's different from a well," Grayling said. "Rivers move. If there's an accident, they can poison everyone downstream. A large percentage of our drinking water comes from rivers and streams. People will be afraid of poison coming out of their faucets. The people who decide our energy policy will be afraid too. Those who are ambivalent about fracking now will never allow it in the future. And the ones who are antifracking will use this accident every chance they get."

"You don't think they're right to be afraid?" Matt asked.

"No," Grayling said. "What happened here was a tragic isolated event. A whole series of things happened that shouldn't have. It's an appalling, one-off accident."

As she listened to Grayling, Yasmin hoped there was a slim chance that he hadn't been lying, that after he had explained his bigger picture he would let them go and then they would find Ruby.

"There's a cost for every type of energy," Grayling continued. "We have to choose the one that has the lowest cost. Hydraulic fracturing gets fuel from right here, under our own land. We can't be held to ransom for it. We don't need to fight wars for it."

"What you need to understand," Jack said, "is that Alaska protects the rest of the U.S. Always has. First against the Commies and now against the Arabs. We provided fuel for America from regular oil wells and then from fracking too. The interior of Alaska's got huge reserves just sitting there, under land that isn't of any use for anything else. Two billion barrels of recoverable oil, eighty trillion cubic feet of natural gas. A bunch of Eskimos isn't going to fuck that up for us."

Matt heard Jack's aggression and pugilistic nature. He was a man who wouldn't back away from a fight or an argument; maybe Matt could use that to keep him away from Ruby.

Jack had started walking towards the aputiak.

"By 'us' you just mean the USA?" Matt said.

"Other countries aren't my problem," Jack said.

"You think you're patriotic?"

Jack stopped walking. "No question about that. Fracking got our country out of recession. Made us independent. Strong. Can't be leaders of the free world if we rely on foreigners for our energy supply." He carried on walking.

"When astronauts first went into space," Yasmin said, "they took photos of Earth. And then everyone could see that it was just one planet, a beautiful blue planet in the darkness of space."

"Animals and birds don't know about countries," Matt said. "Some of them migrate for thousands of miles, all the way across the world. It's just one planet for them too."

"You're fucking tree-huggers now?" Jack said, but he'd stopped walking towards the aputiak.

"Just saying we have a bigger picture than yours," Matt said. He turned to Grayling. "And you haven't convinced me. Not yet."

"The truth is, the reality is, we do have individual territories," Grayling said. "And people fight each other over oil. And we send our boys to die overseas."

"You think fracking will end wars?" Matt asked.

He heard a sound behind him and turned to grab hold of Ruby, put his body between her and these men, but it was just the strengthening wind disturbing a pile of waste containers behind them.

I've got right to the top, because when I went a little bit further my feet were going downward, so I came back to here.

The wind is slapping my face WHACK! WHACK!

I can't see any stars, just the dark and snow coming down and down, like fuzzy cold white blossom.

Up there, above where the blossom snow comes from, are satellites.

I remember Dad in Scotland, telling me what to do. I take Dad's terminal out of the backpack and turn up my laptop screen to the brightest it will go, but it's still hard to see where to put the cable to link the laptop to the terminal. I try to feel for the holes with my gloves but it's super-fiddly. I take my gloves off and just use the thin liners.

I've linked them up and done what Daddy showed me to do. My keyboard isn't freezing because of the special cover.

The terminal is looking for a satellite up in space. On the screen it says "Searching . . ."

I open up Dad's and my blog with the photos and coordinates, which are where the animals died all along the river. When the terminal finds a satellite, I'm going to publish it, even the silly bits with me talking to Daddy because I don't have time to delete them. I hope Daddy doesn't mind that I'm doing this because it's an emergency.

My fingers are getting really cold.

It still says "Searching . . ."

Mum said that a group of satellites is called a constellation, just like stars. But I think there'll only be one or two above me here.

There were no flames in the bonfire; just ash glowing in pockmarked red spots. Yasmin's stomach hurt from needing to be with Ruby; she could feel her fingers trying to grasp at a child who wasn't there.

Matt was arguing with Grayling and Jack, trying to keep their focus on him, telling them that the next wars would be fought over clean water. Yasmin thought that Jack's patriotism was thin and fragile as an eggshell; that it was muscular greed and entitlement that motivated him and, at any moment, he'd cut this short and go to the aputiak, discover Ruby had gone. Jack would kill them without pity or compunction, she knew that, but there was a chance Grayling might stop him.

"Do you know how much water it takes to frack a single well?" Matt asked. "Five million gallons. Which is legally polluted by poisonous chemicals to turn it into fracking fluid. No one knows how to safely dispose of it. That's without any leak into the groundwater, the aquifers, the rivers."

He spoke with conviction, his knowledge of fracking from the villagers' campaign, but his focus was still on the darkness, as if he'd be able to catch a glimpse of Ruby if he stared at it hard enough.

"It's clean water that's going to be as precious as fuel one day," Matt continued. "More so, because you can cut down your energy needs; if it gets desperate you can go back to how we lived before electricity or the car was even invented. Live like the Inupiaq. But water is essential for life itself, and it's global. Wars over water won't be for power, like they are now, but for survival."

"I've listened to enough," Jack said. He turned to Grayling. "I'll start the chopper. You get the terminal and laptop."

Grayling didn't move. It would be Jack who flew the helicopter away from here, Yasmin thought, but she didn't know if Grayling would be his passenger.

"We can't leave them," Grayling said. "They have no shelter. No means of keeping warm."

"But you will leave them, Davey. Just like you didn't tell your pals where they were in the storm."

"I thought I could find them myself and—"

"Still haven't told your pals where they are now, have you?"

Jack was walking towards the aputiak. Grayling didn't reply.

"Davey's the eldest," Jack said. "Eleven cousins, and him at the top. He likes people to look up to him, always has. Even as a boy he had to be admired. The good boy; the good guy; the state trooper. Even his son died patriotically—that's the image, isn't it, Davey?"

Grayling was silent. They reached the aputiak, lit from inside by the qulliq. The pale yellow light caught on their goggles, reflecting tiny images of itself.

Matt saw a gleam of light on metal. Jack was leveling his gun at the aputiak. He and Grayling thought Ruby was inside.

"I never intended this," Jack said, anger in his voice. "But you left me no fucking option."

A sound cracked through the falling snow; metal punctured through the snow walls. Yasmin screamed.

"It's much kinder to do it quickly," Jack said, and Matt thought that he believed his crime would be less if the time taken to die was less.

As he fired again at the aputiak Yasmin wanted the sound waves to vibrate through the dark air and touch Ruby so that she'd know that the man had a gun and to hide.

He fired again and she thought about the tree falling, the sound turning into a mossy tremble, a leaf brushing against Ruby's cheek; she was trying to think calm things for Ruby as if that would help her.

The qulliq inside the aputiak, dampened by falling snow and ice, was extinguished.

Jack switched on his torch. It glinted on the badge on Grayling's arm and then shone on his face. He had barely reacted.

Jack went into the half-destroyed aputiak and found no child; instead a dead husky mutilated by bullets. Matt saw that the dog enraged him.

It's taking so long. I'm thinking of the paint-splattered purple heather in Scotland and Dad's funny Superman T-shirt and being warm, but it's pitch-black-dark and so so cold. I think of Dad up here, all on his own, and I must be brave too.

I've got a picture of a flashing satellite!!

Our blog is publishing onto the Net. All the pictures and the co-ordinates and everything!

But we don't have any followers for our blog. Not one. Nobody even knows about it. No one will see it and help.

I can't see the yellow glow from the aputiak or the orange bonfire dot. I don't know how to get back to Mum and Dad.

Jack made Matt and Yasmin take off their jackets, face masks, and goggles. As he locked their protective clothes in the helicopter, they ran from him towards the hill, because surely that's where Ruby had gone, the place where Matt had sent his emails. Without Arctic protection, they quickly lost body heat and their muscles became weaker and they couldn't run fast.

A searchlight from the helicopter shone out into the darkness. Jack was looking for Ruby. He swung the beam towards the hill. A child was illuminated at the top, silhouetted through the falling snow.

There's a bright light from down the hill, really really bright. I want to think it's Dad or Mum looking for me but I don't think it is.

I open up Twitter. I have to type super-carefully because if I make a mistake in the blog address no one will be able to help us. My fingers hurt so much, like I'm tearing them out of barbed wire, but I can't type in gloves. I remember what Mum told me.

**Words Without Sounds** @Words_No_Sounds – 1m
*653 followers*
Help us. go 2 aweekinalaskablog.com. Anaktue
villagers dead b4 fire. long numbers r longitude &
latitude Add decimal points and minus. Hurry.

I don't know if it's night or day here or at home but somewhere in the world it's day, the part that's twizzled on the string to face the sun. And someone will be awake and read my tweet and be a grown-up and know what to do.

The bright light goes off and it's all dark now.

Yasmin was holding the torch, Matt next to her. She heard Grayling calling to them but didn't stop, stumbling on over the ice and snow. Jack ran past, holding a gun and a torch. The cold was shutting down her body's ability to keep functioning and she felt her mind clouding around one sharp bright splinter of need to protect Ruby. Then Grayling had grabbed her and was giving her their jackets and face masks and goggles. They hurriedly put them on. Grayling continued ahead of them.

My fingers feel so funny, like they're numb and hurt at the same time.

Our blog doesn't have where we are because that was the last email Dad sent of the stars, and I didn't put the stars on our blog. I go into Mum's emails. I'm copying the numbers under the photo of the stars. Dad must know how much she loves stars. Then I open up Twitter and paste the numbers. I try to put in the minus and the decimal, just like Mum did. But I keep making mistakes because my fingers aren't working properly.

Grayling was far ahead of the parents now because he was already properly dressed in Arctic clothes. He'd turned off the searchlight on the chopper to slow Jack's hunt for the child. Now his torch showed Jack a hundred or so yards in front of him. He sprinted over the snow and ice, his chest burning as the frozen air was dragged deep inside his lungs.

When Yasmin had told him that the little girl was asleep inside the aputiak he'd known she was lying. He'd seen the parents' faces and recognized their terror. He'd felt the same when Timothy was fighting in Iraq and he didn't know day to day, hour to hour, if he was still alive. So he'd known all along that their child wasn't inside, that they didn't know where she was. He was a good detective; not hard for him to deduce that the parents were engaging him and Jack in arguments to stop them from going after their daughter.

He was gaining on Jack. Just twenty yards ahead now.

From the beginning of this, he'd lacked integrity and chosen to be blind, chosen to believe that Jack wouldn't hurt them, not because he had faith in Jack's good character, but because otherwise he himself would have been a part of something wicked.

Then Jack had shot at the aputiak, thinking he was shooting the little girl, and there was no hiding anymore from Jack's viciousness or his own culpability. When he saw bullets puncturing through the snow walls of the aputiak, he'd seen that there was no bigger picture; there could be no evil greater than this and therefore no justifying greater good.

He'd felt as if something in him had woken up and stood straight again.

A few paces ahead of him, Jack stopped. He shone his torch at the child, two hundred yards away, and then he took aim with his gun. Grayling stood in front of him to shield her from his bullet.

My bracelet vibrates and I want to take it off. I want to hear stillness. I crouch down so it'll be harder for the bad man to see me. My fingers won't work but I've typed the tweet now.

> **Words Without Sounds** @Words_No_Sounds – 1m
> *653 followers*
> 69.602132, –147.680371 we r here on hill by fracking
> wells help us I think he has gun.

Grayling lay on the snow and instead of pain felt strangely warm. It was snowing down on his face and he felt the land under his body and all around him. Yasmin had been right to accuse him of protecting himself and self-interest. Because in some peculiar way he'd believed that if he cared enough to try to prevent war for oil, broke all the rules and laws, then someone a decade ago, a father like him, would have cared enough too and war would have ended sooner and Timothy would still be alive, his face smiling at something he'd explain to his dad in a minute, not buried in a coffin unrecognizable. Of course it didn't work like that, he knew that; laws of reality didn't bend and change themselves to accommodate his irrational emotional truth. Perhaps it was simply that he hadn't wanted another parent to suffer preventable grief, caustic as battery acid in your throat and gut and eyelids when you tried to sleep, never wanted another human being to know that hurt. *And thou no breath at all.* So he'd chosen to believe Jack, chosen to look at a bigger picture and not at the ugliness involved in its creation. Timothy's beautiful face. Jack had exploited his love for his son and his love for his country: the two loves that made him who he was. And his love had been mutilated into something else. He felt the land scarred around him, bleeding poison.

I'm waiting and waiting for my tweets to post. But somewhere above me in space is a satellite. And Dad's little box is like the catch-your-breath-amazing Tudor mollusk, and I will get a connection and it will all be OK. Because the Internet is like the magnetosphere covering the whole world.

Matt and Yasmin saw the light from Jack's torch, going up the steep slope. They were powerless to get to Ruby before him. Yasmin knew that nobody would come to their aid. No one would come and no one would know. Years could pass, decades, centuries even, without anyone coming here.

My tweets have posted!! I try and do the "Hoorah!!" sign but I can't feel my hands at all. They don't even hurt. I wish they would hurt.

There's a torch coming towards me through the dark. I hope that it's Mum and Dad but I don't think it is.

There's an animal in front of my laptop screen, really close—an Arctic hare, its eyes shiny bright like it's interested in my laptop.

Someone has tweeted me back already! Then another person! And another! That's awesome-sauce fast! That's super-coolio amazing! They are superb lyrebird chicks and baby three-wattled bellbirds!

The hare goes stock-still and I know it's afraid. Maybe the tweets make a noise, like a PING, that scares it, but Dad turned off the sound on my laptop.

The torch is really close.

I don't know where to run.

He's here. I turn my laptop screen at him so I can see him. He has a gun. He takes my laptop.

He's got his gun in one hand, my laptop in the other. He's reading the tweets and the light of the screen reflects on his goggles. I hope there's more and more tweets because then he'll keep on reading and he won't point his gun at me and Mum and Dad might get to me.

He throws my laptop onto the snow. I want to read the tweets but he shoots my laptop over and over and my bracelet vibrates and vibrates and vibrates, making my arm tingle like it's going to be sick, and my laptop is thousands of tiny pieces freckling the snow.

I think he'll shoot me now.

He's turning away from me.

The light of his torch is getting smaller and smaller. It's just a tiny pinprick and now it's nothing at all.

He's gone!

I think he saw that their tweets are like gossip feathers and he could never pick them all up.

I don't have the light from my laptop anymore. No light at all.

Dark dark black.

I think about the night swallowing all the days and I like thinking that, because it's like the whale swallowing Raven, and inside the dark whale his heart and soul were a girl who was dancing.

A light is coming towards me, going up and down because the person is running and I see Mum and Dad.

Dad bends down and hugs me and Mum's taking off her big mittens and she puts them over my hands. She has frozen tears inside her goggles. She blows her breath into the mittens on my hands.

I want to tell them that my words were stronger than his bullets.

And I want to tell them that the superb lyrebird chicks and three-wattled baby bellbirds are making sure everyone knows about the poor people at Anaktue and the animals and they are getting us help.

In the light from Dad's torch, white snowflakes are flickering down from the sky and I think that their typed words to me aren't like feathers at all but snowflakes and they reached us here, falling all around us.

Snow makes no sound when it falls.

We wait here, the three of us, close together for ages and ages. There are stars above us and I think of the baby birds learning the night sky so they can fly home. There's a little new light in the sky, like a slow shooting star, coming towards us. But I know that there's no such things as shooting stars.

Mum's still blowing her breath inside my mittens, all steamy warm.

A ball of snow starts moving, then another and another; Arctic hares are uncurling themselves from the snow. They lollop off across the snow into the dark.

I can feel my fingers again and I have a voice.

It is here, in this bad, that we reach
The last purity of the knowledge of good.

WALLACE STEVENS

## ACKNOWLEDGMENTS

I want to thank the following people for so generously sharing their knowledge with me. Any errors I have made are entirely my own:

Jacob Tompkins OBE—expert in hydrology and MD of Waterwise, and a passionate and brilliant advocator of the importance and value of clean water.

Jimmy Stotts—President of the Alaska branch of the Inuit Circumpolar Council.

Dr. Sebastian Hendricks—consultant in pediatric audiovestibular medicine (specialist for hearing and balance problems in children).

Dr. Amir Sam—senior lecturer at Imperial College and consultant endocrinologist.

Dr. Rob Scott—physicist currently working with the UK Space Agency and the Rutherford Appleton Laboratory's Earth and Atmospheric Science Division.

James Holmes—at the Alaska Department of Fish and Game.

Gerry Gillespie—aeronautical engineer and provider of excellent machine stories.

Jean Straus—journalist and reviewer for Action on Hearing Loss.

The Farnham Astronomical Society.

For their creative help and support, I'd like to thank the following people:

First and foremost, Felicity Blunt at Curtis Brown, who has been a driving force behind this novel. I could not have written it without her imaginative criticism, intelligence, and insight.

I would like to thank Lindsay Sagnette at Crown Publishers for her beautiful and creative editing; and Sally Franklin and Molly Stern for their faith and commitment to this novel. Thank you to Emma Beswetherick and David Shelley at Little, Brown Book Group for their passion for this book.

My heartfelt thanks to Deborah Schneider at Gelfman Schneider Literary Agents Inc., and particular thanks to the remarkable and unique Alice Lutyens, my audio agent.

Thank you to Nora Evans-Reitz and Rose Fox for your patience and help. And a huge debt of gratitude to the talented people who take a typed manuscript and turn it into a beautiful book in a bookshop— Ana Leal, Cindy Berman, and Lauren Dong.

Thank you to my dear and inspiring friends, Nina Calabresi and Bob Oldshue, for introducing me to the poetry of Wallace Stevens in the beautiful setting of Maine.

Last, but far from least, thank you Karin Lewiston, Anne-Marie Casey, Lynne Gagliano, Claire Merryweather, Claire Fuller, Maerisna Hole, and my parents, Kit and Jane Orde-Powlett, for their constant support and for making me leave my study for friendship and fresh air.

Thank you, Cosmo and Joe, who inspired Ruby's kindness and generosity and intelligence. And finally, but most of all, thank you to my wonderful husband, Martin, for sharing the adventure of Alaska and the long journey of writing a novel.

I am indebted to many books, articles, photos, videos, and websites, and in particular to the following:

"Alaska Native Villages Annual Report 2012" (U.S. Environmental Protection Agency).

Maureen Clark, "State Considers Checkpoints, Restrictions on Dalton Highway Traffic in Response to Attacks" (*Peninsula Clarion,* 2001).

"Compendium of Scientific, Medical and Media Findings Demonstrating Risks and Harms of Fracking (Unconventional Gas and Oil Extraction)" (Concerned Health Professionals of NY, 2014).

Debby Dahl Edwardson, *My Name Is Not Easy* (Skyscape, 2012).

Pat Forgey, " 'Fracking' for Oil Likely to Grow in Alaska" (JuneauEmpire.com, 2012).

Bernd Heinrich, *The Homing Instinct: Meaning and Mystery in Animal Migration* (London: HarperCollins, 2014).

William L. Iġġiaġruk Hensley, *Fifty Miles from Tomorrow: A Memoir of Alaska and the Real People* (New York: Sarah Crichton Books, 2009).

Margaret Kriz Hobson, "Shale Oil: Geologist's Alaska Gamble Could Turn into America's Next Big Shale Play," *Energy Wire* (E & E Publishing, 2013).

Kyle Hopkins, "Frozen Landslide Threatens to Devour Dalton Highway" (*Alaska Dispatch News,* 2012).

Nick Jans, *The Last Light Breaking: Living among Alaska's Inupiat Eskimos* (Oregon: Alaska Northwest Books, 1993).

Doug O'Harra, "On the Dalton Highway—Just How Bad Can It Get?" (*Anchorage Daily News,* 2001).

Dan O'Neill, *The Firecracker Boys: H-Bombs, Inupiat Eskimos and the Roots of the Environmental Movement* (New York: Basic Books; London: Perseus Running [distributor], 2008).

Sara Wheeler, *The Magnetic North: Notes from the Arctic Circle* (London: Jonathan Cape, 2009).

I am also grateful to the following websites:

www.actiononhearingloss.org.uk
www.adfg.alaska.gov
www.alaskacenters.gov
www.british-sign.co.uk
www.dec.alaska.gov
www.ecowatch.com
www.handspeak.com
www.iccalaska.org
www.inuitcircumpolar.com
www.inupiatheritage.org
www.nationalgeographic.com
www.worldwildlife.org

The National Deaf Children's Society believes that every deaf child should be valued and included by society and have the same opportunities as any other child. For more information and advice, visit their website: www.ndcs.org.

The first documentary I watched on hydraulic fracturing was "Gasland" by Josh Fox. Since then I've read, watched, and listened to many articles, reports, speeches, and blogs about fracking, but "Gasland" remains the standout piece for me. "The Sky Is Pink" by Josh Fox and the "Gasland" team can be seen on Vimeo and YouTube.

Photos and video of almost every mile of the Dalton highway can be viewed in Google Earth and on YouTube. There are blogs by drivers, tourists, and bikers who have traveled the Dalton Highway and post photojournals. I am grateful to all of them for giving me their literal viewpoint.

The following apps have also been valuable:

British Sign Language Reference Dictionary app
British Sign Language finger-spelling app
Inupiat dictionary app—the many words for snow are evocative of the land where this language is spoken. The first word for snow is *apiqammiaq*—meaning new snow, and then words for different types of snow go all the way through the alphabet to *uupkaagnaq*—packed snow on top and soft snow underneath. The dictionary also gives an Inupiat daily word. Tonight as I write this it is "*qailliaqsruk*—ripple on water; (i) to ripple, be disturbed."

ROSAMUND LUPTON is the internationally bestselling and critically acclaimed author of the novels *Sister* and *Afterwards*. Her *New York Times* bestselling debut, *Sister*, was a *New York Times* Editor's Choice and Target Book Club pick and has been translated into over thirty languages with international sales of over 1.5 million copies. Lupton lives in England with her husband and two sons.

# THE QUALITY OF SILENCE

ESSAYS,
READER'S GUIDES,
AND MORE

# A Conversation with Rosamund Lupton

Q. Relationships are at the heart of your novels (in your bestselling novel *Sister* it was the relationship between two sisters, and in *Afterwards*, also a bestseller, it was the bond between a mother and her daughter). Can you tell us a bit about the relationships you are exploring in *The Quality of Silence*?

A. Much of the novel is narrated by ten-year-old Ruby, and through her eyes we see her relationship with her mother, Yasmin. It's a loving relationship that's made difficult because of Ruby's profound deafness. Yasmin is afraid Ruby will be isolated if she doesn't use her mouth to speak, but Ruby point-blank refuses (she hasn't used her oral voice for over a year) and instead uses sign language and typing (Twitter, for example) to communicate. Alongside their real and perilous journey, mother and daughter also have a personal journey. The climax of this story isn't when Ruby uses her mouth to speak for the first time—although she does—but when Yasmin understands Ruby's decision and listens to her daughter's written voice.

Ruby's other main relationship is with her father, Matt. He understands her and listens to her, while she shares his love of wildlife. Ruby's emails to him and her memories of him, which she shares over the course of the novel, illustrate the strong and loving bond between them.

The other relationship at the heart of the novel is that between Matt and Yasmin. Theirs is a complex marriage. When Yasmin first arrives in Alaska, it's to row with Matt for kissing a local Inupiat woman, and maybe to separate from him. But when she's told Matt is dead, she feels overwhelming love for him. As she drives across northern Alaska, risking everything to find him, her memories reveal an intense romance and a fulfilling early marriage that was then shattered. With no distractions in the polar darkness, Yasmin can see the woman she became on the other side of the world in London and understands why their marriage was failing. While she literally drives a truck to find him, the novel also charts a figurative finding of each other.

## Q. How is Yasmin able to drive a huge truck in such perilous conditions?

A. Yasmin is an astrophysicist because that was my gateway into her character, but it also means she understands the laws of gravity, inertia, and kinetic friction. This knowledge, once expressed as equations in a long-ago classroom, helps her survive the physical reality out on the ice. She also gets practical lessons and help. From the moment Adeeb agrees to drive them, Yasmin studies him because she finds it reassuring to see how he is controlling the vehicle and therefore keeping Ruby safe. When she drives the truck, she puts her theoretical physics into use and remembers, mostly, what Adeeb did to handle this extreme vehicle and road. Yasmin quickly learns from her first mistake, while truckers on CB radio help her along the way. She's no pro—for example, it takes her an hour to put on snow chains.

Her character is also crucially important. When she was still a child, she drove her drunk father home from her mother's grave through an intimidating and busy part of South London. It's that same courage and grit that enables her to drive on the ice road.

## Q. Where did the idea for *The Quality of Silence* originate?

A. It had two starting points, though at the time I didn't realize either would result in a novel. The first was many years ago when, as a nine-year-old child, I started to lose my hearing. At the time I didn't realize what was happening and was only aware that teachers were cross with me for my falling work standard, and I felt left out at playtime. I remember never quite knowing what was going on and a sense of exclusion. Without realizing it, I had been lipreading to get by. I think that, like Ruby, I developed a vivid inner world and an engagement with language that was different from my peers. I had my hearing restored in one ear, but never forgot that time at primary school.

The second starting point was footage I saw of

snow blowing across the Alaskan arctic tundra with the wind sounding eerily violent. A herd of musk oxen were huddled against the blizzard while an arctic wolf hovered nearby, trying to separate a calf from the herd. The snow-covered landscape stretched off the frame and, I imagined, for thousands of miles around. It was in every way different from what I could see sitting at my desk in England, and I wanted to find out more about this extraordinary place.

**Q. What was it about Alaska that inspired you to set your latest novel there?**

A. Alaska has been called the last great wilderness. It is part of the United States of America, though not physically attached to the rest of it, and I find it hard to imagine anything more different from New York City than the Alaskan arctic tundra. As I researched more about Alaska—and visited it—I discovered astonishing beauty. People come from all over the world to see the famous aurora borealis, but even on nights that it doesn't appear, the night sky is astonishing. That near to the North Pole, the stars above you barely seem to move; the Earth is almost literally spinning around you. As an astrophysicist, Yasmin is awestruck by it. I was also fascinated by the animals and birds in Alaska that stay and endure the vicious winter cold. Arctic hares, foxes, and wolves have coats of browns and russets in summer, but in winter their coats turn white to match the snow. As a wildlife photographer, Matt is in love with this place.

But Alaska is brutal as well as beautiful. Over twice the size of Texas and sparsely populated, Alaska can make you feel isolated in a way that's hard to imagine anywhere else on earth. When Yasmin and Ruby are in danger, there's no house for a hundred miles, there's no Wi-Fi or cell reception to call for help. The cold, which can reach minus eighty Fahrenheit, is an adversary as lethal as any human threat. Yasmin, struggling to keep Ruby safe from frostbite and fatal exposure, sees cold as a predator conceived in a place without daylight.

It's November when Yasmin and Ruby set out, which means they're traveling into a night that will last another two months. Almost the entire novel is set in the dark. Yasmin is unable to see who is stalking them, nor the manmade peril in the wilderness. The darkness adds tension and threat to their journey and also impacts them in a subtler way. Without a diurnal rhythm, Yasmin feels trapped in an endless night and becomes mentally disoriented. Matt describes feeling that, out here, there are no days, no turning of the Earth to reach the face of a sun, but a dark night of the soul in which only violent storms break time into different pieces.

Alaska is central to the novel. This story couldn't have happened anywhere else but northern Alaska in winter.

Q. You truly bring the beautiful—yet incredibly harsh and unforgiving—Alaskan wilderness to life. How did you go about researching this setting?

A. Initially I used books, films, and the Internet. It's amazing how much you can discover while sitting in a centrally heated study and how generous complete strangers are with their time and expertise. I would find myself in conversation with an Alaskan wildlife expert who probably had artic foxes and musk oxen outside his window. An Inupiat man was unfailingly patient and helpful, not only with making sure my novel was accurate, but later with the audiobook when he advised the narrator by phone how to pronounce Inupiat words. But at-home, comfy research can only go so far, and I was desperate to visit Alaska. I went in March, when there was some daylight, but it was punishingly cold.

I spoke to truckers about their experiences and realized how like a frontier Alaska feels, with two military bases close to the tiny town of Fairbanks, and Russia only fifty or so miles away across the Bering Strait. I then had an uncannily similar experience to my fictitious heroine when the flight I'd booked from Fairbanks to the far north was canceled because of heavy snow. I ended up bribing a van driver to take me as far north as possible. As we drove along the ice road, I saw the gleaming trans-Alaska pipeline, jarring the impression that I'd wandered through the wardrobe door into Narnia.

As we drove farther north, the road became more perilous. Vast trucks thundered toward us on the unlit, unmarked road, and I realized that nothing in England had prepared me for this. Eventually bad weather forced us to put on snow chains and turn around.

After the road trip, I visited a cabin with kennels, miles from the nearest electricity or phone signal, and went out on a sled pulled by a team of huskies over virgin snow, with animals passing as fleeting shadows through the trees.

I hope I captured something of Alaska in my novel, but the reader would need to stand in a deep freeze to get the full experience.

**Q. Yasmin seems like a loving mother, so why does she put Ruby at risk?**
A. If someone had told Yasmin that she'd drive Ruby over the Atigun Pass with a psycho tanker driver on their tail and an arctic storm closing in, then she would never have embarked on the journey. How she gets to that point was an important part of the story and an exploration of her character.

From the beginning, she is anxious about bringing Ruby with her and wishes she could leave her in Fairbanks, but the town is violent, she knows no one, and she's rattled by the sinister Silesian Stennet. At the same time she's sure that Matt will die in the arctic wilderness unless she reaches him quickly. It's not an easy decision, nor is it something that stays static. She tells herself that if the journey becomes too dangerous, she'll turn around and take Ruby back to Fairbanks. During the novel, this tipping point of danger takes on a physical presence for Yasmin, getting closer to her in the darkness. When she finally realizes it's too dangerous, she puts Ruby's safety before Matt's and tries to turn around. But the tanker driver won't let her. From then on, the journey becomes increasingly perilous.

A more complex answer is that there is an internal

conflict in Yasmin. Most obviously it is the conflict between her passionate love for Matt and her maternal love for Ruby, but just as important is the conflict between her rediscovered courage and her responsibility as a mother. During the story, these two strong character traits compete with each other. She hasn't felt courage and passion since Ruby was born, so she's never had to balance it with love and responsibility for a child. So at one level, Yasmin's journey is a rediscovery of the self she used to be, complicated by the fact that she is now a mother.

Q. *The Quality of Silence* addresses the controversial practice of fracking and humankind's impact on the planet. Can you discuss this further?
A. While I was researching northern Alaska, I read about the Inupiat people, including firsthand accounts of their lives. (For example, *Sadie Brower Neakok: An Inupiaq Woman* by Margaret B. Blackman and *Fifty Miles from Tomorrow: A Memoir of Alaska and the Real People* by William Iggiagruk Hensley.) I admired their fortitude and, in our throwaway culture, I was humbled by their respectfulness toward the land, leaving it unmarked for future generations. At the same time, fracking was edging into the United Kingdom news. Our need to get at shale oil and gas by breaking apart the land was a vivid contrast with the Inupiat way of life.

I read more about fracking, including a persuasive website called the Concerned Health Professionals of New York, as well as many other articles and films, which showed the dangers of fracking to human health.

In the novel—*and this is a spoiler*—wastewater from fracking is contaminated by arsenic, which is present in the fly ash that backfilled the well casings. The toxic waste was then illegally dumped in the river, and the arsenic traveled as a tight plume downstream. Inupiat villagers, hauling water from the river to drink, were lethally poisoned. The story is fictitious, but I wanted it to be a credible fiction. In the real case of the Duke Energy spill in North Carolina (which was not a fracking accident), arsenic traveled twenty miles downstream and that was in a wider, warmer river.

One of the characters in the book is pro-fracking because his son died in Iraq. He believes that young people die overseas in wars over oil. I sympathize with this view, but in the end, I believe, strongly, that the most precious resource we have is clean water. Six hundred and fifty million people in the world don't have that, with terrible consequences.

Rather than write a diatribe, I hoped that the decimated village in the middle of a white wilderness and the poisoned animals half-covered in snow along the riverbanks would be a stark and striking image of the risk of fracking.

Before I started the novel, unsure if I had even the thread of a story, I asked an eminent hydrologist if it was plausible that a fracking accident could kill the inhabitants of a remote village. His reply, with no pause first, was an emphatic "Yes." I was appalled, but I also had a story—one that I thought was important.

**Q. In working on this novel, did you discover anything new about yourself?**

A. I discovered I was something of a chicken. I found the amount of research daunting—fracking, Alaskan wildlife, Inupiat culture, astronomy, sign language—what on earth was I thinking? And then, there was the structure of the novel—a real road that provided a linear structure against non-linear flashbacks to various pasts and an emotional journey that would have its denouement in silence in the Alaskan tundra in a storm. I felt like I was beginning a marathon but already had a cramp. I would have given up were it not for the little things. So, for example, I liked Ruby's tweets, I liked the fact that a ptarmigan's feathers change color in winter to match the snow. And these small things forced me to get off the starter blocks and start researching and writing. It was more of a slow jog than a race, and it took me more than two years to write, but when I finally finished, I knew that I was more of a slow-but-steady tortoise than a chicken.

Along the way, I did change in subtle ways. For example, I used to be a little embarrassed about my partial deafness, and now I am not at all. I don't see it as a disability anymore, and I would love to learn sign language. I also became passionate about the value of clean water.

# Rosamund Lupton on Writing a Deaf Character

The main character in my novel, *The Quality of Silence*, is ten-year-old Ruby, who is highly imaginative, intelligent, and profoundly deaf. The idea for Ruby began many years ago, when at nine I started to lose my hearing. At the time I didn't realize what was happening, only aware that my teachers were cross with me for "not concentrating" and that I wasn't included in other girls' chatter and verbal games. When I remember that lonely time I think of shoulders and backs, a feeling of befuddlement, of never quite catching what was going on, and feeling tired, which I later realized was from trying to lipread from the back of the classroom (where I'd been sent as punishment for my falling grades.) The reason no one had clocked the reason for these low grades was because of my reasonably proficient lipreading, which I'd unconsciously learnt. It was the piercing cry of a cuckoo, which I couldn't hear, that meant my deafness was discovered—there's no lipreading a cuckoo. I had an operation shortly afterward and the hearing was restored in my left ear, leaving me only partially deaf.

Many years later, I was working on the beginnings of a story about a woman and her young daughter's journey across northern Alaska in winter. As I thought about the daughter, I knew I wanted her to be deaf. The novel wouldn't only be an exploration of an extraordinary arctic land, but also the interior landscape of a profoundly deaf child. I wanted her to be the main voice in the book, who would draw readers into her world and show them around and leave them the richer for it.

While I learned to speak prior to deafness, Ruby, who was born with no hearing nerves, never had any hearing and has therefore never heard her own oral voice. She refuses to try to speak with her mouth and instead chooses to communicate in sign language. It's useful to the story—at a critical and dangerous point she and her mother are able to talk secretly to each other in sign—but it's also important in understanding Ruby. Instead of using a voice she herself wouldn't be able to hear, she chooses sign language in which she is fluent and an equal participant in the conversation.

Until I researched sign language, I didn't know about its complexity, richness, and beauty. British Sign Language (BSL) has its own unique construction and grammar and each country has its own different sign language. Ruby uses words from American Sign Language when she prefers them. For example, she likes the ASL sign for "dance," which is making a dance floor with one hand and dancing two fingers on it from the other hand. She enjoys the "visual onomatopoeia" of sign and through her I could write a little about it. For example, the sign for "dawn" is made by using one arm as the horizon and a circle made between the thumb and index finger as the sun rising over it.

I gave a talk recently at a literary festival with a sign language interpreter. When I said that I find sign language beautiful, everyone in the audience, hearing people included, watched her sign what I'd just said orally, and the point was perfectly illustrated. She'd told me beforehand that it had taken her seven years to become fluent at signing. I find myself frequently wishing that I could sign and wondering why it's not taught as a language in schools. Imagine the usefulness of a silent language.

I discovered that it's not only people who are deaf and their families who use sign language. My novel is set north of the Arctic Circle, home to Inuit people, and since at least the eighteenth century they have used sign, including facial movements, to communicate and trade. An Inuit man, Elijah Tigullaraq, explains that raising eyebrows indicates "yes," but there are subtle variations: a slight raising means slightly yes, a large movement means definitely. In sub-zero temperatures it's useful to be able to keep the lower half of your face covered.

The terrible drawback of sign language for Ruby is that she only has one friend who understands sign and the other children at her school find her strange and are cruel to her. She experiences painful loneliness. Two-thirds of young deaf people surveyed in the United Kingdom last year said they were bullied because of their deafness. Reading about their experiences vividly brought back my own. Then, as now, the noisy playground and lunch hall are places that are hardest for deaf children to follow a conversation and join in—places where children are meant to have the opportunity to make friends.

But since my time at school there has been a seismic change in how children communicate and connect with each other, at least away from school. When Ruby's father buys her a laptop—to her mother's worry—Ruby has access to email, Twitter, and blogging. She has a new way of talking to people and expressing herself—one in which she is as loud, fluent, and vocal as a hearing person. One of my first readers was my audio agent, Alice Lutyens, who is herself profoundly deaf. Her wholehearted positive response to the portrayal of deafness in the novel—which meant a great deal—was given by email. It's the way we always communicate. At one point in the book, Ruby says that she wants the typed social media world to be the real world because that's where she can be most fully herself. The speaking-listening denouement in the novel is not when Ruby uses her mouth to talk for the first time (although she does), but when her mother learns to hear her daughter's written voice.

Although Ruby can't hear words she does experience language at a sensory and imaginative level, which she expresses as tweets:

**Words Without Sounds** @Words_No_Sounds — 12m
*650 followers*
ANXIETY: Looks like a chessboard with the squares
quickly moving about; feels sweaty and shivery;
tastes like prickly ice cream.

Having found deafness excluding and negative as
a child, I loved inhabiting Ruby's world with her.

# A Reader's Guide for *The Quality of Silence*

1. When Yasmin learns of her husband's death, she refuses to believe that he is dead. Did you believe in Yasmin, or did you think she was being stubborn?

2. Ruby has very different relationships with her parents. They both love her tremendously but have different opinions about Ruby using her computer to interact with the outside world. Which parenting style did you agree with more?

3. Yasmin ultimately puts her daughter Ruby at risk, taking her on this dangerous journey in freezing temperatures. Did you ever think that she was being a bad mother? Or did you understand and sympathize with her because it was an extreme situation?

4. Ruby describes how she conceptualizes words as colors, shapes, and ideas. What did you think of this? How do you think Ruby's deafness impacted her narration of the story?

5. How do you think Yasmin is able to drive a massive truck on the treacherous Alaska roads? Do

you think people are able to go beyond their normal capabilities when faced with life or death situations?

6. Rosamund Lupton's descriptions of the Alaskan wilderness are vivid and beautiful. Was it easy to imagine yourself there with Yasmin and Ruby?

7. The flashbacks interspersed throughout the story illustrate the relationship between Yasmin and Matt. Did you enjoy reading these flashbacks? What do you think they added to the story and understanding of the characters?

8. The debate of fracking arises in the novel, did you have an opinion of this practice before the novel? Do you have one now after reading *The Quality of Silence*?

9. The fellow truck drivers that Yasmin connects with on the radio system are very nice to her. What did you think about this community of truckers? Do you think they should have done more to stop Yasmin or was the information and support they gave her helpful?

10. Did you ever guess or speculate who the truck driver stalking Yasmin and Ruby was? Were you surprised when the driver's identity was revealed?

11. Discuss the ending. What did you think of the crime and the motivation behind it?

12. Twitter serves as a lifesaving tool in this novel. Do you think Twitter or other forms of social media have this capability to save lives or at least send out an S.O.S. in the real world?

ALSO BY NEW YORK TIMES BESTSELLING AUTHOR
ROSAMUND LUPTON

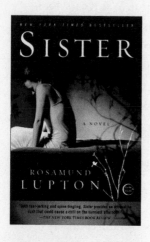

"Both tear-jerking and spine-tingling, *Sister* provides an adrenaline rush that could cause a chill on the sunniest afternoon."

—THE NEW YORK TIMES BOOK REVIEW

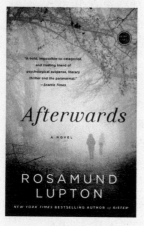

"As much an homage to the mother-daughter relationship as it is a crime novel . . . There are so many twists, turns, and heartbreaks in this tragic, tense novel."

—USA TODAY